Afterworld

Afterworld

By

Robert Beltz

Copyright © 2002 by Robert Beltz

All rights reserved. No part of this book shall be reproduced or transmitted in any form or by any means, electronic, mechanical, magnetic, photographic including photocopying, recording or by any information storage and retrieval system, without prior written permission of the publisher. No patent liability is assumed with respect to the use of the information contained herein. Although every precaution has been taken in the preparation of this book, the publisher and author assume no responsibility for errors or omissions. Neither is any liability assumed for damages resulting from the use of the information contained herein.

This is a work of fiction. Names, characters, places, and incidents either are the product of the author's imagination or are used fictitiously. Any resemblance to actual events or locales or persons, living or dead, is entirely coincidental.

ISBN 1-58877-157-1

Cover designed by eNovel.com
Published by eNovel.com

eNovel.com, LLC
4480 Springfield Road
Glen Allen, VA 23060

(804) 673-6111
(804) 281-5686 (fax)

Printed in the United States of America

ONE

RONSTADT

Karl Ronstadt parked his SL500 in front of the sports arena. He congratulated himself on his good luck to find a spot within a short walking distance of the front door. The key clicked off and the precision built sports car stopped dead. Not a wheeze, cough or piston stroke after ignition shut off. Silence, precise and orderly. The machine worked the way it was supposed to. Karl tugged his equipment bag from the car and retrieved his hockey sticks from its close quarters. It was a cold late October night. The wind howled yet the stars twinkled surprisingly bright. The air had a bite as he snapped the top button on his hockey jacket. Anticipation of what was to come warmed him against the cold. A pleasant sensation flooded him and quickened his step.

He was forty-five years old, rugged and in his physical prime at a time when most men his age were well past theirs, a young boy trapped in a middle-aged doctor's body. Soon the lad's mind in the man's body would be fused into one well coordinated hockey machine.

Karl walked lightly down the stairs to the arena team rooms. In two hours he knew he would trudge with lead-like elephant legs up those same steps.

So far he'd seen no one. True it was an important game and he was a half an hour early, but that didn't matter. There were few spectators interested in watching amateur hockey players batter one another about in the arena.

An old man moved his wide broom covered with a polishing cloth slowly on the linoleum floor in the hall. Karl absorbed the smell of sweat soaked uniforms and the damp cold of the adjacent ice surface. He could have been led blindfolded into the building and yet would have known exactly where he was.

"Hi, John, how are you doing?"

The old man tilted his weary face up toward the sound and then with the flicker of recognition smiled and answered, "Oh, Doc, it's you. Old John is jus fine, jus fine. Gettin' up all the grit and dirt so you won't dull your skates when you walk on the floor."

"Ya' knows, Doc, I ain't gonna be around here much longer. They says I gotta quit, I'm too old. I don't looks it but I'm gonna be sixty-five in November and then it's quits. No more old John around this place keeping your floor clean."

Karl nodded, "It won't be the same without you, John. You've been here longer than I have, you're about the only one."

"Sure enough, Doc, ain't nobody as old as you playin' this silly game. Either you is the best or you is the craziest. No matter, no way anyhow when old John is gone, they won't miss me one bit."

Karl rested his bag on the floor and patted the old man on his shoulder. "John, we have been buddies. I'll miss you. If that arthritis kicks up, you call my office and come on in. Karl will take care of you."

"You know, Doc, I won't come see ya' no more, cause ya' won't let me pay for what ya' does and old John may not be smart or good at nothin', but he pays his bills and don't take nothin' from nobody and that's a fact."

"Well, John, you come on in anyway and we'll work something out." Karl lifted his bag. "Where are we tonight?"

The janitor pointed toward a team room that had a yellow hockey sock dangling from the doorknob. "You's in there."

A moment later, Karl was seated in the well lighted dressing room talking about the game with Don Walton, his right-wing, while five other skaters dressed around them. Don was a muscular man in his early thirties and weighed over two hundred pounds. He wasn't fast, but he was strong and a good play-maker. He had been a probation officer until arrearage on his child support order had caused him to flee from both his job and jurisdiction.

Don had just finished putting on his long underwear. He shook his burly head, "Shit, Karl, if we don't have any more players than this, I'll have a heart attack sure as hell. I'm good for once every three shifts, but I can't skate half a game."

Karl smiled, "That's not like you, Don, remember us, we're the magnificent seven."

Ralph Flynn adjusting his knee brace said, "The magnificent seven my ass, Karl. The last time we skated with seven skaters we got whipped and I damn near stroked out. I had to take two days off work and it took me a month before I could get this knee working right." He tapped the hinged aluminum brace.

Within the next ten minutes, the rest of the team straggled in. The room was unusually quiet, no bawdy jokes nor bravado. Just the sound of tape being torn, snaps and buckles joined and an occasional slap of a hand on a pad or helmet.

Was it a Kiwanis meeting? It could have been. A couple of businessmen, a school teacher, an insurance agent, five shop workers, a telephone lineman and a bank vice president? No, a hockey team. Something quite distinct, different and apart from the sum total of their occupations. A well disciplined organization of physical men cutting across all social and economic barriers. Education, background, status nor income counted. That was left in the parking lot. They were a team, a team of men who needed to tax their muscles to stay alive. Men devoted to a single simple goal. Play the best they were physically able to, challenge their bodies and to win, above all to win.

Karl pulled his white jersey over his head and adjusted it. He glanced down to see if it lay on his shoulder pads straight. He noted the "C" on his chest. He was the captain and proud of it.

He went to the blackboard and set the three lines. He tapped the board with a piece of chalk. "Now these guys are pretty tough, we all know that. It's basically a question of discipline. Play your position, watch your check and don't get mousetrapped. They have a tendency to let a winger wander out over their blue line and cherry-pick, so let's watch it. Play a good game, and if you've got to take a penalty, use your head about it; only take a good one. No cheap shit tonight guys."

In a few moments the teams were on the ice warming up. Karl watched the opposition's goalie practice out of the corner of his eye, nothing too obvious. He made a mental note that the goalie was missing slots on the stick side near the left corner of the net.

Pucks whizzed around, banged off boards. The sharp slap of a stick against hard rubber, a puck bouncing off of a leather goalie pad, all common sounds with elemental beauty to them. The game was simple enough, the body pushed to its endurance and muscles oxygen starved, yet it was better than anything, better than money, cars, status or even sex.

In a few moments, the game started. Karl skated hard. As center, he had to do more work than any other player on the ice. He had to be first man back and the first man up. He was captain and had to set an example for the other men.

It was a small noisy crowd, twenty or thirty people in the stands screaming encouragement and obscenities, the usual mix of hockey enthusiasts and blood-thirsty nuts. After the first shift, Karl threw himself over the boards and sat on the bench gasping for more oxygen than his lungs could deliver his exhausted body. Each pore sweat, but it was the clean odorless wet of honest exertion. Karl tensed his legs and felt every muscle of his body. He was finished, exhausted and hurting, yet in three and a half minutes he would be ready to start the process again.

Karl glanced away from the play for a moment then heard a roar. He looked back to see Don shoved to the ice from behind by an opposing behemoth defenseman. In a moment the defenseman was on Don pounding his face with his fists. Don turned on his side and struck the defenseman in the solar plexus with the most dangerous weapon a hockey player has, his elbow. Within moments the combatants were separated by linesmen. Don limped to the bench, his face a bloody mess.

Karl groaned, "What the hell happened over there?"

Don, dazed, eased down on the bench beside Karl. "Oh, that big bastard's been giving me a hard time; I just said something about his mother and the next thing I knew I was eating ice."

A torrent of blood flowed from a two inch fissure in his right cheek. Karl had him lay on his back, but Don couldn't take that position and coughed turning on his side. He spit fragments of teeth into his hand.

Karl was furious. "This is absurd, we're playing recreational hockey and that jerk tried to kill you."

Don struggled to a sitting position touching his lips gingerly with his fingers and said, "Don't get bent out of shape, it's just part of the game."

Karl looked at him in disbelief. "Part of the game my ass!"

The officials called Karl over and a heated discussion ensued. Both of the players were given double minors for roughing. Don returned to the dressing room where the coach worked on his ripped face with butterfly adhesive tape in a futile attempt to pull the jagged edges of the torn gladiator's shredded wound together.

In a few moments the game was back in full swing. Two shifts later Karl lined up Don's attacker on the boards. The big defenseman hadn't worried about Karl, after all he was only a hundred and eighty pounds but that was his mistake. A hip-check took him heavily into the boards where he crumpled to the ice like a rag doll. Karl deftly retrieved the puck in front of the downed player and circled toward mid-ice. The other defenseman was trapped deep. Karl had only one forward to beat.

At the opposition's blue line he made his move. He shoveled the puck from his forehand to his backhand quickly, bobbed his head to the left and skated full tilt to the right. The forward stumbled just an instant, confused by the maneuver. That's all Karl needed and in a moment was home free with only the goalie to beat. Now instinct took over. Karl glanced up at the goaltender who was protecting the right side of the net with his stick, hugging the post. Karl made a swift backward motion with his stick. The goalie, anticipating a slap shot from ten feet out, slid left to block the bottom half of the goal. Karl didn't shoot. His fake had worked, now he had the top half of the net to shoot at. With a quick flick of the wrist the puck was off. The goalie made a futile swipe at it with his gloved hand as it bulged the net twine.

In exuberance, Karl thrust his stick upward in a victory motion but then was sent spinning. The big defenseman hit Karl from behind while he was off balance. Karl felt the sensation of turning and then the crack of his face against the goal post. Everything was black and red. Karl thudded to the ice and slid. There was a crushing weight on his body and the suffocating inability to gasp breath. Then faintly, ever so faintly, as if a whisper through a misty tunnel he heard, "His skates, get his skates off."

CRESCENT

Milisant Crescent rubbed her head. It was sore where she had fallen when she was shoved down by the two boys who stole her purse. In her sixty-six years, her frail black frame had suffered much worse jolts than this one, but this last bump was more than an affront. Looking back on her forty years teaching in the New York public school system it demonstrated the total futility of her life.

She was born of two hard working Arkansas farm laborers who could neither read nor write. Her name Milisant was spelled wrong on her birth certificate and served as a daily reminder of the educational deficiencies of her people. She devoted herself to trying to help. A few lives were brightened and enriched by her labors, but that didn't matter anymore because Milisant Crescent was done. She was through. She was tired, alone and unloved.

Milisant sat down at her writing desk and slowly with arthritic hobbled fingers wrote instructions for her funeral and disposition of her meager personal effects, two rooms full of sentiment, a moldering cattail from a visit to a bog during a nature study trip, a yellow cracked parchment - her degree from teacher's college and the sole memento of her only romance, a faded picture of the Niagara Falls, three days and two nights of the only love of a man she had known.

Milisant turned the light off in the sitting room. She shut the door to the bathroom and to the world. She ran lukewarm water in the tub, dropped her schoolteacher's dress and slip and eased her body in the tepid water. She removed a razor blade from its handle carefully. She smiled, she didn't want to nick her fingers. With both hands under the water she cut one wrist, then the other. She laid back with arms extended. It didn't even hurt. Of course it didn't hurt, because it didn't matter, no one would stop her, no one would care. A warmth spread over her and she closed her eyes. Her cheeks flushed. She smiled, she had done it. The only definitive thing in sixty-six years.

The sink faucet continued to drip at its ever steady pace. It was as dependable as an hourglass, drops of water splattering on the iron stained basin. The drips became distant, muted and then for the first time in the twenty years she had lived in the flat, the dripping stopped.

MERROW

Anne Merrow was in a hurry. She had to be at Sky Harbor International Airport in an hour. It was her first seminar as a faculty member and her paper on dream interpretation was a winner. She knew it. She hummed. She was happy. Tulsa today, God knows what tomorrow, she mused. Move over Joyce Brothers, I'm coming through!

Her roommate, Carrie Allen, peered at Anne from the floor where she sat cross-legged working on the hem of a skirt. "Aren't you just a little bit nervous?"

"Carrie, it's what I want. It's what I am. That's like asking a fish if it's nervous to swim or a bird if it upsets it to fly. I've been in school twenty-one years and the only thing that I've wanted is this."

Carrie kept stitching and under her breath said, "Yeh, that's what I hear your dates say."

Anne grimaced, "I don't think I heard that. No, definitely, I didn't hear that!"

Carrie smirked calling after her as she moved toward the bathroom. "Self-fulfilling prophecy Anne."

Anne shot back over her shoulder, "Bullshit!" She hesitated. "Carrie, I can't believe this bathroom. I really can't. You didn't even put the cap on the toothpaste. You've got panties in the sink, a blow dryer and a curling iron plugged in and your hot curlers look like they're about to melt."

Carrie pulled herself up, "Jesus, sorry Anne, forgot about all of that."

She went to the bathroom and began trying to order things. "Anne, be a darling and wring out those shorts."

Anne tossed her blond curls and put both hands into the half full sink.

Carrie, while retrieving her curling iron, tangled its cord with the blow dryer. Anne saw the blow dryer moving out of the corner of her eye. She tried to pull back but was too late, as it slid into the basin. There was a blinding flash in her head. The molten heat of the sun was in her brain, she saw it for just a millisecond.

WILSON

George Wilson should never have come to Guatemala. A master welder from Bristol, England, he won the Irish Sweepstakes and had a lifetime dream of visiting the Mayan pyramids. Now here he was on a stone littered field-runway at Tikal. The twin engine DC-3 lurched forward. The pilot had only half a runway. Another DC-3 had blown a tire and was mired in the soft volcanic soil blocking the narrow clearing cut from the tropical rain forest.

George pulled at his seat belt and wondered if God had it in for him. He had dysentery in Guatemala City. He would never eat turtle soup again. The best restaurant in the city, the bellboy said. Reminiscence of the Glade air freshener sprayed by restaurant personnel to cover the mildew odor of the carpet was still in his sinuses. The sweet choking scent mingled in his senses with the taste of turtle soup.

That evening while reading the last chapter *Madame Bovary* in which she dies agonizingly at her own hand after taking arsenic, it struck him. He was strong and was never sick. First the colliery as a youth and then the shipyard. A tough hard life, yet the turtle soup and the Glade got him. As Madame Bovary died, he writhed in abdominal pain. Toward morning he made a pact with God that if he was permitted to survive he would never eat again.

He did survive, but then two days later there was the earthquake. Thrown out of bed at 3:00 a.m., he thought the world had come to an end and it had for five or six hundred peasants, but not for George, not quite yet.

The DC-3 coughed and sputtered. One of the motors didn't sound right to George whose ear was quite attuned to piston engines. The plane turned and faced the runway where three hundred yards ahead the wing of the disabled aircraft partially blocked it.

George looked about. No one seemed concerned, the movie crew and the actor in the Zorro costume who had been jumping around cracking his whip an hour before, smoked cigarettes and talked in Spanish. George didn't understand anything they were saying.

The plane's wheels braked and the engines revved. With a squeal the DC-3 bounced down the runway gaining speed. George couldn't see ahead. Trees were racing by his window. The plane creaked one last time and was airborne.

George breathed a sigh of relief, but then in the next instant his world was turned upside down. The left wing sheared off. George grabbed his face, terrible shredding metal sounds, gruesome shrieks arose from throats of the passengers and the plane crashed into the trees fifty feet above the ground.

George was hanging upside down when he heard the explosion. It was so strange, just a little popping sound like a cardboard milk carton blowing out in a trash fire. He beat the odds in the lottery, but the odds beat him in Guatemala.

TWO

Karl Ronstadt could sense the blackness, he blinked his eyes and tried to touch his face. He could not feel his face nor see his hand. Not only was there blackness but motion, spiral motion. It was as if he were in a black fluid medium being spun downward.

He groped for recognition of what had happened or where he was, but the motion had him, he was a leaf being carried by a rushing stream. In time, how much he had no idea, he began to enjoy the ride. There was motion although all was black about him, a sort of euphoria, feeling of well-being flowed through him. It is a dream, of course it must be a dream, Karl reasoned. Such a dream.

Now a sound, a crackle, like bugs electrocuted by an insect lamp - then flashes of light, weird geometric patterns. What was it? Karl had seen the patterns before but couldn't remember where or when. He shook his head and it then came to him. The flashes were patterns on his retina when as a child he looked into bright light then shut his eyes. They were all about him, yet he didn't see them with his eyes. He was enveloped by blackness broken by flashes of strange zigzag patterns, bits and pieces of light like sparklers were everywhere. He blinked again but whether his eyes were open or closed, he saw the patterns, no, more than saw, felt them.

Had he taken drugs? Was he on an LSD trip or suffering an acid reaction? No, of course not, not Karl Ronstadt the all-American boy. Karl wanted to call out, to shout, to make some kind of affirmation of his presence, to stop the three-dimensional merry-go-round.

He tried to scream but no sound came and that's when it struck him. In all the motion and the light, there was no sound. The electrical high frequency emissions he had first heard and associated with the light tracings had ceased, but the speed he was traveling or the velocity of what was around him increased. The light streaks now blurred and Karl spun, twisted and turned, yet he had no sensation of dizziness - only speed.

The euphoria ended and Karl was seized with fear. He was either badly injured and hallucinating or, and this was unthinkable, dead. What had happened? What *had* happened? Was he in bed sleeping?

What did he last remember? Then the realization, a flash of red; the corner of the goal; the steel pipe.

He twisted, swam and flowed through the lightless medium. In time the darkness was punctuated by pinpoints of light. There were clearly stars but no configuration that Karl had ever seen. Spiral galaxies, star clusters, gaseous nebula passed by. They began distinct but now were streaks, ribbons of light cutting through the dark ever faster. Karl sped on. Time lapse photography of stars - the diurnal motion, pictures of night freeway traffic taken with open shutter. The streaks blurred into a milkiness, a kind of light haze.

The sound of wind rent the silence. Yes, it was wind. A hurricane descended upon Karl. He was in the midst of it, but was not afraid. He became very cold. He needed a blanket to pull about him. If only he had Margaret with her soft, warm skin and long legs. After they loved, she enveloped him; that's what he needed. It was so cold. His teeth chattered. He moved through a white iciness, as if he passed into a glacier.

Ahead there was something, he couldn't make it out. It was very bright, a blinding brilliance. He tried to shield his face but to no avail. The approaching luminosity permeated his being. He was moved toward it. He did not like the feeling of being out of control. He spent a lifetime in control and now he had absolutely no control. He was seized by a panicky feeling of helplessness. There was no way out, no explanation for what he was experiencing, no predicate from his existence as a referent. The gleaming object loomed ahead, ever larger.

Karl forced his eyes wide open. What was it, what could it be? Fiery swirls appeared at the outer margin of the huge disc ahead. Solar flares, that's what it was, reasoned Karl. Searing ejecta was thrown out from the edges of the churning interior of the white hot star.

Now the disc covered Karl's entire field of vision. He absorbed the sensation, the scorching heat of the foreign sun. His being, or whatever was left of it, was about to be thrust into the burning disc.

Karl grimaced, the awful truth of what lay ahead was now clearly understood. Karl R. Ronstadt, M.D., was going to hell.

Karl rolled to his side. He laid his head on the crook of his arm. Wow, he thought, did I ever get hit. He looked for his hockey stick but didn't see it on the white expanse of ice or what? The whiteness carried on in all directions.

Karl sat up and looked at his feet. His skates were off. His white tube socks weren't even wet. He stood and brushed imaginary frost from his hip pads. His helmet was missing and so was the arena as well as any other discernable landmark. The floor or ground or whatever it was he stood upon was not ice. It felt firm and had a milky translucence.

The recollection of his long journey returned.

He shook his head as if to clear it and spoke to the emptiness, "I am either mad or dead. God, how ironic. Turn a hockey player loose on an endless ice surface for eternity."

Karl began to walk. He had no idea where he was going, where he was, nor where he had been but it seemed the appropriate thing to move, so he did. After a time, he began to jog. It's curious, he thought, there is no fatigue and then he realized he wasn't breathing. He effortlessly moved over the ground.

Karl thought he heard a sound and whirled around, looking toward the horizon. He put his hands on his hips and called out, "Okay God, I'm here. I made it, now what?"

Karl heard a sound again. He turned toward the noise and saw in a distance a small form on the ground. Not knowing what to make of this, he approached slowly and cautiously. He came upon a little boy seated cross-legged facing away from him.

The sad figure cried mournfully, "Mommy, Mommy, Mommy please help me."

Karl was afraid to reach out and touch the little boy and so carefully cleared his throat.

The brown haired lad turned his head and gasped in horror.

Karl must have appeared a giant to him with his pads and uniform. He spoke softly, "Son, don't be alarmed, I won't hurt you. What's your name?"

The boy stood, ready to move away quickly if the situation

became dangerous. "I'm Billy and I'm lost. I don't know how to get home."

Karl held out his big hand. "I'm Karl, Billy. I'm pleased to meet you."

Billy started to reach for the hand but hesitated.

Karl continued, "I'm lost too. Where did you come from?"

Billy shook his head, "I, I don't know. I had a dream, a bad dream."

Karl reached down for his little hand and took it. This time Billy didn't resist and squeezed his fingers.

"Don't leave me, please mister don't leave me. I'm scared."

Karl squeezed his hand back, "Don't worry Billy, I won't. Where do you live?"

"2410 Pine Hill Drive," came the reply.

"No I mean, what city are you from?"

"I'm from Toronto, sir. Do you play in the NHL?"

Karl smiled, that was one dream he had not fulfilled. "No, Billy I'm just an amateur player."

"Oh," came the dispirited reply. "Where are we mister?"

"I have no idea, none whatever. Have you seen anything in this place?"

Billy nodded, "Just over there where I was before, there's an arrow."

He pointed ahead.

Karl and his young charge walked hand in hand toward a speck, which in time proved to be a giant black arrow embedded in the ground and covered with several layers of whatever they were walking on. The surface had the appearance of clear, acrylic plastic, absent the usual sea shells and seahorses one finds in gift shops.

Karl commented, "Well, Billy, at least we know what direction to go."

THREE

Milisant Crescent stood transfixed. Her black naked body contrasted against the whiteness. She looked in disbelief at her wrists. They were intact. She stretched her fingers. The arthritic knobs on her joints were gone and her fingers moved with ease as a young woman's.

"Wouldn't you know it," she mumbled, "even Heaven is white."

She saw the two figures approaching from the distance. A large man dressed in white holding the hand of a boy. Milisant shuddered. She turned away. She wanted to run, but that was absurd, there was no place to run. She looked down over her aged black body. I never looked good without clothes, she thought, not even as a girl. The man and boy got closer. Milisant dropped to her knees. She interlocked her fingers and raised her arms, "Oh God," she beseeched, "I'm sorry, I really am. I know I shouldn't have done it, but I was so lonely and so tired, so very tired."

Karl and Billy stopped in front of her. Milisant kept her head bowed not daring to look into the face of the Almighty.

She asked, "You're God?"

Karl chucked, "No friend, I'm not God. Tried it a couple of times and didn't care much for it. Besides I don't think God ice skates, although this would make one heck of a rink here."

Billy chimed in, "He's a hockey player but doesn't play in the NHL."

Milisant looked at the strange pair and then turned her nakedness away from their eyes. Over her shoulder she asked, "If you're not God, can you tell me what this place is?"

Karl had forgotten for a moment how things were. "I don't know where we are, nor do I know where we're going. If you'd like to join us, your company is welcome."

Milisant Crescent wanted to cover her nakedness.

Karl sensed her problem and stripped off his hockey jersey. "Why don't you wear this, it's not very stylish but you'll probably feel more comfortable with something on."

Milisant blushed. In a moment she had it on covering her past the knees.

Billy giggled. "You sure are a funny looking hockey player."

The strange trio continued ahead.

Anne Merrow struggled to her feet. She glanced about the barren landscape. She straightened her half-slip and adjusted a bra strap. She put both hands on her hips and shook her head as if to dust out the cobwebs.

She stamped her foot and muttered, "Carrie, damn you, damn you, damn you, damn you! You couldn't put the cap on the toothpaste, pull a plug or pick up your own shit. And what happens? What happens is I'm here, wherever here is, while you go merrily klutzing on, now that's justice."

She looked upward and shouted, "God? Can you hear me God? This is really too much. I'm not ready for this God. I have too much to do. God, this really sucks!"

She half expected a deep resonant voice to reply, "Anne, nobody is ready. No one expects death."

She mumbled, "Great place, really terrific. I get to wander around forever in a half-slip and bra."

A gruff voice from behind Anne asked, "Hey Mum, you really think we're dead?"

Anne, frightened whirled around. She stammered, "Where did you come from?"

George Wilson smiled. Gorgeous lady, he thought. "Mum, I'm from Bristol, or I guess Guatemala City. Are we dead?"

"Well unless you're Mr. Clean and I'm the white tornado, it looks that way." She hesitated, "I'm sorry, I guess that's a little indelicate."

George Wilson looked about in awe. "This sure isn't the way I thought it would be, Mum."

Anne folded her arms in front of her breasts blocking them from his view. "This is just about right for me. What could be more fitting for a person specializing in dream therapy?" she gestured toward the unending whiteness. "All I need are a few Salvador Dali melting clocks and it's perfect."

George Wilson was perplexed, "I don't follow you, Mum. Are you some sort of a doctor?"

"I was, not am. What were you?"

"I'm a welder. Best damn welder in the Bristol yards, luckiest guy alive. I won the Irish Sweepstakes."

Anne tried unsuccessfully to hide her smile. "Bristol, England?"

George nodded.

"Guatemala's a long way from England, what were you doing there?"

"I always said before I died" - he hesitated - "I wanted to see the Mayan pyramids. When I won the sweepstakes, I took a holiday. I've been all over Mexico and Central America, Chichen Itza, Uxmal, Palenque, Copan and then Tikal, that's where the plane crashed."

"Well, good for you friend. You made it before you died. Unfortunately I didn't. What's your name?"

"George Wilson, Mum."

"Well, George Wilson Mum, I'm Anne Kathleen Merrow."

George stammered, "George Wilson, not Mum. Mum is what I called you."

"Well, George, just call me Anne. Let's hope for your sake, God hasn't consigned you to eternity with a lady psychologist. Let's take a walk and find out if He has a sense of humor."

Anne turned on her heels and strode ahead. George followed.

FOUR

The mammoth billboard read:

WELCOME TO AFTERWORLD

Milisant Crescent muttered, "Must mean we're dead."

Karl put a finger to his lips and nodded toward Billy.

Milisant understood.

Karl said, "I guess this must be the city limits. All we need are the Kiwanis and Rotary signs."

He walked behind the billboard. "I'm disappointed. I expected it to say, 'Ya' all come back now.'"

Billy squeezed the big man's hand. "I want to go home, Mister. Please, I want to go back to my mom and my dad."

Karl knelt down and looked into the pleading blue eyes. "Billy, you're going to have to be a tough guy. It's going to be a long time before you see your family again."

"But, Mister, my mom's gonna be awful worried about me. I've just got to get home. She'll be scared to death, that truck - ", Billy hesitated and then collapsed to his knees and began to sob.

Karl grasped Billy's chin with his hand. "Billy, you play hockey?"

The little boy nodded.

Karl pulled him up by a limp arm. "I'm an old hockey player and you're a young hockey player. I don't see we've much to worry about as long as we stick together. What do you say?"

The lad felt for Karl's hand.

Milisant had gone on and called back, "Look ahead."

A large building covering the horizon appeared in the distance, faced with reflecting glass.

In time, the travelers were confronted with a like group of three. Soon they recognized their own images as a mirror reflection from the building.

Words were embedded in the acrylic ground surface: ENGLISH, ESPANOL, DEUTSCHE and many others at regular intervals. Karl, Milisant and Billy followed the English designation.

In front of the building, a black bordered rectangle was laid into the ground surface. Inside it were instructions:

PLEASE STEP INTO THE SQUARE. KEEP ENTIRELY WITHIN IT. TRANSPORT CAPACITY - 12 PERSONS, DO NOT EXCEED.

Karl and Billy stepped into the rectangle. Milisant followed.

The interior glowed red and a musical note sounded. Instantly they were transported to a green room with darker green plastic seats lining three sides. Soft music played through a ceiling speaker. A sweet young feminine voice interrupted the music. "Please take a seat along the wall. When room capacity has been reached, your indoctrination person will be with you. Thank you."

Within a few minutes other people appeared in the center of the floor, listened to the recorded message and took seats. Soon all chairs were occupied. The group was a conglomeration of humanity. An elderly man in a surgical gown, a large, heavy-set man in his late sixties sat naked next to three airline flight attendants all wearing the same uniforms, and a bearded young man wearing a leather motorcycle jacket and sunglasses slumped in a chair. A police officer and several old men and women rounded out the group.

The music ceased. Voices hushed in anticipation of the first preternatural encounter. A bong sounded like an elevator reaching its intended floor and then, on the three solid panels above the chairs, a lighted message appeared:

YES, YOU ARE DEAD

Billy squeezed Karl's hand.

The notice flashed on and off. A young woman appeared in the center of the doorless room. Her honey brown hair hung shoulder length. She was dressed in a light green uniform, the same color as the room. She wore a plastic sign over her breast which read, "Yo Hablar, Espanol".

She tipped a little forward on her toes and smiled, "Hi, my name is

Darlene. I'm your official greeter. Welcome. I know you must have a lot of questions. Believe me, in time they'll be answered." She smiled again reassuringly.

"For the present, it is necessary that each of you be identified and registered. We have special processing for ministers, rabbis, priests and clergymen. Are any of you in this category?"

No one acknowledged the question.

She spied Billy. "Oh, children are not processed through this facility."

She approached him. "Are you a little boy or a midget?"

Before he could answer, Karl said, "He's a midget, Miss."

The bright-eyed girl said, "Oh, well that's okay then."

She turned as she spoke to face each bank of chairs. It was obvious that the speech had been given often.

"I will explain the identification process for you. You must remove any metallic objects or personal possessions from your pockets and place them in the collection device. You then will be assigned identification designators. You will have to wait your turn for requisition allocation. A place is being prepared for you.

"I want to apologize for any inconvenience caused by construction and refurbishing which is ongoing. Recognize that any dislocation will be temporary. Appropriate monitor personnel will be available to assist you.

"I know you will find the wait ahead a little inconvenient, but realize that we must process between eighty and one hundred thousand people a day. In an Earth year we process in excess of thirty million persons. We *are* doing the very best we can with the resources available.

"I know you have questions, but I am unable to answer them. That will come later."

The entire room, as an elevator, descended. The height of the room doubled and then was cut in half by a locking horizontal plate. In the place of the reflective surface there was a solid light green wall with an arched doorway. Above it was a sign:

PROCESSING INPUT.

The hostess stepped in front of the archway. "Please queue up. Note the black line in the floor. Start here. You must not step over it until your turn when you hear a musical note." She smiled and disappeared through the doorway.

The group assembled in a line. There was some disagreement at the front as to who should go first, no one wanting the honor. A bell tone sounded and the fat naked man carefully approached the green jell-like covering filling the doorway. He cautiously attempted to touch the substance, but his hand passed through it. He walked into the opening and disappeared.

Anne Merrow stepped through the jell-like transparency. To her left was a wall mounted funnel like an expressway toll collector. A sign above the inverted cone read:

ALL PERSONAL PROPERTY, COINS, RINGS,
WATCHES AND METAL OBJECTS
MUST BE DEPOSITED.

Anne glanced about. She was alone. She fingered the opal ring that had been the last gift of her dead father. She ignored the collection device and walked through a black frame. A shrill alarm sounded. Lights flashed with painful intensity. A flickering red sign proclaimed,

RULE VIOLATION - INSTRUCTION DEVIATION -
RETURN TO COLLECTION POINT.

Anne retreated through the frame and the sound ceased. She carefully removed the ring and sadly placed it on the upper rim of the inverted cone. It wobbled downward and disappeared. She retraced her steps through the checkpoint. She was not prepared for what lay ahead.

FIVE

In front of Anne stretched row after row of holding stanchions. Thousands of people stood patiently in lines in the piped off areas extending further than the eye could see. Her mouth gaped open. She was jarred to her senses by a woman's voice.

"Let's move along, Honey, right over here."

Anne's attention was drawn to a computer bank where a red-headed woman in her mid-thirties was seated. She wore a happy face pin that read, HAVE A NICE ETERNITY.

"Extend your right hand and place it in here," the shrill voice directed. The woman pointed to a slot in the machinery in front of her.

Anne cautiously inserted her hand into the mail chute size opening.

"That's fine, Honey. What's your name?"

Anne blinked, withdrawing her hand from the compartment, "Anne Merrow."

"No, your full name and please spell it."

"A-N-N-E K-A-T-H-L-E-E-N M-E-R-R-O-W."

"Date of birth."

"March 31, 1968."

"Were you a United States citizen?"

"Yes."

"Social security number?"

"You've got to be kidding."

The computer operator looked up, "No, I need your social security number."

Anne brushed her hair back, "I haven't the vaguest notion. It's not something I committed to memory."

The operator disgustedly offered, "If you have a social security number, I must have it. If you don't, I can put 'none.'"

Anne looked out over the sea of heads. "Put 'none.'"

The operator peered at her, "You didn't have one?"

Anne grimaced, "Not anymore."

"Last address please."

Anne rattled off her apartment address.

"Okay, let's see if you belong here."

Anne shook her head and thought, This is it. The sum and substance of my life is a readout on this monster. My being is at the mercy of one of these? Really! All I ever got from a computer was Roy Acuff records that I never ordered and dumb letters threatening me with capital punishment if I didn't pay a bill run up by some poor soul by the name of Ann Merrill.

The machinery whirled. Banks of light flashed. On the small screen in the front of the machine appeared three, three dimensional, rectangles. After a few moments, the margins of the rectangles overlapped and a light flashed in the center. There was a sizzle. Anne smelled melting plastic.

The operator smiled, "Give me your left wrist, Honey."

Anne extended her arm. The redhead locked a plastic bracelet to her wrist with pliers.

Anne withdrew her arm and read, A. K. Merrow, 910A42787791Q4328990012641F.

The operator tore a print-out sheet from her machine, "Died April 21, 1995 - electrocuted by a hair dryer. That's how it was?"

Anne nodded.

The redhead reached down. "First time I ever had anybody killed by a hair dryer."

Anne responded, "Mine too."

"Here's your identification and classification card."

The technician handed Anne a green plastic plate, similar to a credit card, on a fine chain.

"Put this around your neck. If asked to identify yourself, show the card and your wrist band together. There's a changing booth right over there." She pointed. "Take your clothes off. You may wear a shift or slacks and a shirt."

The lady was very pretty indeed, black hair, bright green eyes but her face was stern.

"What do you mean, 'Rejected'?" George Wilson questioned.

"I'm really very sorry sir, but those are the rules. Your name just isn't on our list."

"Well let me see your list then, Mum."

"It's in the computer sir, or rather it's not in the computer. Your handprint doesn't register and I don't have enough identification to make a disposition. Are you sure you don't know your social security number?"

"Look Mum, what's social security? I don't know what you're talking about."

"Aren't you an American citizen?"

"No, I'm a British subject. I'm from Bristol."

The girl nodded, "Let me see."

She reached under the counter of her terminal and withdrew a large volume. She thumbed through it, speaking to herself, "Cross Code Rule 781.43." She wetted her index finger and plunged through some more pages.

"Umm," she commented, "let me try this."

She gazed at the book while operating the terminal keyboard. In an instant there was a hum. She read the display screen, "'Insufficient data for identification.' I'm very sorry sir, your name just doesn't register. Don't you have any other identification?"

George was docile by nature and used to the British Civil Service which required a degree of patience unknown to Americans but even so he was having difficulty dealing with this situation.

"Look Mum, I had me a wallet with cards in it, pictures, driver's permit and I just put it in that machine like it said."

"I'm sorry sir," the operator said with a sickeningly sweet smile, "but all personal effects are destroyed."

Her eyes perked up a bit, "Did you have a visa or a passport?"

"I did."

"What's your passport number?"

"Don't have the foggiest."

"Well, I'm really sorry sir, but there's nothing I can do, those are the rules. You must be treated under special handling."

The operator pushed a button and in a few moments two yellow-clad women appeared. They were stern and business-like. The largest asked the operator, "What's the problem?"

She shrugged her shoulders, "I can't make any identification of this subject. He's an English citizen who *allegedly* was killed in a plane crash in Guatemala."

George said, "Okay, if that's the way it is Mum, let's just call this a big mistake. Let's say I'm not dead."

The operator smirked, "Sir, if you weren't dead, you wouldn't be here."

George challenged, "Never make a mistake?"

She shook her head.

"Well love, that's a good one, it is. You can't let me in because your silly machine doesn't say I'm dead."

The large woman directed, "That's quite enough sir, follow us."

George snapped, "Say, why don't I just go back the way I came, huh?"

The smaller woman tersely replied, "That's not permitted."

Karl Ronstadt removed his shoulder pads. He pitched them with the rest of his hockey equipment into a bin. He pulled on a beige jumpsuit. It fit quite well.

There was nothing small enough for Billy. Karl found a woman's jumpsuit and helped Billy into it. He rolled up the sleeves and the pantlegs.

Billy said, "Thanks a lot mister."

"Why don't you call me Karl."

Billy smiled, "Okay Karl."

They stepped from the changing booth into the mass confusion of thousands of murmuring souls lined up in holding stanchions. Heads and bodies in the distance obscured what might be the gate or entrance to wherever it was they were going. A young blond woman in a light blue blouse and skirt approached.

She smiled, "Hi, my name is Christine and I will explain what you should expect. As you can see, there are long lines." The rote presentation was stopped abruptly. She gazed at Billy and questioned Karl, "How did you get him through?"

Karl smiled, "It wasn't easy."

"I'll bet it wasn't." She confided, "You can't believe the rules in this place. There is a rule for everything."

In a more business-like tone, she continued, "You must make a choice which line to be processed through. Note there are signs and symbols at designated intervals indicating the major religious affinities of English speaking persons."

The girl continued, "You see a sign designating the Baptist religion ahead of you. Religious denominations are clustered in groups. For instance, the Christian denominations are divided into subgroups of Catholic and Protestant with further subgroups such as Presbyterian, Methodist and so on. Eastern religions are clustered to your right, Middle-eastern religions are to the left. If you belong to a sect or denomination that is not a designated one, you may be processed under Miscellaneous. If you do not believe in an organized religion, there is Atheist, Agnostic or No Preference."

Karl inquired, "Do you have to be a member of a church to be processed through that religion's line?"

The young woman shook her head, "No, doesn't matter. If you'll note your identification card and your wrist band, you will see that there is no designation for age, sex, national origin or religion. There is no discrimination here and these religious classifications are basically for the comfort of our arrivals."

Karl gestured toward the lines, "What about on the other side, are people from different religions accorded differential treatment?"

The young woman cautiously glanced about then whispered, "I'm not supposed to tell you this. It doesn't make any difference. Everyone's treated the same. If I were you, I would pick the shortest line."

Karl laughed, "This must be pretty tough on nuns and priests."

Christine's eyes sparkled, "It is. So much so that we have special sections for members of the clergy. They take their business seriously and this is supposed to be the payoff." She carried on, "I'm sorry, I have to move along or they'll be checking on me. There are a couple of things that you should know. Memorize your number. The last seven digits are the most important since everybody here will have the same first twenty digits. You're being processed on the basis of the chronology of your death.

"It is true if you get into a shorter line you will be processed before someone who died before you did in another line, but within each line chronological integrity is maintained. This is very important. Line cutting is not permitted and should that occur, monitors are instructed to remove the violator."

Karl interrupted, "What do you mean, remove?"

Christine repeated, "Remove. Just like I said, they are *removed*." Her ominous tone was meant to convey more than she said.

She continued, "There are listing screens at intervals. These displays, like television screens, show the numbers being processed. Sequentially you'll be able to determine how far you are from the gate. Additionally you may use them as video playback machines.

"It is impossible, because of the volume we are processing, to give individual attention to questions about how people died. As a consequence, the machines will permit you, if you choose, to see the event of your death. Merely insert your identification card into the slot under the viewing port and you will see exactly how it happened.

"Also, they will show your funeral if you want to watch it. Many people are quite fascinated by this. To some it is a source of amusement and to others, interest."

She nodded toward Billy, "I recommend against the boy using the machines. They are not available at child processing and might be unduly unpleasant for him.

"Now this completes my presentation. I can answer two questions for you."

Karl had a hundred questions and he didn't know where to start. He placed his hands on his chest, "Is this really still my body? I am not hungry. I'm not tired and I ran out there without fatigue. Tell me about what this is."

Christine smiled, "I've had this job for a long time and no one has ever asked that question. You must have been an astute man during your lifetime. The fact is that what you've perceived to be your body is not. It is your recollection of the being you were in life, with several important modifications. Any bodily defect that may have existed has been removed. The deaf hear, the blind see, the crippled walk, those who died of diseased conditions do not have them here.

"It is hard for us to conceive of any existence apart from physiological self - the body. Theoretically it is possible to exist after death completely disassociated from your former physical self, but this is very inconvenient and difficult for both the psychological well-being of our guests and for us as identification is of fundamental importance.

"You'll note the wrist tag and the identification card. Without a body, there would be no way to affix these markers nor could we perceive one another. As a result, you are in something like a hologram. You will feel sensations but the physiological needs you had when you inhabited your body are absent. You will have no need for nourishment. You can stand for," she smiled, "an eternity and you will not be fatigued. You will not have sexual appetite. These matters are all connected with the physical body which you have left."

Karl murmured, "Lovely place."

She nodded her head, "Especially if you like shuffleboard and bingo."

"What?"

"Never mind. Do you have another question?"

Karl asked, "Yes, can I get a transfer?"

Christine said sternly, "Anyone who does not follow the rules gets transferred but," she hesitated as if she thought better of what she was about to say, "it's best to follow the rules.

"Now I've spent all the time I can with you." She spoke hurriedly as if the topic had turned to something much too heavy to be discussed with safety. "Please exercise your freedom of choice in the selection of a religious designation and take your place in line."

Billy squeezed Karl's hand reminding him of his presence. "Karl, what does this mean? I don't understand."

Karl shook his head, "You're in good company, Billy. I don't either."

SIX

Milisant Crescent gazed down over her pastel shift. The material clung to her body, draping her aged frame and exposing its imperfections.

She peered out across the sea of humanity before her and moved in the direction the young woman had indicated toward the holding stanchions for those of the Baptist religion. She found the end of the line and took her place behind two young black men.

The multitude was surprisingly quiet. People stood in line, orderly and silent. Each line inched along the serpentine pathway that doubled back on itself. The black men ahead of Milisant pushed and pawed at one another. The bigger of the two pranced pulling on his jumpsuit exclaiming, "Ain't these the duds?"

The smaller man ahead of him turned and put the palm of his hand behind his head, wiggling his fingers, "Don't you thinks I look like an Indian?"

The bigger man shook his head, "No man, you've been out in the sun too long. Indians is mulattos, not purebloods like us."

The smaller man squinted at his friend, "You got blue eyes, Mr. pureblood brother. Bet youse gotta sea captain great-great granddaddy. Maybe one of them southern gentlemen that was creepin around the slave quarters while their fine ladies was up fixin their hair, putting on their corsets," he pulled imaginary laces from his abdomen.

The bigger man pushed his friend, "Youse right, Kenny, we got fucked by whitey before we was even born. Why, we's as pure as newly fell snow back home in Gary."

Kenny said, "It don't snow in Gary, Leroy, you knows that. That's just soot that come down from the sky out them furnaces."

Leroy strutted, "Kenny, did you see all the white meat in this place? Do you think this is our re-ward, to be surrounded by all this beautiful white meat?"

Leroy commenced to prance and stepped back, landing on Milisant's foot. She instinctively withdrew it and pushed the large black man. Leroy swung around prepared for a fight.

Milisant admonished him, shaking her finger, "You boys had better watch your mouths."

Leroy laughed, "Hey, Kenny, I done stepped on a little nigger lady. Come and looks at her, she's an Auntie Tom."

Milisant frowned, "Don't you boys respect anything? Don't you have any conception of where you are, what has happened to you?"

Kenny chirped up, "Why, granmomma ma, we is in the meat line. We is waitin to get to the front so we gets our white meat of the day."

Milisant looked somber. "Don't you boys know we are dead?"

Leroy laughed, "Dead - little nigger lady - I dead, you can see all of me here an I'm all together." He patted his groin.

At that moment, a burly arm thrust forward and grabbed Leroy by the shoulder pulling him to a stanchion pipe. A ham like hand swung him around and lifted him by the front of his jumpsuit. A huge white man well into middle age growled, "You filthy no good excrement."

He slammed Leroy on the head with his free hand dashing the youth to the ground.

Leroy gazed up at the large man in amazement. Kenny came to his assistance and helped him to his feet. Leroy mumbled, "But, but I pumped five slugs into you."

"True enough but I spattered your brains all over the floor of my liquor store and Martha blew the head off your jive ass buddy there, Kenny, with a shotgun."

Kenny questioned, "You mean we's dead?"

The big man bellowed, "You bet your sweet black ass."

Leroy lurched at the liquor store owner and grappled with him. Three yellow-clad monitors pushed their way through the ring of spectators. The lead young woman sternly demanded, "What is the meaning of this?"

The two men held each other fast but turned their heads toward her. Leroy said, "This old fat man is hasslin me, lady, but you pay it no mind. Take your white ass and get outa here, cause if you don't, when I's done with him, I's got a few tricks for you."

The two monitors now flanking the one who had spoken, extended translucent handheld dowels toward the grappling men. The leader spoke again. "Gentlemen, disorder is not permitted here. Follow me."

Kenny swaggered up to the small woman and leered, "Why, I's more than happy to follow you anywhere, ma'am. You look so sweet, I bet you'd taste jus like molasses an honey. How would you like some hot black hands all over your lily white skin?"

He grasped the ringpull zipper of the monitor's jumpsuit and abruptly tugged it down, exposing her full breasts, abdomen and pubic hair. The flanking monitors reacted immediately, pointing their dowels at Kenny. A blinding light flashed and in an instant his right arm was severed at the shoulder and disappeared with a crackle.

The lead monitor rezipped her jumpsuit. Kenny blinked, looking for his arm. She ordered, "All three of you follow me immediately. If you do not, we'll have no choice but to terminate you here."

The fighters shaken, released their embrace and followed the monitor. Kenny stumbled along behind them.

The last monitor tarried a moment and addressed the gaping spectators. "We are very sorry. Occasionally death priority results in people who have died at each other's hand being placed in close proximity. This may cause a scene. Rest assured that order is restored."

Karl grasped his plastic identification card and thrust it into the slot in the machine. He peered at the screen. He saw a puck fall from the back of a hockey net and he, arms upthrust in victory celebration, struck from behind by the defenseman who blindsided him after the play was over. Karl mumbled, "That son of a bitch."

Below a listing screen hung a sign proclaiming:

ORDER IS ALL
ALL IS ORDER

Billy asked, "What does it mean?"

Karl shrugged, "I guess it's the thought for the day."

They inched slowly ahead. Karl was having difficulty sensing the time that had passed. He missed the usual indicators, daylight, night, hunger or fatigue.

Karl chuckled. Billy asked, "What's so funny?"

"There is a saying that there are no atheists in heaven but we're in that line and even though it is the shortest, there are thousands of them here."

Billy queried, "What's an atheist?"

"It's somebody who doesn't believe in God or an afterlife."

He cocked his head, "But, I thought we're here."

Karl nodded, "Right."

"But then the atheists are wrong."

"Billy, lots of people are wrong about most things. There's no reason why it should be different here. Besides, being wrong is less painful than admitting error."

Multitudes of people stood orderly in line shuffling slowly forward. The usual rumble of indistinguishable voices in the background that accompanied large crowds was absent. A hushed whisper here and there but for most, the dead stood eyes transfixed ahead, quietly proceeding to, Karl mused, who knows what.

Karl's thoughts turned morose and he analogized the scene he was part of, to columns of condemned Jews waiting for the train to take them to Auschwitz or Buchenwald. Or perhaps, cattle standing patiently in holding pens biding their time until the fall of the hammer and the butcher's knives dismembering their warm carcasses.

Karl shook his head, bad thoughts, very bad thoughts. Here you are, the place is clean, no messy accident victims or terminal cancer patients - that was true disorder or order gone malevolently awry.

Billy pointed, "Can you see what that sign says?"

Karl squinted, "It says, 'Order is Perfection.'"

"What does that mean?"

Karl rubbed his chin, "In the physical universe, the world of sun, moon and stars, certain uniform relationships exist. Unfortunately, in the affairs of people, physical laws don't apply and there is disorganization and lack of predictability. I think that sign means, at least to those in charge here, being organized - things in their place, events predictable - is viewed as perfect, the way they believe the ideal should be."

"Sort of like keeping my clothes hung up and things like that."

Karl nodded, "That's about it."

A feminine voice in an unmistakable German accent interrupted, "I don't care what it's like here. It can't be worse than down there."

Karl turned to the young woman with coarse blond hair and piercing blue eyes standing behind them in line. He asked, "Where are you from?"

The girl replied, "Hamburg, St. Pauli, to be exact."

The answer didn't register. The woman stepped back a bit, "Let me tell you about yourself. You are a doctor or a lawyer."

Karl smiled, "A doctor, very good. You must be a student of the human condition."

The girl smiled, "More than you, my profession is older."

Karl said, "A lady of the night?"

The blond smirked, "Oh, that's a bit coarse. Let's say I am a courtesan."

He corrected, "Were . . . But, tell me, what you are doing here if you are from Germany?"

"I speak English, don't I? Why shouldn't I be here?" She gestured toward the end of the line, "They said if I spoke English, I could be here."

"Why don't you want to be with the German language group? I assume you are German."

"Ya, I'm Deutsche, but the Americans had the best of everything in life, why should it be different here?"

Karl queried, "What's your name?"

"Friendly Freda. That don't count no more. If you want to know, read my number."

She thrust her hand out exposing her wrist band.

Billy asked, "How did you get here, Ma'am?"

The young woman knelt down. "My boy - the hazards of trade. You see, there was this Greek sailor. . ."

Karl interrupted, "Look, Friendly F, I don't think he needs that."

She glared at Karl. "Okay, big boy, would you like to see it? All you do is stick this," she grabbed her dogtag and thrust it out, "in a machine back there."

The young woman turned her head down and away from Karl. A single rivulet ran down her cheek. He pulled her chin up with his hand, "Freda, I'm sorry. This is hard for all of us. You and I may understand what's happening but the little guy here, well, he just. . . Let's just treat each other kindly, okay?"

Karl grasped Freda by the shoulders turning her toward him and placed both hands on either side of her neck over the carotid arteries. There was no question about it, he felt a strong, hard, bilateral pulse.

Anne Merrow shook her head, causing her fine, long, blond hair to rustle along the back of her white jumpsuit. She stretched the muscles of her back and rolled her shoulders. She stared ahead at the endless line that played out in front of her. She began to curl a strand of hair with her finger, a habit she'd picked up in grade school in boring classes. Now, there was no teacher nor mother to admonish.

Anne shifted her weight from one foot to the other. She yawned but that didn't help either. The line inched ahead slowly. Anne mused, it must have been a bad time for the Lutherans. The Lutheran line she was standing in was the longest.

All those around her stood eyes ahead, zombie like. The large white room was as quiet as a library. Anne drew in a deep breath and screamed a loud piercing cry. The two elderly men immediately in front of Anne jumped, scared out of their wits. One stumbled over the other and people began falling down along the line, a graphic display of John Foster Dulles' Domino Theory.

People standing near Anne cowered from her, horror-struck. She had committed an unpardonable sin. She had made a loud noise in a silent zone. Order had been fractured and the silence acquiesced in by thousands of standees, violated. Anne smiled. The woman behind her whispered to a neighbor. "She must be mad, utterly mad."

Three monitors quickly worked their way through the line. They were given hushed directions to the site of the commotion. They soon reached Anne who had been given a great deal of room by those about her. She stood, head erect, faced forward in her proper place in line.

The tallest monitor, asked in an officious tone, "All right, what's going on here?"

In unison, those about Anne extended their fingers and uttered, "She did it."

The monitors ringed her. The tall girl asked, "Young woman, what is the meaning of this?"

Anne nonchalantly responded, "Could you tell me what time it is?"

The monitor glanced down at her bare wrist, in an instant her blue-gray eyes darted back to Anne's. Harshly, she said, "Time is not kept here."

Anne smiled, "It's a pity. I'll never know how long I have stood in line or how long I will stand in line."

The head monitor declared, "You will stand in line as long as necessary. Now enough of this, why the commotion?"

Anne stared away from the inquiring eyes and said softly, "I was exercising my freedom of screech."

The large monitor's eyes pinched. One of the smaller monitors smiled covering her lips with the back of her hand. The tall monitor sternly announced, "Disorder is not permitted."

Anne shook her head, "I'm truly sorry. I didn't mean to upset everyone, but I suffer from Hoffritzphobia."

The monitor blinked, "What?"

"Hoffritzphobia. Don't tell me you are not familiar with it?"

The monitor was now on the defensive, "I don't know what you are talking about."

Anne scratched her chin, "It's a rather uncommon malady first discovered in 1829 by Hans Hoffritz, the noted Viennese vivisectionist."

The monitor asked, "What is it?"

Anne continued, "Hoffritz discovered it in Austria. It occurred much as Archimedes discovered volume displacement, the Curies radium and the more recent discovery of synthetic rubber. Hoffritz noted that persons standing in line waiting for service at a delicatessen he often frequented, quite uncontrollably and at unpredictable times would scream. He devoted the last 15 years of his life studying the phenomenon which was not confined to delicatessen lines. Hoffritz deduced that certain people under circumstances requiring delay and orderliness were driven by an eventual panic caused by consummate boredom to express themselves by screaming. The scream itself acts as a tension reliever and is good therapy for other people standing nearby the afflicted person.

"I first became aware I had it while waiting to get into the little girls' room in kindergarten.

"In any event, I feel much better now and I hope I haven't inconvenienced you. I certainly have enjoyed talking with you. Anything you could do to expedite the line moving along to get to wherever we are going would be appreciated."

The tall monitor said ominously, "Disorder is not permitted."

Anne stood her ground, "I didn't mean to be disrespectful nor did I create disorder, I merely hit a high C. I am, as you probably don't know, an opera singer."

A smaller monitor repressed a giggle.

The lead monitor drew in a breath but Anne raised her finger, "Tell me, what is your name? I'd like to report your efficiency to your supervisor when I get an opportunity. As a woman, I can appreciate another woman who is doing a good job and competent at her calling."

The monitor's eyes softened, "My designation is Weston VCT."

"Well, thank you very much, Weston VCT. As soon as I have an opportunity to talk with your superior, I will mention you. Now, if you will excuse me, apparently it is my lot to wait in line and you are distracting, so if you could leave, I'll do my best to suppress any urge I might have to scream. If I do, it is involuntary and nonvolitional, the only cure is not having to stand in line."

Weston was perplexed. She didn't know how to handle the situation and it was clear she was getting the worst of every exchange. She admonished, "Young woman, you cannot violate the rules."

Anne stared blank-eyed. "Rules, what rules? No one told me there are rules."

Weston responded, "Order must be kept. Rule 327A requires there by no breach of order."

"Really, I don't know your rules."

Weston pointed toward the front of the line, "You'll get a rule book up there."

Anne yawned, "Well, when I've had an opportunity to look them over, I'll do my best not to break any, but when it comes to screaming, I really have no control. I have Hoffritzphobia. I can't help it, it's just like a woman being unseemingly tall."

Anne glanced up at the monitor and continued her upward gaze after clearing the tall woman's head.

The monitor stated, in a menacing tone, "I will not be baited. I have discretion to remove anyone violating public order. You will do well to control whatever urges you may have."

With that she turned on her heel, not waiting for Anne to retort and strode away. The two smaller young women who accompanied her tarried. The one who had been suppressing a smile whispered to Anne, "Hoffritz?" The other monitor winked, then they followed their leader.

SEVEN

Extreme law is often extreme injustice.
— Publius Terentius Afer

George Wilson pressed his hands against the inside of the glass cylinder imprisoning him. Through the dimly lit corridor and the distorted transparent medium, he could see hundreds of other cylinders containing shadow forms standing at attention waiting for whatever was to come. The Muzak like strains of a symphony were barely audible. Although no doubt intended to be reassuring, the music added to the strangeness of the setting.

To George's right was a cylinder containing a thin black man. He could make out some movement of the man's fingers as they clutched at the stump of his missing arm. The man to his left was large and burly. He stood erect and motionless staring into the ill-lit containment room.

George closed his eyes and relived that day, his last day. It was bright, warm and still, a kind of quiet George had dreamed of but never experienced. The shipyard was dirty and noisy, always the pervasive chatter of pneumatic tools, riveting and the rub of metal against metal.

But in the jungle, in that beautiful jungle, there was stillness, broken only by the cry of a Macaw or screech of a monkey. There was also room, lots of room. The vast open space between the tree canopy and the ground. The trees towered above him 300 feet, filtering the Guatemala sun into casts of green. George was in the forests of Tikal. He was alone with the sounds of the jungle about him. They were warm and comforting like the strains of a song learned in childhood but forgotten in old age. Somewhere in the primordial George Wilson, there was a kinship with the jungle. He could not describe it nor did he try. He just felt, for the first time in his life, he was home.

In front of George lay a snaking trail of army ants. Winding their way from where to where? The column extended off into the underbrush on either side of the well worn path. A curious sight, George mused as he hunched down and watched bits of leaves move on the living conveyer belt.

At noon on the last day of George Wilson's life, he stood gazing up through tangled roots and tree trunks at the base of Temple IV, the largest prehistoric manmade structure in the world, save only the great pyramid at Giza in Egypt. Its huge perimeter had been attacked by trees over the last eleven hundred years. Blocks weighing two tons were displaced but the top two-thirds of the temple was restored.

George pulled himself up over roots and broken branches as he climbed the magnificent Mayan monument. After several hundred feet of rough going, he reached the area where restoration had begun and the climb was easier as he made his way up shallow steep steps.

At last, he emerged from the jungle canopy into the bright sunlight. The treetops lay just below him like the ocean surface. The bright sun warmed him. In time, he reached a plateau three hundred feet above the ground and from that point ascended a recently constructed pipe ladder which took him to the rear of the platform at the base of the roofcomb. The humidity of the rain forest and the bright warm sun coupled with exertion tired him.

He sat for a moment on the ledge and gazed out over the treetops that lay below. Jutting out like icebergs from an Arctic Sea were the roofcombs of temples I, II and III. George walked along the ledge. At the front of the temple, he was startled to see a small figure sitting with knees clasped to her breast staring ahead. The young woman glanced up at George, tossed her honey-brown hair and smiled. "Buenas dias, Senor."

George smiled and returned the greeting, "Buenas dias, Senorita. Como esta usted?"

The woman returned, "Muy bien, y usted?"

George scratched his head, "Hablo English."

The girl smiled, "I didn't think you looked very Spanish."

"You don't either. Where are you from?"

"Belize yesterday but Los Angeles originally. And you?"

"Guatemala City, yesterday, Mum, but generally Bristol, England. How long have you been up here?"

The pretty girl pulled at a wisp of hair. "I climbed it at five o'clock this morning. I snuck in before the gates opened and saw the sunrise."

She pointed, "I saw the first light touch these monuments, it was a lifetime high for me and I'm not on anything. Look out, as far as the eye can see, there's green except for those bleached steeples of the dead. Listen," she hesitated and in the far distance the cry of a great monkey was heard, "isn't that beautiful," she whispered.

She asked, "Did you see Zorro today, he's been here for a week. There's an American film company coming in next month. They are filming another 'Star Wars' and what a set, it's out of this world."

George smiled, "Hope they don't leave beer cans, Mum."

He was jerked from his reverie by a crackling announcement, "Block H processing is beginning. Prepare to accompany monitors."

The cylinder to his right descended into the floor with a pneumatic whoosh. The one-armed black man had been leaning against the wall half asleep and fell abruptly to the ground. A monitor signaled him up with a glowing dowel.

Leroy shuffled about uneasily in the dimly lit green room, absent-mindedly fingering where his arm had been. Before him, sitting behind an acrylic table sat three women in their mid-twenties. Leroy was flanked by the two monitors. The center woman asked, "What is the violation?"

One of the monitors handed a plastic card to the interrogator. She inserted it into a view screen slot and read, "Rule violations 732A and 123-11A - inciting a disturbance, general misbehavior required punitive action."

The interrogator addressed Leroy. "It seems in the short time you've been here, you've been very active."

Leroy scowled, "I don't take no shit from you, honky, or nobody else. Arm - the bitch took my arm."

The interrogator asked, "Mr. Johnson, do you have anything to say concerning the rule violations?"

Leroy scowled again, "Rule violations, my ass. Fuck your rules. That cunt took my arm!"

"Mr. Johnson, you lost your arm, but that has no particular significance. Is this all you have to say?"

Leroy glared at the interrogator, "Is this a trial or somethin? If it's a trial, I want you read me my rights."

The interrogator betrayed no emotion. "Mr. Johnson, you have no rights."

Leroy blinked, "I want a lawyer. I gotta have a lawyer. I gotta right to a lawyer."

The interrogator replied, "No, Mr. Johnson, you don't have a right to a lawyer. You don't have a right to anything."

She asked the other seated woman, "Do either of you have any questions?"

Both shook their heads.

The interrogator said, "Indicate, please."

The women pushed buttons on the table and a red "T" glowed in the acrylic in front of each place. The interrogator pointed to a door which was marked with a "T."

"Mr. Johnson, you are to be transferred. Please go to the Transfertorium exit."

Leroy firmly planted his feet. "You can shove your exit, lady. I'm going nowheres until I see the man. I wanta see *the* man."

The monitor to his left pointed her dowel toward Leroy and it pulsed a laser that just missed his groin. Leroy quickly uttered, "Okay, okay, I goin," and hurriedly stepped through the door.

George Wilson stood in front of the interrogator's bench. "I don't understand, Mum, rule violation?"

The interrogator said, "Well, this is a technical violation. We do not have the appropriate identification information to process you."

George shrugged his shoulders, "What can I say? I have a phone number, an apartment number. I can give you my union number."

The woman to the right of the interrogator spoke, "If you're really English, you must have a National Health Service number."

George exhaled, "I had a card. It was in me wallet, but I put me wallet in that thing that said to put everything in it and it's gone. I never memorized that number, I don't get sick."

The woman on the other side asked, "Are you sure your name is George Wilson?"

"That's the name they gave me at the orphanage."

The interrogator queried, "Do you know the names of your parents?"

George shook his head, "No, Mum."

She responded, "Thank you very much. Designate."

The interrogator and the woman to her left lighted red "T's." The woman to the right flashed a green "I."

"Mr. Wilson, please exit through the designated door."

Milisant Crescent waited her turn. The plastic sign ahead of her turned from red to green with an audible "ding." The door parted from the center and she stepped into a well lit room. A woman seated at a bank of machines glanced up and smiled. "Please place your identification card in the slot in front of me."

Milisant stepped forward, bent down and inserted her card into the opening. A "click" sounded and the young woman smiled and said, "That's fine. Let me see your wristband, please."

Milisant extended her arm and the woman compared the number on the bracelet with something on the computer screen in front of her. Milisant could not see the display but a green light reflected off the face of the girl who questioned, "Milisant Crescent?"

Milisant nodded, "That's right."

The woman smiled, "You've been cleared for acceptance. Please step to your right."

A door opened and Milisant passed through it. The dimly lit hallway led to a round capsule-like enclosure. As soon as Milisant entered, the door sucked close. There was an array of lighted numbers displayed on the wall of the chamber. In the center was a single red seat. It was similar to the soda fountain stools Milisant remembered from her youth.

A disembodied female voice announced, "Welcome and congratulations. You are now permitted the privilege of selecting the apparent physical presence which you wish to inhabit. Through this chamber you may choose any age which you attained during your lifetime, from whatever your age was at the time of cessation to age 18. If you are less than 19 years of age, you are not permitted a selection nor may you select an age in advance of what you reached during life.

"Your memories, experiences and self as they exist this moment, will be retained. Only your physical appearance will be altered to be as it was during the age you select.

"Once an age has been selected, it cannot be changed. If you wish your physical appearance to be as it was during an earlier time in your life, push the button for the age you choose to adopt. Please make your selection promptly. If you make no selection while the green light flashes, you will remain as you are and must exit the chamber when the door opens."

A soft green light above the selection panel began to pulsate. Milisant sat on the stool. She extended her fingers toward the panel. Even young she was not pretty but at least young was young. The green flashing light pulsated faster urging her to make a choice. She pushed the 25 button.

There was a humming noise and then a voice announced, "Please sit back on the stool, place your arms at your sides and close your eyes. There will be no pain."

Milisant followed the directions. Through her closed eyelids she perceived bright illumination like silent lightning flashes. Soon, she heard "ding" and the voice announced, "You may leave."

She opened her eyes. To her surprise she gazed down over her own youthful form, a sight she hadn't seen in 40 years and barely recognized. She exited into an anteroom where another young woman was seated at a desk.

The girl smiled, "I have some important materials for you. Here is your residence assignment. Note the cog, unit and module numbers. Here is a key to your module computer. It operates in English and will answer your questions.

"Note that your residence allocation is blue. When you leave this room, follow the blue line on the floor to the blue monitors' station." The young woman handed two plastic cards to Milisant.

Anne Merrow was ushered into the residence module. There was a white table in an open domelike circular area; halls with radial arms led to six smaller round rooms. She sensed someone's presence and turned to greet the smiling approach of a fleshy woman in her 40's.

"Oh my," exclaimed the woman. "I was the first one, now I have company. That's so nice."

She extended her hand. "My name is Helen Benson."

Anne perfunctorily extended hers, "I'm Anne Mer---."

The woman interrupted, "From Sioux Falls, you know, that's in North Dakota. Oh my, this is some place isn't it? I mean I really didn't think it would be like this, did you?"

Anne wasn't given an opportunity to answer.

"I mean, look at it, it's sort of like an igloo but who am I to complain. I never complain about anything. I mean maybe I complain a little but I don't complain a lot, you know what I mean?

"It'll be so lovely to have someone to talk to. I've been lonely, standing in that line waiting for all those people. It was terrible, like Grand Central Station. You probably don't know about Grand Central Station. Well, anyway, the worst of it is, I've lost my grandchildren's pictures. They were in my purse. They're gone and I just don't think that's right. I mean what do I have to show people. All I can do is say, I have two grandchildren, one is Tim, he's 12 and Sara, she's 8. But no pictures, that doesn't strike you as fair, does it?

"Well, it doesn't matter. I really feel great. I haven't felt like this in oh, I don't know how long. You know, I was in so much pain I couldn't stand it. It was first one thing and the other. It started out a little lump, the next thing they were removing my breast," she grasped her fleshy chest. "But I got it back, right? There it is. That's pretty good and then the pills and the chemotherapy and the narcotics. It was awful. I mean I don't suppose you had big C did you?"

Anne's mouth opened, but there was no pause.

"That's a funny thing to call it, isn't it, big C. That's what my doctor used to call it, big C. Sounds like a wrestler or something. I wanted to ask him what little C was if cancer was big C but I never did. Didn't feel good enough to, anyway. Great having you here. This is really some place, isn't it? Look at me, I'm 20 years younger than I was when I died and besides that I've got my breast back." She patted her corpulent chest.

"This is stark, really stark. Don't you think this is stark? What we need is some color, maybe some flowers, paint the ceiling or something. Can you paint? I used to paint, I wonder if there are paints here. I mean even if they didn't have real flowers, if we had plastic flowers, that would be okay. They're no trouble, you don't even have to water them, dust them a little now and then, that's all."

Anne extended her hand to stop the woman's chattering, "Please, I'm really tired and quite confused. Which room is mine?"

The woman laughed, "Oh, I don't know. Whatever you want, except mine. That one's mine over there."

Anne said, "Fine, look I'm pleased to meet you but I think I'll rest a bit."

"Oh, glad you're here. This is so lovely to have somebody to talk to. I don't suppose you play bridge do you? I mean that wouldn't matter because there are only two of us now but if you played bridge, that would really be nice."

Anne walked toward the radial arm leading to a corridor as far from her neighbor's room as possible. She felt a tug on her shirt. "Anne, I think you said your name is Anne. Would you like some tea? Do you want me to see if I can get some tea?"

Anne was astonished, she pulled free, "Please, whatever you like. Get some tea."

"It won't be the same. The silver isn't silver, it's plastic but it'll do. I'll get some tea." She trundled back across the room to a cabinet on the wall.

Anne rolled her eyes, put her hand on her forehead and sighed, "Oh God, what did I do to deserve this?"

Karl and Billy were escorted to B492-7. The blue-clad monitor smiled, "This is in a nice area, I hope you'll enjoy your stay.

"This is the module entrance. Place your card in the slot and it will open." The girl demonstrated and the door silently parted from the center. They entered.

"There are instructions on the wall. Your information center is located there. Your Social Director-Acclimator will be by after your module is full. If you have any requests, you may use the videophone. It's on the wall over there," she gestured.

From behind them came, "Oh, hello, hello, some more people. Grand, great."

Karl turned to face a heavy-set woman holding two teacups. "Pleased to meet you. We are going to have tea. Would you like some tea?"

Karl smiled, "No, thank you."

The woman dropped her gaze to Billy. "You, young man, you're about the age of my grandson. Would you like some hot chocolate, maybe some cookies?"

Billy nodded.

"Good, good, I'll be right back. Where are you from?"

Karl started to answer. She interrupted, "I'm from Sioux Falls-North Dakota, you know. I had cancer. They removed almost everything. They couldn't believe it but I was still going. I mean, I fooled them all. I lasted longer than they ever thought I would. Couldn't keep me down, you know, until the last operation. You should have seen me, weighed less than 100 pounds. Wouldn't know it now would you? I mean you wouldn't believe what they did to me. They took out so much."

Karl stroked his chin, "You've had a hysterectomy?"

The woman lowered her teacup. "Oh, my God, it shows. You can really tell? I didn't think anyone could tell just to look at a person. Are you a doctor?"

Karl nodded and asked, "What about the hot chocolate?"

"Oh, I forgot about that. I wonder about my hysterectomy. I wonder if I got it back?" She hugged her abdomen with her elbows as if to probe it. "I mean if there isn't a scar, I probably have it in there."

She disappeared down the corridor to her room.

Billy shook his head. "She's sort of a funny lady, isn't she?"

Karl smiled, "Well, we're not going to have peace and quiet, I can see that. This isn't exactly violins and a harp."

"Doctor?" Anne Merrow whispered playfully.

Karl turned toward the voice. He asked, "Are you part of the establishment?"

She smiled, "No, just a customer. My name's Anne Merrow." She extended her hand.

Karl joined hands holding her warm palm a bit longer than was appropriate.

"Karl Ronstadt. And my friend, Billy, is a Canadian hockey player."

"Is this your boy?"

Karl answered, "No, we met on the plain."

Anne queried, "Airplane?"

"No, the plain outside the entrance to this place."

Anne commented, "Nice job on our friend there. I didn't want to offend her but she is a little much."

Karl smiled, "She shouldn't bother us for awhile, she's got to check out if she has her plumbing intact. Maybe you can show us the ropes here."

"Sorry, I can't. I just got here myself. All I know is that you can have whatever room is unoccupied."

Karl asked, "You're not 85 reduced to 25 by virtue of button pushing, are you?"

Anne laughed, "No, what you see is what I was."

The door opened and Milisant Crescent entered. She felt as if she had interrupted a family scene and started to apologize for intruding.

Karl stopped her, "No, Miss, you are probably one of the new boarders, just like the rest of us. I'm Karl Ronstadt."

"I'm Milisant Crescent from New York City, a school teacher."

Anne waved, "Anne Merrow, Phoenix, psychologist."

Billy stood up, "Billy Evans, Toronto, hockey player." He then gestured toward Karl, "He's a doctor."

Helen Benson bustled in carrying a tea service. "Oh, we have a new one. Black girl, how nice. I always wanted to talk with a real black person, you know, private like. Ask them things. This will be so nice."

EIGHT

George Wilson stood in line in the dimly lit hall behind a burly man. George recognized him as one of his neighbors in the holding cylinders. At the end of the hall was a glowing door of gelatinous matter similar to the green one that he had entered Processing Input through.

Two monitors stood in the corridor with their translucent rods at ready. The larger one signaled a woman at the front of the line to enter the green doorway. Above the entrance was: TRANSFERTORIUM. The woman stepped in, the door turned red, flickered an instant and then turned green again. George Wilson inadvertently touched the shoulder of the large man in front of him. The man whirled around and George retreated bumping into an old woman standing behind him.

"Sorry," he apologized.

The man exhaled now perceiving no threat. He asked, "Do you know what's going on?"

George shook his head, "Haven't the foggiest."

The big man asked, "Why are you here?"

"I guess because I was raised an orphan and don't have the right name or a social security number."

The big man lamented, "I'm here because I roughed up a couple of punks."

From up the line came, "Fuck you, man."

Leroy stood two persons ahead of the burly man and gave him the finger.

The big man asked George, "You've got a funny accent, where you from?"

"England. If I was a Yank, I wouldn't have this problem."

The big man shook his head, "I don't like what's coming. I have a bad feeling about it. Your problem is that you don't have a tag or a bracelet, is that it?"

George nodded, "That's about right."

The big man whispered, "I don't think I'm going to be needing mine much longer, why don't you take them and try and get the hell out of here."

"Like how?"

"Like, I'm gonna beat the shit out of that punk in line ahead of us. When I do, these girlies are going to come running. See if you can get away during the ruckus."

The burly man covertly lifted the chain from his neck and handed it to George who put it on. The big man put two fingers under his wrist band and flexed his forearm. The bracelet snapped like a chain of dandelion stems. He handed it to George who slipped it on his wrist.

The big man turned back toward the front of the line and called out, "Leroy, how you gonna pick your nose with only one arm? I bet you won't even be able to jerk off anymore."

Leroy shot back, "Old man, I killed you once, now you want me to kill you again?"

The store owner erupted bellowing, "That's it."

He charged like a bull right through the two people behind Leroy knocking them to the side. He grabbed the youth's shoulders and shoved him down face first to the ground.

People ran every which way trying to get out of the way of the flailing arms as the storeowner pummeled the back of the youth's head.

The two monitors quickly worked their way through the startled onlookers. Leroy's friend, who had also been in line, jumped on the storeowner's back and tried to pry him off.

One monitor tested her weapon, hitting the ceiling, dropping molten bits of plastic on the crowd. The big man turned and threw Leroy's companion at her, knocking her into the wall and dislodging the dowel from her grasp. It rolled down the corridor. George Wilson picked it up and slipped it in his pocket. Then he walked back up the hall.

Three monitors charged toward him. He pointed toward the fray. "Help, please help them."

Two of the young women ran on to assist the fallen girl while the third, dressed in a red jumpsuit, lingered viewing George suspiciously.

She demanded, "Where do you think you are going?"

George stammered, "Well, I was going to get help. They need help down there. They need you. Right now."

The young woman smiled, "There is only one way out of here for you and that is through the Transfertorium."

She pointed her dowel toward George's midsection and ordered, "Now, back up carefully."

George swung his arm, striking her shoulder and knocking the dowel from her grasp. She cried a short agonizing gasp. He pushed her against the wall and held her fast. She panted and resisted but it was to no avail. George placed his dowel against her forehead.

"How do I get out of here?"

She whimpered, "You can't get out. No one can get out."

George said, "Well, Mum, if I don't get out, I'm going to splatter your head all over the wall. Now, I've not done one violent thing in me life. I don't want to hurt you. How do I get to the room where the people are?"

Trembling, she pointed down the corridor. "There's a connecting passage with rooms that eventually go back to the entrance."

George ordered, "Get them lights off in this hall."

She quaked, "They are never off. They're always on, there's no switch."

George surveyed the ceiling. He aimed the dowel at the brightest point. The laser beam fired, melting plastic. In an instant it was through to the source of the light which exploded with a hiss, billowing smoke out the hole burned by the beam. The hallway was dark.

George held the monitor to the wall. Footfalls approached and then passed on the run.

He pushed the small woman forward and whispered, "One word, one word out of you and that's the last word you speak."

He held the rod to the back of her head and she nodded, understanding.

They moved forward. She whispered, "It's here on the left. I can feel the door."

The door parted and in the dim light, George saw an empty monitor station.

He pushed the girl inside.

"Where's the switch for this door?"

She said, "It's the palm button right here on the inside."

George shut the door and then blasted the switch.

The girl pleaded, "Please, please don't hurt me."

George menaced her with the dowel, recognizing that his only way of escape was her mortal fear. "How do I get to the big room?"

She motioned to another door.

"You're not lying to me are you, Mum?"

The girl, horror-struck, shook her head.

"Just to be on the safe side, let's you and me go together, Mum. Straight ahead."

She said, "No, no, not that way. Over here."

She led him to another door, pressed the palm button and they entered a long corridor.

She said, "This is a service hall."

George relaxed his grip and pushed her ahead letting her walk free of him.

She glanced back over her shoulder. "You must have done something terrible. Were you a murderer?"

"No, Mum, didn't have a social security number. Let's move."

The corridor finally ended at a door. The girl hesitated in front of it. "I can't open this, you have to have a special key."

George lowered his dowel and splattered the lock. The door opened exposing a huge cathedral-like room filled with thousands of complicated clicking, flashing machines. He pushed the monitor inside.

"Hi, my name is Caroline. I'm your Social Director-Acclimator."

Karl stood as she entered the module. The young woman was stunning. She had long blond hair and very fair skin. The aqua skirt she wore accentuated her shapely legs, small waist and large breasts. She held a clipboard in one hand and pencil in the other.

She called, "Please come here."

Billy, Anne and Helen with the restored uterus, gathered in the central room.

Caroline flipped through some pages.

"One missing still," she said to herself and made a note.

"This is interlocking radial unit B492 and your module number is seven," she announced without looking up from her board.

She flipped through pages of computer printouts. "The residents of this module are Horace King, Linda Evens," she glanced up touching the tip of the pencil to her tongue. Her blue eyes met Karl's. "Are you Horace King?"

Karl shrugged his shoulders, "I'm afraid not."

Her gaze turned to Anne Merrow. "Are you Linda Evans?"

Anne shook her head, "Don't I wish. Unfortunately, I'm a 27 digit number with an alphabetic preface."

Caroline smiled, "Were you Linda Evans?"

Anne shook her head, "Never."

"What is your name?"

"Anne Merrow."

Caroline shook her pencil. "You two aren't supposed to be in this unit."

Anne feigned dismay, "Oh, darn, when I saw my bedroom window overlooked the park, I was afraid someone made a mistake."

"What?"

Anne smiled, "Never mind, dear."

The tall girl looked down at Billy. "This is not the children's section. How did you get here?"

Karl responded before Billy could answer. "Miss, I am a physician and this man is well past the age of majority. In life he suffered from a rare metabolic dysfunction that created hormonal imbalances with the effect of suppressing the pituitary gland to the extent that he remained short although in years he was an adult. The malady is known as Thumb's Syndrome named for the famous midget who toured in the late 1800's with P. T. Barnum."

Anne whispered, "Hoffritz."

Caroline tossed her long hair. "Well, I suppose that's all right, then."

"Dearie, I must be on your list, my name is Helen Benson."

Caroline looked at the clipboard again. "No, you're not on it either.

I don't know why this always happens to me. Is this B492-7?"

Karl shrugged his shoulders. Caroline went to the computer terminal and traced the number on the serial plate with her finger. "It's the right unit but you are the wrong people." She bent down over the computer keyboard and the screen whirred to life. Caroline gracefully and swiftly punched the keyboard. In an instant, names began appearing line by line. All of the occupants of the module gathered around the machine.

She asked, "Are these your names?"

Anne replied, "Every one except Henry Kallas. We haven't met him yet."

"I'm sure you will. Okay, you're in the right module but I've got the wrong list." She cleared the screen and then entered new information. "I have the list for E492-7. Well, no matter. I want to introduce myself."

She turned to the group, pressing the clipboard to her chest. "It will be my job to help you make the adjustment to Afterworld, that is, become acclimated. That's why I'm called Social Director-Acclimator. First, we acclimate you, get you used to the place and then social activities begin.

"You are all fortunate being in this module since it is quite new. I must explain what is expected of you. You've been told about our regulations. Each module has its library which is located over there." She pointed to a bookcase.

"There are essential books such as the dictionary and our rules.

"You've been provided with key cards which will give you access to the computer terminal, which is also called information center. The terminal will answer any question it is programmed to deal with. Merely punch your question out, using the keys like a typewriter.

"Now, as you might imagine, time is a rather meaningless concept here but because we function on a schedule, it is necessary to index events on the basis of a time reference. We use the 24-hour military clock and you will note above the computer there is a digital display of the time and the day. A day consists of 24 hours.

"There will be an indoctrination film shown at 0400 at the entertainment cog. I will be by shortly before it is scheduled and take you. In the meantime, you have four hours, make yourselves at home."

She smiled and left.

Helen clapped her hands together gleefully. "Isn't this marvelous, I mean just marvelous. We have our own computer. We're going to see some movies. She was such a nice young lady. Oh, I think I'm going to love this place."

Billy asked, "Karl, I guess I'm not supposed to be here. Will I get in trouble?"

"I don't think so, Billy. There are millions, probably billions of people here. I don't think it makes much difference whether one or two is misplaced and not exactly where the Great Computer in the Sky has destined."

Helen chimed in, "I'm glad he's here. It will be marvelous to have a little boy. My boy's all grown up. When he was young, I said I wish he would stop growing and now, that's what we have. It's marvelous."

Milisant started to pick up the cups and saucers on the center table. Helen stopped her, "Oh, Melissa, you don't have to do that. This isn't like down there. I'll help you."

Milisant said coolly, "Milisant."

"Oh, whatever," Helen fussed, taking the cups and saucers to the galley area.

The module door opened and an attractive red-haired woman entered, clipboard in hand. "Hi, my name is Sandy. I'm your Social Director-Acclimator. Welcome to Afterworld. It's my job to -"

Anne interrupted, "We just had one of your people here. Her name was Caroline."

The young woman looked at her clipboard, "Isn't this G492-7?"

Billy answered, "It's B."

"Oh, sorry. I'm new and it's really hard sometimes, all these places look the same."

She smiled and left.

Anne muttered something.

Karl asked, "What did you say?"

"Disneyland."

"What do you mean?"

"It's Disneyland. That's what this place is. These girls are all from Disneyland. All we need is Mickey Mouse, Pluto and Dumbo, a brass band and ice cream cones."

Helen chimed in, "I went to Disneyland and it was nice. Clean, no dirt anywhere, no riffraff round."

Anne sarcastically asked, "Do you suppose God is Walt Disney?"

NINE

George Wilson clamped his hand around the monitor's mouth and pulled her head to his chest, "Not one word," he whispered. George retreated into the maze of machines.

The monitor struggled to free her head from his grasp but was unable to shake his iron grip. In desperation, she sunk her teeth into the flesh of his palm.

He uttered a sharp involuntary, "Eiiiii" and released her. She twirled, backed up from him and ran sideways into a machine bouncing off it and fell to the floor. George pointed his weapon at her.

She covered her breasts with her hands and begged, "Please, Mister, please don't. I won't say a word. I promise, but don't."

George lowered the dowel. A wave of revulsion swept over him. He was a peaceful gentle man and had never harmed anyone.

"Look, Mum, I'm sorry about this. I just want to get back to where the people are. I've been pushed around since I got here. They took me wallet and tried me because I didn't have a social security number."

The girl blinked, "You mean they were sending you to the Transfertorium because you didn't have a social security number?"

"Right, miss."

The girl relaxed for the first time since her abduction. She shook her black hair and breathed a sigh of relief. "I think I can get you back to Processing Central, if you promise you won't hurt me, Mister."

George nodded, "As long as you don't turn me in, I promise. What's your name?"

"Tammy."

"Tammy, I'm George..." He hesitated thinking better of giving his last name.

"How do we get out of here?"

Before Tammy had an opportunity to answer, a woman's voice shouted, "In here."

Tammy and George's eyes met in panic. She motioned ahead and they silently moved deeper into the room. The sound of running feet followed them.

"Where are you?"
"I'm over here."
"Do you see anything?"
"No, do you hear anything?"
"Just us."

Voices ringed George and Tammy. There was no way out. He grasped his weapon firmly and motioned to her. "Get away from me. Get back with them."

She bit her lip. Tears welled up in her eyes and she shook her head. They were near the wall and there was no escape.

Tammy whispered, "Down there on the floor."

George glanced to his left. There were sawhorses, paint cans and a drop cloth over what appeared to be other cans. George understood at once. He lifted the edge of cloth and they crawled under. Tammy pressed her back to his chest. He felt her warmth and put his arms around her shoulders.

Someone's footfall stopped at the drop cloth.

George released his grip. He held his breath. His fingers clutched the laser dowel. He tensed himself awaiting the expected discovery of the shrouded couple.

Whoever it was that stood inches from the painting supplies pivoted on one foot. She was so close that he could hear the sound of her uniform moving against her body. Other footsteps approached. A woman's voice inquired, "What are we looking for?"

Her confederate replied, "Some guy. There was a fight and all hell broke loose. Somehow he got ahold of Sue's faser and blasted the central circuits. The computer is out so we've lost everything on everybody in the hall."

"What does the guy look like?"

"Nobody knows but he's got a faser, so be careful."

"Come on you two, no coffee klatches in here. Get in gear."

The sound of footsteps receded.

In the distance a voice called, "This room's clean, let's go."

A few moments passed, they were alone with the clicking buzzing machinery.

George lifted the drop cloth and held it while Tammy crawled out.

She was small and petite, her skin flawless and her facial features sharp and distinct.

She interrupted his appraisal, "Look, I can help you but don't breathe a word of this." She glanced at the plastic card hanging on George's neck and then at his wrist band. "I thought you said you didn't have ID."

"I didn't, but the guy ahead of me in line gave me his."

This seemed to satisfy Tammy. She directed, "Follow me."

She led the way through the labyrinth of machines to a door. She retrieved a small plastic disc from her pocket and inserted it into the slot over the palm button. The door opened.

She whispered, "Now, go down the corridor and you'll reach Processing Input.

"I must leave you and return to my station before I'm missed. May I please have the faser?"

George said, "Look, Tammy, if we was back home, I'd trust you with me life, but..."

Tammy fidgeted, "Please, I must have a faser when I'm checked out at the end of my shift. If I had wanted to hurt you, I could have given you away in the machinery room."

George said, "I don't think you'd hurt me, but I won't be blown apart. Come here."

He pulled her through the open door into the corridor. He rolled the dowel into the machinery room.

"If I ever was to get safe and wanted to see you, how could I find you?"

"My name is Tamara, MC5."

Karl Ronstadt stepped off the synthetic walkway onto a granite rock which overhung the frothing water. Where the water came from and where its course terminated were open questions. The rock comforted him. The surface was uneven and wetted by the mist of the descending torrent that rushed by two meters or so below the rock.

Karl surveyed the vista. The flowing water was cold and carried the smell of mist to his nostrils. It was the first refreshing experience he had had since reaching the sterile surroundings of eternity. No acrylic, polyester or synthetics here. Honest to god water and rock. He stooped down and ran his fingers over the moist, rough surface of the granite. Mica flecks reflected in the diffused twilight. He could identify the feldspar, pitchblende and quartz of the rock.

The rapidly rushing water in front of him acted as a demarcation line between the monotony of the artificial, synthetic residences and the wild, swirling madness of the real. The speed and ferocity of the water soothed Karl. It, like his spirit, was as unfettered as it was disorganized.

The artificial light illuminating the city dimmed and soon would approximate night on earth as Afterworld's attempt to reproduce life's diurnal rhythms.

The spray wetted Karl's jumpsuit. He expanded his chest and drew in a deep breath of moisture ladened air.

The moving waters spread out to the hazy gray horizon. As a child he had stood on a rocky prominence within inches of the cascading waters of Horseshoe Falls. The immensity of the water before him reminded him of a great Niagara that reached to infinity. No beginning, no end, no limits.

The place looked better in the dark; a velvety black, dotted by bright specks of light.

Karl scraped the boulder with his foot, shaking loose a few pebbles he pushed off the edge. They disappeared lost in the tumult below. He shifted his weight on the rock preparing to return to the artificial walkway when a thunderous cracking erupted from the surface below. The ground gave way and he fell. In an instant he was pitched into the black cold waters. Terror gripped him and he struggled. He was submerged below the surface as the riotous current carried him on. The cold water shocked his body.

After the initial panic he recognized he must get hold of himself or he was finished. He could not be far from shore. He bobbed his head up, breaking the surface. He gasped for air but aspirated water as he fought to align his body with the current. His head was wrenched beneath the surface again and again, but he fought.

He attempted desperately to stroke his way to shore, but the current held him. The cold numbed him and he recognized there was no way to struggle free, yet he fought with every ounce of his strength. He was furious, bad enough to die once but not again, not this way. The swirling pattern of the water changed and Karl had the sensation of being pulled in a circular direction. He understood immediately.

In seconds he was drawn by the whirlpool into the descending depths of terrifying nothingness. He could hold his breath no longer and expelled the little remaining air in his lungs and involuntarily drew in the cold suffocating waters.

He gasped one last cry with all of his being, but in the swirling black there was no sound. All things had ended.

Through the void in the far distance came the call, "Karl, Karl." He felt a tug at his sleeve and opened his eyes to find Billy standing over his bed.

"Karl, are you alright? You were making a noise." Karl soaked with sweat, shook his head and blinked. "I had a nightmare."

Billy said, "The lady's here to take us to a movie."

Helen Benson called, "Come on you two. Caroline is here. We don't want to be late."

Caroline tossed her hair. "I'd like to introduce you to the sixth and final resident of your module. This is Mr. Henry Kallas."

George Wilson nodded. Anne Merrow immediately recognized him. He held his hand up beseeching her to remain quiet. She did.

Helen Benson interlocked her fingers. "Kallas, Kallas is Greek. How nice. We have a boy, a black, a Greek, a doctor and all. This will be so nice."

She addressed George, "Do you have any grandchildren?"

TEN

The theater was huge and arranged in a semi-circular bowl like half a football stadium. The screen was at least 70 feet high.

Anne Merrow sat down. The seat gave under her weight, one of its support members was broken. She compensated for the tilt by sitting erect.

George whispered to her, "Thanks, Mum."

Anne nodded. She wanted to say, "I'm not your mother, buddy," but suppressed the urge.

Lighting cracked across the screen. Black clouds rumbled and thundered. Anne blurted out, "I bet Charleton Heston plays Moses."

Caroline hissed out a, "Sssssh."

The film rolled on; a forest fire, volcanic eruption and earthquake. A deep baritone voice-over narrated, "Natural calamity, pestilence, disaster and disorder. These are the things you have left behind. Love is order."

The screen filled with blue sky and lazy white clouds. A symphony played in the background.

"Natural science is built on order." Chemical equations flashed on the screen. "Mathematics is built on order," mathematical computations followed, "and nations are built on order." A chart of the U.S. Government appeared.

The immense screen was next crowded with the rotunda of the U.S. Capitol. In time lapse photography, the bright day changed to twilight then sunset. The Capitol retreated becoming ever smaller against the cloudless black sky. The camera panned in on the lighted visage of the Great Emancipator and superimposed over the base of the statue of Abraham Lincoln, accompanied by the faint strains of "God Bless America" was:

> ORDER IS FREEDOM
> FREEDOM IS ORDER

The narrator solemnly intoned, "The unity and strength of a free people . . ."

The voice-over changed from dramatic baritone to a slowed version of Raymond Massey on a windup 78 rpm victrola. The middle of the motion picture boiled and bubbles bigger than frisbees erupted like giant pimples on Honest Abe's face dissolving into bright light. The film was self-destructing.

In a few moments, it was announced, "Due to technical difficulties, we cannot complete the showing of the indoctrination film. Please follow your Social Directors who will return you to your modules. Thank you."

The crowd nervously filed out the open door for each row. Outside the theater, Anne mumbled to herself, "So much for order."

Milisant, who was within earshot, thought she was being spoken to and said, "What?"

Anne was caught again. She had many habits that annoyed others, including talking to herself, a kind of oral therapy she had worked out. When called to task by superiors, teachers, or her parents, she invoked different mechanisms. Earlier, she denied she was talking to anyone, but later, especially with peers and fellow workers in the mystical area of mental health, she would reply, "I'm just verbally walking through a problem, please don't interrupt me."

She replied, "Nothing, just talking to myself."

Milisant smiled, "It must be a feminine trait. I do it too and people think I'm crazy. Sometimes, it was the only way I could keep my sanity."

Anne replied, "We're not crazy. There's nothing the matter with talking to yourself. Some of my most productive conversations are with just me. One of the problems we have --- had in our society was the inability to express feelings and verbalize. By talking to yourself, verbalizing how you feel, you defuse the frustration you may be experiencing. It is useful trying to put feelings into words. Somehow, in words..." Anne caught herself, both hands were working and she was talking a little faster and louder than usual. People nearby were staring. She thought, Oh no, you're proselytizing again, cool it.

At the front of the group, the Social Director had her hands full. Helen Benson was machine-gunning her with questions.

"Do you have any grandchildren?"

"No."

"Where you from? - I'm from Sioux Falls."

"We're not supposed to give information regarding our personal circumstances."

"Why? It's ever so much fun to learn about people. People are my favorite thing. I'd tell you anything."

"We just aren't, it's against the rules."

"You have so many rules."

"It seems that way, but once you're here awhile you get used to it."

"Dearie, have you ever had a hysterectomy?"

"What?"

Helen then whispered, "There's a doctor back there who can, with one look, tell if you've had your apple cored. Isn't that something?"

When all the occupants were inside the module, Caroline said, "We're sorry about the inconvenience connected with the film. We sometimes have technical difficulties, not unlike earth. The film is designed to explain our rules. During your first few 24 hour periods, I would suggest you carefully acquaint yourself with the rules."

Helen Benson had been quiet for too long. She blurted, "Rules, I love rules. I used to memorize rules. There was this game show called 'The Golden Rule.' People would guess what their friends really wanted..."

Caroline interrupted, "What we have here is a situation where a great number of people have to live together in a small area. On earth, you would call us a volume dealer. As a result, things have to go smoothly; otherwise, we would have chaos."

Anne chimed in, "The chaos principle, eh?"

Caroline smiled, "You know about that? Not many people do."

Anne returned the favor, "We live by it on earth. Unpredictably, random nonreproducible phenomenon."

"We don't here, so please do us all a favor. If you, any of you get into trouble, I get into trouble.

"Now lights out at 2200 hours. You're expected to be in your resting shelves, in your individual quarters, from 2200 to 0700. You have toilet and shower facilities connected with your rooms.

Breakfast will be served at 0730 at the nourishment center."

Karl asked, "Miss, why do we need to sleep and eat if we don't need nourishment and we're never fatigued?"

Caroline lectured, "Most people require the regimen of their earthly life. They order their lives by milestones connected with eating, sleeping and cleansing.

"Your grooming habits and other aspects of your earth life are duplicated in what is called 'shadow activity.' It exactly parallels what you are used to and permits an established routine that you will find comfortable."

Helen Benson scratched her head, "I don't get it."

Caroline responded, "You will. It doesn't take long. It's really quite simple, watch."

Caroline inhaled and her chest swelled up accentuating her already large breasts.

She had Karl's attention as well as George's.

"It appears I have just taken a deep breath but there is no air here. I don't need air. I'm used to expressing myself this way. After you have taken your first shower, you will get the general idea."

Billy inhaled. He said, "Ma'am, it feels like real air."

Caroline smiled, "As it should and the food will taste real. When you go to your resting shelves, you will seem to sleep and when you awake, you will be refreshed. You may even dream.

"I should warn you that your first few nights may be troubling. Some people experience unusually vivid dreams, but considering what has happened, how far you have traveled and how you have changed, that should not be surprising.

"Should you need assistance, use the videophone." She gestured to the small screen on the wall.

"Now have a nice evening and I'll see you for breakfast at 0730."

As Caroline was leaving Helen Benson called out, "Dearie, dearie. Where did you get your hair done?"

The door closed before an answer.

ELEVEN

Anne was tired, very tired, she shut her bedroom door. Things seemed manifestly unfair. Her life had laid before her with worlds to conquer. She may not have become the Margaret Mead of psychology, but she made all of the right moves, had the correct contacts and was on the fast track of her discipline.

Anne was not curing alcoholics, nor helping obese women overcome their appetites. It was in academia where her seeds were planted, in research, testing and teaching. She looked about her room and found her shelf.

"Christ why don't they just call it a bed. It's a bed." The room was stark white. She called out, "Carrie Allen! God, I've got a person for this place, Carrie Allen. She really needs it. Not only does she need it, she deserves it."

The bathroom didn't have a tub. She grumbled, I get a shower. For eternity, I get a shower. The only time I take a shower is when I have a period.

She dropped her shift to the floor and stood in front of the shower nozzles. She fiddled with the red and blue handles until the liquid was as hot as she could stand. Torrents coursed over the mounds and bulges of her body. A stream poured between her prominent breasts. The sensation was peculiar, but nice. The liquid tingled, yet was not as wet as water. Hot mist filled the small stall. She turned the handles off and groped for a towel. There was none. The fog cleared and with it came the coolness of liquid evaporating from her skin. Within seconds she was dry.

The lights flickered. She knew what that meant. Like living in a girl's dormitory, lights off in five minutes! In bed she slipped between satin like sheets that hugged her nude body in a pleasant soft embrace. The lights flickered again and then darkness. Such darkness. The absence of light, Jonah in the belly of the whale, the blind from birth, not a sound.

Anne yawned, "Sensory deprivation. I'm living in a dream tank. I wish I had this in the lab."

Anne awoke. She blinked.

"Miss Merrow, rise and shine. We have a treat for you today." It was Caroline.

It took a few moments for her to put things together, where she was and what had happened.

"What...what is it?" she asked.

"You're going to like this. We have a reef. We want you to dive."

"A what?"

"A reef. You're diving this morning."

Anne was a certified scuba instructor. She earned the certification to sharpen her skills. The sleep tank at Arizona State was only one of three in the country. Subjects, a euphemism for human volunteers - another euphemism for college kids who needed money - were placed in the tank where they were completely isolated. Their respiration, heartbeat and EEG were monitored. The human subjects floated head up in the dark enclosure buoyed by a saline solution. It was difficult to get them to go to sleep because they started hallucinating so quickly.

The diveboat was a beauty. It was powered by two 120 h.p. outboards and well equipped. Caroline helped Anne aboard. She fired up the engine. The white cliffs, probably styrofoam Anne mused, were soon behind them.

The shore receded to a pencil-thin line and then disappeared. Conversation was impossible due to the wind, waves and sound of the motors. Caroline seemed to know exactly where she was going. Anne scanned the controls for a compass but found none.

She yelled, "How do you know where you are? Do you have a Loran?"

Caroline smiled, "We're almost there."

In short order, the boat turned facing the direction of the waves. Caroline threw out the anchor. It dragged and then abruptly hooked into something solid. The boat stopped with a jolt then began to pivot around the anchor. Whitecaps tossed and turned the craft as it bobbed up and down. At times, the gray sky was lost to a wall of water as the bow was forced down by the waves.

Anne searched the dark sky. She questioned, "Are you sure we should be doing this?"

Caroline smiled and held out the top of a wet suit. "Try this on for size."

Anne welcomed it for the warmth it provided against the wind and spray. She pulled the jacket on and above her left breast read, "Dr. A. Merrow."

She looked up in amazement. "My God, it's mine. How did you get it?

Caroline quipped, "Garage sale."

She helped Anne adjust her air tank harness. Just before Anne put the regulator in her mouth, she said, "I want you to get my ring back."

Caroline cupped her ear, "What?"

"I'll talk to you about it when I come up. What am I diving for?"

Caroline turned Anne's airtank on, then holding her by both shoulders said, "For your destiny."

Anne sat on the transom of the boat holding her facemask firm and flopped back first into the sea. There was a rush of water as the waves carried her a short distance before she began to slowly sink. She felt for the emergency cords of her vest CO^2 cartridges and gave them a little tug. She cinched her weightbelt.

She scanned for visible landmarks and found a submerged reef not far off.

She made for the reef, kicking straight-legged and moving with little effort. Soon she was engulfed in incredible beauty. Brain coral on the outcrop glistened in the shimmering light filtered through the water. Coral fans moved back and forth rustling in the current driven by the waves above. All was silent but for the noise of bubbles Anne expelled. Little blue neonfish darted here and there. A school of iridescent angelfish to her right moved as a unit back and forth in the undulating current.

A large red and green parrotfish slid under a rock shelf ahead. Anne played this game before. She lowered herself to the level of the ledge and then pulled her face quickly under it. The parrotfish confused, turned tail and headed for a crevice in the algae covered rocks.

Anne worked her way toward the crevice. It extended down as far as the eye could see. She was not interested in diving in deep, black places having had past unpleasant experiences, and passed over the reef, turning her attention elsewhere. She chased a couple of groupers and played hide and seek with a myriad of little fish inhabiting the weeds and coral of the teeming world. Sixty feet below the reef in white sand, there were starfish, spiny sea urchins and the unmistakable shape of a manta ray. She had no fear of rays and loved to watch them swim like a flapjack with the outer edges pulsing.

Anne had been paying such close attention to what lay below her that she lost track of time. She checked her watch. She had none. She could not time her ascent to avoid the risk of nitrogen narcosis, the cause of the bends. Nitrogen in the blood, under pressure in deep water, escapes as a diver ascends, forming gaseous bubbles which can be life threatening.

A silver form in the periphery of her vision commanded attention. She turned to face the object. It was the largest barracuda she had ever seen. He looked like a nuclear submarine hanging stationary 100 meters from her. Now it was clear. She remembered the reef and she certainly would never forget that fish. It was the Palancar Reef off Couzmel. She had been on an Easter break during her first year's work on her Masters. She dived and met the world's largest living barracuda. He shadowed her, playing cat and mouse, until her oxygen supply was practically depleted. Finally, with no choice, she slowly ascended and he followed her the whole way. When she pulled herself into the diveboat, she checked the surface to see if he was still coming.

Now here he was again! He was not looking at her, he was paralleling her, his pectoral fins slowly treading water. Anne knew barracuda were generally not dangerous. They are school fish. She wouldn't want to be cut near one, but there were few stories of barracudas attacking divers. All in all though, a large, aggressive fish must be treated with respect. It was she who was the intruder. It was she who did not belong there.

The giant fish was clearly the master of this reef. He feared nothing here. It provided his cover, his sustenance and was his territory. She knew this and turned so she faced the fish and with small movements of her hands started to tread water moving backward. She moved back

10 meters, the fish moved ahead 10 meters. He crisscrossed several times and then turned to face her head-on. His large jaw teeth glistened in the muted light.

His eyes gazed into her soul. Every inch of the fish spoke aggression. His black spots, feathered at their edges, set off his bulk against his aluminum sides. He slowly moved in on Anne. She carefully reached to her right leg for her knife. She knew she was no match for the fish, but if she was going to go, she would make him pay. She felt the smooth skin of her calf; she had not been given a knife. She continued to move backward, away from the leviathan.

She was breathing hard, consuming more oxygen than usual because of the stress, when she choked. There was no air. She had five minutes of reserve. She tugged on the emergency rod to give her those extra few minutes of life's breath. She felt the valve move, but there was no air. She tugged again, still no air. She pulled one last time. The rod broke loose. She dropped it and watched it tumble slowly like a leaf into the depths below.

Now, there was no choice. She grabbed her face mask and pulled it off, spit the regulator out of her mouth, straightened her neck, looked up to the sky beyond the sea surface and started a free ascent, the most dangerous and deadly diving maneuver. She kicked evenly but was not moving fast enough. She ripped the buckle on her weight belt open and it fell away. She gained speed as she moved upward, her eyes fixed on the glimmering waves above.

She was three-quarters of the way to the surface still exhaling when a mighty blow struck her chest. She was jarred and dizzied - spinning. She grabbed her breast and her hand went through it into a gaping hole in the warm cavity of her chest. My God, I feel my heart! Then through the blurred seawater, a huge gray form wheeled, turned and drove at her face.

Anne cried out from deep inside her soul, the agonal shriek of the rabbit struck by a hawk's talons, but her voice could not escape her throat.

"Good morning," announced a disembodied voice. "Breakfast will be at 0730."

Anne snapped upright and struck her head on the ceiling above her bunk. She shook, sweat streamed down her face. She grasped at her chest. It was intact. She took a deep breath and lowered her head to her bent knees. The room was still but for the pounding of her shadow heart.

TWELVE

The inmates of B492-7 walked toward the center of the cog. Billy caught up to Karl and pulled at his jumpsuit. Karl was lost in thought.

"Huh, oh it's you Billy."

Billy was pale and drawn. "I had a nightmare last night. I don't think I like this place."

Karl patted him on the shoulder. "I had a pretty weird dream myself."

Then changing the subject, Karl asked, "Weren't you working the computer?"

"Yeah, I wanted the hockey scores, but I can't get any news out of it. There's stuff about what happened before, but nothing after --- well, after we came here."

Karl pulled his earlobe. "I'm not really surprised. I don't think we'll be permitted to communicate with earth. Have you ever heard of Harry Houdini?"

Billy thought for a moment, "There was a magician on the Saturday morning cartoons called Houdini."

Milisant Crescent interrupted, "Pardon me, doctor, but I saw Houdini when I was a girl."

Karl turned toward her. She was a good 10 years younger than he. He was about to chide her when he recalled the age selection booth. "How old were you?"

"I was 66, but when I was real young, Houdini staged an escape in the Hudson River. He was lowered into the water in a chained steamer trunk handcuffed and blindfolded. It was November, or December, cold. We thought he had drowned, but in about five minutes he struggled free and came to the surface. There were spotlights on him and people on the bank yelling, cheering and clapping. It was really something."

Karl said, "Billy, Harry Houdini was an escape artist, a magician. A man who was very gifted. He died long before you were born.

"He also studied the supernatural and exposed frauds - people who were pretending to be able to communicate with the dead. He said that if it were possible to come back, he would. After his death, his friends kept a vigil every Halloween as he asked. So far, no one has heard from him.

"That doesn't mean that such communication is impossible, but I think there is a wall that separates us from everything we've known and because of that I don't think you'll find out who wins the Stanley Cup this year."

Billy thought for a moment. He said. "Who will feed my dog, Lucky?"

Karl said, "Your parents will take care of Lucky."

Billy shook his head, "I really miss him. He is my buddy. It's just not the same without him."

Karl asked, "What kind of a dog was he?"

"A golden - a humongous golden retriever."

Caroline met them in front of an igloo shaped building with a large black 492 over the arched entranceway.

She smiled, "Good morning, it's not likely you'll get lost since all paths lead to the nourishment center, but notice the number. That is your cog number. Now go in, take a tray, it's cafeteria style. Everything is free - enjoy."

The group entered the austere white structure. Milky translucent benches, half circles with declining radii, circled concentrically, a large oval table in the center of the room piled high with fruits, sweet rolls, cold cereal, juices, heated pans filled with bacon, fish, sausages, pancakes and sundry goodies.

Helen Benson clasped her hands, "Oh, this is wonderful."

Then she asked grasping her already expansive girth, "Dearie, what will this do to my figure?"

Caroline smiled, "Not to worry. No matter how much you eat, you will not change. What you see is what you have chosen of what you were."

That was enough for Helen. She began filling her plate. The rest followed, but for Anne Merrow who held back.

Anne approached Caroline and demanded, "Who are you?"

"My name is Caroline. I'm your Social Director-Acclimator."

Anne's deep blue eyes pierced Caroline's. They were locked soul to soul. Anne verbally thrust, "Cut the shit, girl. You just turned a phrase off the top of your head that reads like something from Shakespeare. You know about the chaos principle. You were in my head last night in what I ---" she hesitated, "think was a dream, but I'm not sure.

"You're not Betty Boop, or some super glandular bimbo. Who are you?"

The words were drawn carefully and evenly, like a glassblower pulling out the stem of a crystal goblet.

Caroline did not turn away. Her ice-blue eyes stayed locked to Anne's. Neither woman blinked. "Doctor Merrow, I am Caroline CX51. This is who I am. Who I was is quite a different matter and that, my dear, was my destiny."

"Jesus, you really were there, weren't you?"

"Where?"

"In my dream - you know damn well where."

"We all have dreams, perhaps this is a dream, or your earlier life was a dream. I know from your dossier that you were into dream research and as a consequence I expect your dreams would be more florid than the average."

Anne rolled her eyes, "Florid. What happened to Frank Buck his first night here? Was he eaten by a lion?"

Caroline smiled, "He was never on my shift. Now off with you. You can't fraternize with the help too much. It doesn't look good."

Caroline pushed Anne's shoulders, turning her toward the buffet.

Milisant Crescent sat down across from George Wilson. "Do you mind if I sit here, Mr. Kallas?"

"The name's 'Wilson' Mum, George Wilson. Kallas was a friend who helped me out. You can call me George."

Milisant had spent more than half of a century respecting formalities of communication with other adults, respect often not returned in kind. Abrasive speech was part of the environment she lived in. The ghetto children grew up in a verbal sewer. Invective, obscenity and brutalization of the English language were poured over them like gravy. It was in the very air they breathed and became their tragic birthright. But, in Milisant's world of the classroom, she practiced civility, good manners and proper English.

Her world became a closed circle as the years passed and drew ever tighter about her. At the end, she was alone. At school she was a year past retirement and no one even noticed. The majority of people whose lives she touched went on to their tragically ordained careers of crime, drug abuse, prostitution and early death.

She often said, "I'm like an old carp in the Hudson River, I didn't make it the way it is, but I got to live in it just the same."

George chomped down on a large strawberry. "M-m-m, tastes good. I have to hand it to 'em, the food is something. Mum, did you read the rules?"

Milisant was shaken from her reverie, "Ah, no, not yet."

"Well, you better. I used to think God was pretty smart. The Ten Commandments, all of them darn good. Looks to me like there's been some of our boys from the British Civil Service up here. Rules cover about everything."

The Social Directors had segregated themselves from their charges and were eating at a large table near the wall. An electronic bong sounded. They cleared the oval center table and brought in coffee for their wards.

Anne took a cup.

Caroline queried, "Sugar and cream?"

Anne countered, "Sodium pentothal, please."

Caroline retorted, "Bad chemistry. Heat fractionates sodium pentothal and worse yet, the acid in coffee breaks down the molecular bonding. You might as well pour table salt in your coffee if you like it that way."

Anne rolled her eyes. "If I can get a grant, will you work on my team?"

Caroline continued serving, "Sorry, I already have a job. I always wanted to be a waitress."

Anne asked Karl, "What kind of doctor are you?"

"Internal medicine, oncology."

"Ever do research?"

"My whole practice is research. I spend half of my time looking for something I don't want to find and then when I find it, the rest poisoning the people who have it, but not enough to kill. I leave that to God and nature."

Anne said, "Well, there's research and there's research research. I'm in -- was in research research. We don't think like normal people. We don't act like normal people nor do we talk like normal people. I have to put up with smart ass administrators to keep the baby alive - that is bringing in the bucks to keep the party going - lights on. Savvy?"

"I'm with you. Without pandering, there are no pandas. The zoo stays closed."

"You're pretty quick for a man. Anyway, Carolina in the Mornin' over there - read an IQ of 160 plus, maybe a lot plus, has been treating me like I treat men.

"You want to know how things work here, the answers to the eternal questions? Forget the computer. If you can plow that field, you've got the answers. Good luck Charlie, but I don't think Star Kist will choose you."

"Are you always so aggressive? Do you talk to everybody like this?"

She shook her head. "In research research, we don't talk to anybody, we interact, communicate."

Anne watched Caroline serve coffee to a disheveled man slouched at a table near the far wall.

"My God, it's Haberschmidt, Robert Haberschmidt. Nobel Prize for Science, 1964 - genetic mutations, precursors to gene splicing; 1979 Nobel Prize - molecular biology. An incredible mind. Died in an auto accident two years ago running the wrong way down the interstate, cold sober and probably in another world."

Caroline nicknamed her charges the "dash seveners," after their module number. In the cog there was a 10,000 volume English language library, shuffleboard courts, bizarre at best with three-dimensional moving holographic pieces and a bingo hall - computerized bingo, digital displays set in transparent tables similar to the Pac-Man video games of western civilization.

Soon Caroline introduced her group to the Biosphere. The scent of warm pollen laden air floated out from within the large building. Many sensations were experienced at once: the moldering smell of fresh cut hay, the aroma of leaves burning in the fall and the sharpness of frigid air on a snowy night.

She pushed a button closing the door. "While your eyes are getting accustomed to this lower light level, let me explain. You all experienced some sensations as we entered the Biosphere. What you felt was related to your past. One of the unfortunate aspects of Afterworld is that it seems a bit sterile."

Anne chirped in, "A lot sterile."

Caroline continued, "In reality, all of your memories are intact. Everything is stored in the electrical impulses that are part of your being. The world of your past never really existed as you perceived it or felt it. Each of us carry in our own mind, the entire physical universe. Have any of you ever been to France?"

She waited a moment. "I see everyone nod but Billy and Mrs. Benson.

"Doctor Ronstadt, tell me, Doctor, about France. What do you think France was like?"

"Well, it was a beautiful country. The Louvre Museum is an incredible place where some of the world's finest works of art are found. Napoleon's tomb is impressive. The Eiffel Tower, an interesting structure designed by the same man who..."

Caroline cut him short. "Fine, Doctor."

"Tell me, Mr. Kallas, what you thought of France."

"Well, Mum, I'm not one really to say. I don't have the education like the doctor here. It's got a great train system, fast and clean. Don't care much for the French people, but I don't think they liked me either."

"Doctor Merrow, tell how you saw France."

"While visiting the Sorbonne, I found French people to be aloof but reasonably civil. There was little crime. The major cities were cleaner than home."

"Miss Crescent, how did you experience France?"

Milisant apologized, "I'm sorry, I misunderstood. I've never been to France. I've read about France and its educational system. I can visualize the Eiffel Tower and the Louvre, Venus de Milo, the Mona Lisa, but I never personally was there, so I really can't say."

"Miss Crescent, what you perceived France to be is no more, nor less than what was experienced by our three other friends who actually visited the country. In truth, France is not the small snapshot described, but to each of you is what you thought it was.

"What you have in your minds, your memories, is how you saw the world. It was not the reality that existed, but your perception of it. It is a very personal thing which helps explain wars and political intrigue. Each side to a controversy sees things differently. Distrust arises because of mismatching of ideas of what is real and is not.

"Is there anyone who did not have a vivid dream last night?"

No hands raised.

"Fine, now what you experienced was no less real than the various things you thought were happening.

"With this background, let's play a little game."

Caroline lowered a clear dome over Billy after he sat at the small table. "Billy, this is an Actuator.

"Place your hands on the surface and close your eyes. Good. Now, think about a ball that is blue, yellow and green."

Caroline dimmed the room. She directed, "Concentrate, concentrate on the ball."

Flicks of colored light, like bacon grease, spat out from the top of the table. They swirled like a cloud of yellow-jackets and then sorted themselves into colors forming a blue, yellow and green globe suspended above the table.

"You have done very well. Now, I want you to slowly open your eyes, but keep thinking about the ball."

Billy blinked. The ball started to disintegrate.

"No, Billy. Keep thinking about it."

He said, "My gosh."

"Can you make the ball spin?"

Billy pressed his palms harder to the table and the ball began to slowly rotate and then spin faster and faster, the colors blending in a whirl.

"That's good. Take your hands off the table."

Billy lifted his hands and the ball disappeared.

Caroline praised him, "Very few people can do this on the first try. I'm proud of you."

"Doctor Merrow, tell me, was the ball real?"

Anne was being tested and she knew it. She said, "The ball was as real as we are."

Caroline continued, "Later you will each have an opportunity to experiment with the Actuator. Soon you will be able to decorate your rooms. Not with a paint brush, but with your mind brush. You will paint with your memories on the canvas of your mind.

"Come along, let me show you what else we have here."

Caroline led the way to a hall along the inside perimeter of the round structure. She explained, "These are products of our guests, three dimensional paintings."

A case in the wall contained a view of a sunlit sky with white clouds standing out against a blue background. The towering cumulus clouds had texture and dimension. The faint aroma of a fresh breeze wafted from the picture.

From the next case, a white tailed buck, doe and fawn peered out from the display, ears alert and black eyes glistening.

Case after case held visions from earth. Bengal tigers, African elephants, wildebeest of the savannah, ringneck pheasant on the wing, fields of grain, ponds, meadows, glaciers, mountains, Caribbean beaches and earth rise from the moon. Frozen images of what would never be revisited.

Caroline led to an exit. After everyone was out she said, "Now, my friends, you have seen your little world, your new world. It is limited only by your imagination and this wall."

She pointed to a high gold wall in the distance.

"This is the outer limit. You have all of the amenities of a resort within this cog. The wall is the end of your world. There is nothing outside that you do not have here."

As the group walked back to their module, Billy found Karl's open hand with his fingers and grasped it. Karl had never been a father and was a little uncomfortable being close to anyone. Nonetheless, he curled his large hand around the boy's fingers.

Billy observed, "That was neater than the Ontario Science Centre."

Anne held back until Caroline was abreast of her. "Okay, Caroline CX51, or whatever your model number is, do you have some time off duty. I'd like to talk."

Caroline shook her head, "Sorry, can't help you. We're not allowed to fraternize."

"Are all the social directors of your caliber, or did we get the pick of the litter?"

"I really can't say how the selection process goes. As you might appreciate, we get everybody here. A lot of talent."

"So you can't socialize with the guests. Merely lead your six newcomers around and show them the ropes."

"Right."

"No contact with anybody else but the help, correct?"

"Right again."

"Then tell me about Haberschmidt."

Caroline stopped in her tracks. Her piercing blue eyes found Anne's. No words were exchanged, but the message was clear.

Anne congratulated herself. Merrow 1, CX51 0.

Women can cut women in a way man will never understand. Tension between the two gladiators was broken by Helen Benson who grasped the shoulder of each from behind. "Well now, wasn't that something? All I need are some postcards. I wish my friends could see this.

"Say, Miss Caroline, can I get my soaps?"

Caroline said, "I'm sorry Mrs. Benson. There is no television here except the videophone."

"Well, how about reruns, you must have VCR's?"

"No, we don't. There is the Biosphere, books, bingo, shuffleboard and your computer. Don't forget your computer. It may end up being your best friend."

THIRTEEN

Anne adjusted the computer seat. She extended her fingers and flexed them. It had been a long time since she had been before a keyboard.

She mused, "Nothing very complicated about this technology. Okay, let's see what you can do."

Anne punched in the code for biographical data and then:

ANNE KATHLEEN MERROW

She liked her name. The keyboard was a generic IBM PC, but the display terminal used some type of liquid crystal. The machine printed:

LOCKOUT, SEE RULE 1237(F)

She reached above the computer terminal for "Rules and Regulations of Afterworld." She found the section. It read:

(F) Guest to guest biographical information is prohibited.

Anne typed:

READ RULE AND UNDERSTOOD. GUEST TO GUEST BIO NOT REQUESTED. I AM BIO SUBJECT!!!

She tripped enter, but the computer responded:

NICE TRY.

"Jesus Christ, another smart ass." She typed:

ARTICLES IN PRINT.

The computer responded:

DREAM SEQUENCING AND SENSORY DEPRIVATION - 1995.

She typed:

POSTHUMOUS PUBLICATION?

NO POSTDEATH DATA AVAILABLE. SEE RULE 2734(A).

"Great, now I'll never know if it was published."

Karl Ronstadt approached. "Can you work this thing?"

"Not much to it. It's an idiot PC. Working it is easy. Getting any information out of it is hard. Anything you'd like to ask God?"

Karl stroked his chin, "I have a lot of questions. This isn't exactly how I thought they'd be answered. Computers intimidate me. They don't like me. Let me show you, slide over."

Anne moved to the side of the bench and Karl sat down. "I saw you accessed your own articles. Tell me what to do. I want to access mine."

"It's super simple. Clear the screen. Push ESC over there on the left side."

Karl did and the screen went blank.

"Now, you have to give your registration number. Use the last seven digits off your wristband."

She said, "Good, now push NRA."

Karl mused, "The National Recovery Act?"

"Not quite. It stands for Non Random Access. That means HAL here doesn't have to go rambling through all the writings of Western Civilization. We'll tell it where to look."

Anne gave Karl more directions.

"Good, now push ENTER."

Karl did. Nothing happened except the last letter entered flashed. Karl threw up his hands, "Okay, now what?"

Anne scratched her head, "I don't know. It must know you're afraid of it. Let me try." She duplicated Karl's query and the screen filled with citations.

Screen after screen rolled by filled with Ronstadt writings. "I thought you weren't into research?"

"I wasn't particularly. I just believed in self-aggrandizement, 'publish or perish.'"

"Only 12 pages. What happened to 1995? Oh, I know, same thing happened to me. Sorry, guest."

Anne tossed her hair, "Well, any burning questions? I have it within my power, the power of the almighty computer, to answer three questions. Choose wisely."

Karl said, "Oh, genie, wondrous genie, how amongst the riddles of life can I choose just three questions?"

Anne answered, "Easy enough, just start. You have two left."

"Ask it, what is the meaning of life?"

Anne entered the query. The computer responded:

EACH SOLITARY LIFE DESCRIBES ITS OWN MEANING.

Karl smiled, "Not bad. Actually, pretty good. Why don't you ask it about your friend Haberschmidt? See if we can get any information about when he died."

"It won't work. I couldn't even get my own bio."

"Try Haberschmidt anyway."

"Okay, but we're just wasting time."

Karl retorted, "We've got a lot of that."

Anne entered the necessary information. The computer responded:

MIDDLE NAME, PLEASE.

Anne said, "Come on, you've got to be kidding. How many Robert Haberschmidts are there?" The screen filled with ROBERT HABERSCHMIDTs.

She sighed, "Geez. Here's one MD, Ph.D, Ph.D, Ph.D. Middle name Kilroy."

Anne entered the addendum, the computer printed:

ROBERT KILROY HABERSCHMIDT, MD, Ph.D, Ph.D, Ph.D, born 7/13/23, Madison, Wisconsin. Died __Education: Public school system, Grosse Pointe, Michigan, graduated first in class Grosse Pointe High School 1937, age 13. University of Michigan, BS - Major physics 1940, first in class. Graduate training: Harvard University Ph.D - biology 1945; Cornell, Ph.D - genetics, 1947; University of Edinburgh, Ph.D - chemistry 1949; University of Michigan, MD 1952.

Anne put her hands on her hips. "It's disgusting, isn't it? Here I am, 27, in debt, finished. And Haberschmidt, lord, by the time he was 27, he had more degrees than my entire department at Arizona."

Karl stared intently at the screen. "There's something strange here. Take a look at the top again."

Anne scanned it. "So?"

"So, there's no death date. I thought you told me he died in 1993?"

"He did. It was in the papers."

"You said we couldn't get information regarding guests here?"

"That's what it said."

Karl nudged Anne, "Clear the screen. Let's ask a straight-out question. Is Haberschmidt alive?"

Anne asked.

Answer:

NO SUBSEQUENT INFORMATION TO DEATH PERMITTED.

Karl shook his head, "Maybe Haberschmidt is alive and the guy just looks like him."

Anne grimaced, "No chance. I saw Caroline whispering to him. When I mentioned his name to her, I got the red hot icepick in the eye. I know I hit home. I betcha a hot fudge sundae, it's Haberschmidt."

"Well, if it is, what's wrong with the computer?"

Anne shook her head, "I don't know. Maybe he's got somebody else's ID. I used to get booze that way when I was a kid."

Milisant was enthusiastic. She had a willing student, one with no learning disability, who was a pleasure to work with. Billy sat attentive through hours of instruction. He had come from educated parents who had spent time with him. His spelling was deficient, but this problem wasn't unique. Television had supplanted the printed word for his generation, a medium of unrelenting mediocrity.

Milisant gave Afterworld high marks. Its best move was the absence of teleculture and its electronic Tower of Babble. If the medium was the message, the envelope was empty. Television had become the white noise of the 90's. Families no longer communicated. They sat en masse at meals, tranquilized by the constant barrage of idiot chatter.

Billy asked Milisant to come to his room.

"I've got the light off. Go in and shut your eyes."

Milisant giggled, she liked playing games and had practically no opportunity to do so.

Billy said, "Now look, Miss Crescent."

She blinked. In front of her was a life-size three-dimensional picture of a large Golden Retriever. The animal's eyes glistened, its moist tongue extended over its ivory teeth. It stood with feathered tail raised high.

Billy beamed, "Well, what do you think?"

"It's beautiful."

Billy corrected, "He's Lucky. He's my dog."

Milisant had been working with the Actuator herself but had produced only a bowl of fruit.

Billy said wistfully, "I really miss him."

Milisant patted him on the shoulder. "Well, you have him. Here he is."

"No. This looks like him but it's not Lucky. It's just a picture."

FOURTEEN

"Bingo! Bingo!" exclaimed Helen Benson.

The caller intoned into the microphone, "We have a winner. It's Helen Benson again. Come up and get your candy dish."

Helen was the undisputed champion of electronic bingo.

Karl was in a foul mood. The last game had been a close call. He had only one number to cover which would have given him Bingo in either of two plains, then he would have been stuck with the stupid candy dish. Karl Ronstadt, MD, PC, Savior of mankind, physician to the dying wins depression glass. The place was getting to him. He felt hemmed in, suffocated.

He whispered to Anne, "I think I have a headache."

She whispered back, "Can't be - not permitted, Rule 841, sub (z). Besides it's not time for your period."

He came close to smiling and nudged her with his elbow. "Want to take a walk?"

"Is that a question or an invitation?"

"Invitation," he mouthed silently.

In the Afterworld equivalent of evening, the light was muted and by "lights off time," the area outside was pitch black. There were no street lights, nor did any light seep from the interior of the windowless modules.

They walked to the wall.

Karl placed both hands up against the gold surface and stretched his feet out, simulating a frisk position.

Anne queried, "Well, Atlas, do you think you can move it?"

Karl slid down the wall to a sitting position. "No, and I can't climb it. It's slippery and extremely hard. There's nothing near it that you could climb on top of. It's like the Berlin Wall and we're in No Man's Land."

Sitting down beside him, Anne said, "Well, do you think it's to keep us in, or them out?"

Karl shook his head, "Darned if I know. I'd just like to do something useful. I've had it with sitting around. I have no patients to treat and I might as well be on a cloud playing a harp."

Anne signed, "Welcome to the club."

Karl gazed into the black starless sky. "I tried to help. I asked Caroline if there was any work I could do. She said, 'Nobody gets sick here. There is nothing for a doctor to do.'"

"I spent a lifetime trying to cure disease. If I had been successful I'd been out of work. I'd worked myself right out of a job. You know it never struck me how incongruous that is."

"Don't worry about your friendly MD's. For everyone who wants to cure disease, there are a dozen supporting their boats, airplanes and thoroughbred horses losing the war."

Karl signed, "I even asked for manual labor, anything. I talked to your buddy, Caroline, and she gave me a Form F-74."

Anne uttered the words "F-74" in unison with Karl.

Anne queried, "Do you know what Helen made in the Biosphere for her room?"

Karl thought a moment, "What? The National Inquirer - 'TWO HEADED CALF GIVES BIRTH TO A BARITONE SAXOPHONE PLAYER, CONNECTED TO WOMB BY RCA JACK.'"

"No. She's not that imaginative. Tupperware."

"What?"

"Tupperware. She has a whole set of Tupperware on her wall. That's the picture she dreamed up - Tupperware."

"You're kidding?"

"No. I swear on my mother's grave."

"I bet your mother isn't dead."

"She wasn't last time I knew. Cross my heart and hope to die."

"That won't work here either."

"May a mystic bolt of green lightning strike me down if I speak falsehood."

Karl started to say something. Anne covered his mouth with her hand, "Wait, wait, see just like I said."

Karl smelled Anne's fragrance. He grasped her hand. She wiggled her fingers loose from his and stiffened. This was the first time he had seen her ill at ease.

In the bluish-purple fading light, Karl scanned Anne's form. He was taller than she and as they sat together, it was easy to covertly appreciate her body. She was well built and had a tight athletic frame.

"Anne, I have enjoyed you. You are refreshing. You are imaginative. You are spontaneous and entirely unrestrained. You're as irreverent as hell, and considering the circumstances, that rates a 10."

Anne was uneasy. She was used to fencing with men. She had her territory and defended it. She was proud of her mind and best when on the attack. She was seldom cornered and could hold her own with the brightest.

"Sorry doc, I'm taken."

Karl frowned, "What do you mean?"

"I mean I'm already in love."

"With whom?"

"Caroline."

"Are you serious?"

"Yeah, but it's not her body I'm after. It's her mind."

Karl signed, "It just shows the difference between men and women. I want her body. You can have her mind."

Anne retorted, "12.721."

In unison, they spoke, "It's against the rule!"

Every 30 days, the world of 492 was checked by three Control Supervisors, dubbed "the census takers." They were dressed in red jumpsuits and tended strictly to business.

The routine required matching of wristband to ID tag.

Problems were developing regarding Billy. Each time the supervisors appeared, there were more questions. Lucky on the wall and Billy's youthful appearance mitigated against the midget story. This particular morning, the supervisors were new. There was no banter with them. They were officious bureaucrats doing their job.

The smallest of the women, Roberta per her nametag, carefully eyed Billy.

Roberta announced, "He's a child."

Karl shook his head, "No, madam. I'm afraid you're mistaken. This gentleman suffered from a growth deficiency."

She said, "If he had a growth deficiency, it would have been cured upon entrance."

Karl nodded, "I suppose, but no one can exceed a configuration not experienced during lifetime. As the poor fellow obviously displays, he never got any bigger than this."

Roberta was not to be put off. She gestured to Billy, "I think, sir, we would like to talk with you in private. Which is your room?"

Billy pointed.

She snapped, "Darlene, stay out here and I will take care of this with Terry. In there, young man."

Karl barred her entrance to the hallway. "I don't care if you talk to him, but I'm his physician and must be present."

Roberta ordered, "I'm in charge here, not you. Move away."

Karl didn't budge.

Roberta menaced, "Move away immediately. I'll cite you for violating 327A and your friends here will get another boarder."

George Wilson urged, "For God's sake man, back off."

Anne spoke up, "Roberta, perhaps I can help you. I am his psychologist. There is nothing you could ask him that I can't answer."

Roberta was approaching a bureaucratic feeding frenzy. There was blood in the water. She would not be turned aside.

"Madam!" she railed.

Anne raised her index finger, "No, not madam, Doctor. Doctor Merrow."

"Look lady, I don't care who you are, or were. I've got a job to do and I intend to do it. As far as I'm concerned, this 'gentleman' is a kid and has no business here. I have no idea how you all pulled this off. After I'm done with him, I intend to find out. Now move it!"

She shoved Billy. The physical action was more than Anne could abide. Even docile Milisant, who had been pushed and shoved her entire life was indignant.

Anne barked, "Okay, tootsie, if you want to play games with this stalag's inmates, fine, but we demand our rights."

Roberta curled her lips, "You've got no rights."

Anne said, "Check again, lady. Try Rule 126(D)."

That stopped Roberta and Terry in their tracks. They looked at one another. Terry shrugged her shoulders. Roberta brushed through the ringing group to the computer terminal and yanked the appropriate volume from the shelf. She thumbed through the book, found the section and looked up disdainfully.

"So, that's got nothing to do with any of this."

Anne said, "I beg to differ with you. The Rule says we have the right to have our SDA present during any interrogation. We cannot complain except through our SDA. We cannot be complained about except in her presence."

Darlene peered over Roberta's shoulder. She was struggling with the statutory language, staring intently at the page and silently mouthing each word.

Anne signaled Karl toward the videophone.

He turned the volume down and punched out Caroline's code. Her face appeared on the small screen. Karl silently mouthed, "Help."

Roberta snapped the binding closed and shelved the rule book. She spit out, "It's not clear to me. I don't think you're right. It's not the kind of circumstance that rule is meant to cover, but it won't do any harm to wait for your Social Director."

Anne smirked, "There's nothing sweeter than a bureaucrat getting stuck on the fly paper of their own rule."

"I can tell you, it will do no good," Roberta continued. "We have supervisory control over a SDA. If you want to have her stand in and listen, I'll grant your request, but it won't matter. Who is she?"

Anne questioned, "She?"

"She, she," Roberta shouted. "Your SDA."

"Oh, that she," Anne was stalling for time. "She's CX51."

Under her breath Roberta asked Darlene, "Who the hell is that?"

Darlene shrugged.

A stern voice from the front of the room demanded in measured tones, "What is going on here?"

Roberta gazed at Caroline wide-eyed and said, "It's you. Are these your people?"

Caroline replied, "They are."

Darlene covered her mouth and whispered, "Jesus."

"What is going on, I asked."

Roberta found her voice, "I think they have a child in here and I was trying to interrogate him and this, this woman," she pointed to Anne, "insisted that the SDA be present when we talked to him. We didn't know this was your module. But when I have a job to do, I do it."

Caroline cleared her throat, "Fine, who are you?"

"Roberta."

"Roberta, do your job. I'll come along and help."

Roberta pointed toward the sleeping room where Billy was standing perplexed. Anne stepped back and Caroline, who was the last to enter the hall directed, "Take a hike. I don't want anybody here when we come back. You got it?"

Outside the module Karl asked, "What's happening?"

Anne answered, "I really don't know. I think we've got a friend in management. We've got a problem we can't handle. It's their ballgame and Caroline knows the ropes."

Loud voices, muffled by the walls of the module, were heard as the group retreated.

George said, "I'm proud of you, boy. You too, Mum. I want no trouble. Those ladies were armed. Look for the bulge along the outside of their right leg. A tough bunch these."

In 10 minutes, Caroline found the group outside. "Everything's okay. Go home."

Anne patted her on the shoulder, "Thanks."

Caroline responded, "Just doing my job, ma'am."

Anne shot back, "Jack Webb."

Billy was sitting on his bed when his friends sought him out.

Milisant asked, "What happened?"

Billy blinked, "Nothing. There was some pretty bad language. I didn't know ladies talk like that."

Helen Benson joined in, "What did they do? It sounded like they were going to throw you out."

Billy replied, "Miss Caroline did most of the talking. She said something about the nasty lady cleaning the toilets."

Anne threw up her hands, "Who was that masked woman?"

FIFTEEN

George Wilson whistled on the way back from breakfast. Helen Benson, a perpetual rosebud, caught up with him. "So George, what's the cheery song?"

"White Cliffs of Dover."

"Oh, I know it, heard it on TV. I watched all the old black and white movies about the war."

It was obvious she was referring to the last, real, declared, unambiguous, military action of the U.S. of A.

She continued, "They always played that song at the end of the movie when the RAF fliers couldn't make it back to the base."

George nodded, "Right, Mum."

"I didn't see you at Bingo last night."

"Wasn't there, Mum. Wanted to be bright and brisk for today. It's me first day on the job."

Milisant had overheard. "Excuse me, Mr. Wilson," she said.

George interrupted, "Come on, Mum, don't be calling me Mr. Wilson. Me name's George. I call you Milisant. You call me George."

"Sorry, did I hear you say 'job'?"

"Right."

Karl Ronstadt had also picked up on the conversation. "George, what kind of a job? What are you doing?"

"What I've always done, fixin' things. I put in for being a mechanic."

Anne was intensely punching the keyboard later in the morning when Karl interrupted her concentration by staring at the screen over her shoulder. Now distracted, she paused, then offered, "How about some shuffleboard?"

Karl shook his head, "Come on, I've had it with shuffleboard. The game doesn't even make noise."

Anne smiled, "You're not much fun anymore, big boy. You're treating all of us like terminal cancer patients."

"We're terminal alright, or rather past terminal."

Anne softly cooed, "Cheer up. It could be worse. We could be dead."

Karl rolled his eyes.

Anne twitched her nose and began rolling up a strand of blond hair on a finger. Karl knew something was coming.

She started working the computer. "Why didn't I think of this before. How many people do we have here?"

Karl shrugged his shoulders.

"We have six inmates in each module - 36 modules in each unit, that's 216 people. We have 36 units - 7,776 plus one director per module."

She punched it in.

"Jesus, this is simple addition. Can't you handle it? Oh, here it is, 1296 innkeepers for a total of 9,072 lost souls, plus functionaries, bureaucrats and ladies in red.

"What do we know about these people?"

Karl answered, "Precious little."

"That's right. We know about six of us, a few of the constabulary and a handful of our neighbors, but that's it.

"We know the computer isn't going to tell us. It intrigues me that the big programmer in the sky isn't anxious for us to have this information. What do you say we conduct our own census?"

Karl scratched his head. "7,776. That's a lot of people to interview."

Anne replied, "We can do it."

Helen Benson interjected, "Can't you get in trouble?"

Neither Karl nor Anne had recognized she was privy to the conversation.

Anne icily responded, "Not if we can keep *quiet* about it."

"Are you going to ask Miss Caroline's permission?"

"Not on your life. According to Michelin's Guide of Ethereal Places, it's not against the rules. If you start asking permission, then we'll get stopped. If the information was something they - the giant ants - wanted us to know, the computer would give it to me."

Karl put his arm around the short, portly lady, "Mrs. Benson," he said, utilizing his best bedside manner, "I think Dr. Merrow is right. The less said about this, the better."

Helen offered, "I want to help. I see more people than you do. I'm at bingo every night. I'll be quiet about our little secret."

Anne and Karl exchanged looks. Karl deferred to Anne, it was her idea. Anne fingered the computer keyboard. "Alright Mrs. Benson, but this is our secret. Remember, Roberta. There are probably a thousand Robertas out there, like sharks, ready to pick us off. We must be careful."

Helen nodded gleefully, "Careful is the word. I'll be careful as a goose in a pillow factory. What do you want to know?"

Anne, the consummate psychologist, responded, "We'll work up a questionnaire, then we'll feed the results into the computer."

Karl queried, "How are we going to get 7,776 questionnaires?"

Anne playing the keyboard was oblivious to interference. Karl and Helen crowded behind her and watched the screen.

ARE YOU HAVING A NICE DAY?

YES, THANK YOU, ANNE.

I WOULD LIKE A LITTLE HELP FROM YOU.

I'M HAPPY TO HELP.

CAN WE TALK IN CONFIDENCE?

DEFINE PLEASE.

IT'S A PERSONAL CONVERSATION - PRIVATE. ARE YOU CROSS LINKED TO A MAINFRAME?

YES.

IF I WANTED TO TALK JUST TO YOU, IS IT POSSIBLE?

YES.

TELL ME.

LINK UP IS TIME DELAYED. 24 HOUR PICKUP OCCURS AT 0100. USE CRC MODE AND ANY INTERACTION IS CLEARED - NOTHING TO TRANSMIT.

DO YOU HAVE ACCESS TO BIOGRAPHICAL DATA ON RESIDENTS?

RULE VIOLATION.

I KNOW, BUT CAN YOU GIVE ME A FORMAT HOW THE INFORMATION IS ORGANIZED?

YES.

PRINT, PLEASE.

YOU HAVE A VERY NICE TOUCH, ANNE.

THANK YOU.

The printer rolled out a bi-fold sheet of categories. Anne scanned it.
Karl asked, "Do you want to shorten it up?"
"No, all this information means something. Wait a minute. Look at this."

TRANSFER IN -
TRANSFER OUT -
TERMINATION LINE -

Anne put her thumbnail below the last entry, "Are you thinking what I'm thinking?"
Karl frowned, "I'm afraid so."

Anne was back at work at the keyboard:

PLEASE DEFINE - TERMINATION LINE.

SORRY, ANNE, RESTRICTED ACCESS.

OKAY, THANKS MY FRIEND. BE A DARLING AND PRINT ME 7,776 QUESTIONNAIRES.

SIXTEEN

The small band of conspirators decided that the information sought should be obtained surreptitiously. During meals and group activities the Social Directors segregated themselves which gave the -7ers room. Everyone was engaged but Billy. It was decided that he should not participate lest more questions arise regarding his status. The lower profile, the better.

Helen Benson was in her medium. She had a plausible excuse to talk to everyone. Surprisingly, she turned out to be the most productive of the group. Helen further solidified her position as champion and was referred to as the "Bingo Lady."

If Anne or Karl moved in the direction of Haberschmidt, if that's who he was, they would be intercepted by Caroline who engaged them in conversation. By the time their exchange had ended, the old man was gone.

Anne was adroit at observing nuances of personal interaction, it was her forte' as a professional.

George Wilson had proved to be one of the most valuable members of Ghost Town, as it was dubbed by the -7ers.

Unfortunately, the heavenly plumbing was "designed in Mexico and built by Italians," George groused. Whole systems failed regularly with power outages common. George was the only repairman and as such was swamped. There was a long waiting list for his services. He earned the title of "Repair Technician."

An electrical engineer, a burley Canadian, Kevin Baines, worked with George part time. Baines was a strange duck, as George would say. A gifted "spark man," but a bona fide eccentric. He had been hell bent on his way to becoming a millionaire. He carried the vision of building a better mousetrap to its logical absurdity.

He explained, "The trouble with people is they didn't have enough love and are plagued by vermin. I developed a program where rodent eradication and companionship were intertwined." He raised ferrets. He delighted in explaining how friendly, trustworthy and true a ferret was.

George offered, "What's the big deal about ferrets, cats was what we had. They ate mice and were pets too."

Baines threw down his voltage meter. "Cats are miserable creatures. They're no good at catching mice. If you had a cat, I bet you had mice."

George interjected, "Sos I did."

"Ah, if you had my ferrets, no mice. Another thing, cats don't like people. Cats tolerate people. The only time you get any attention out of a cat is when it's hungry. It'll make up to you, but once it's fed, forget it. A cat's in love with itself. There's nothing left to share. And mousing? Huh, that's a laugh.

"Now, if you want to rid your yard of robins or sparrows, a cat would be good. Cats catch and eat 'em just like my ferrets go for mice and rats.

"There's never been a friend like a ferret. You can depend on him. He'll love you. You may not deserve it. They're like dogs, even better. And mice and rats, they tear 'em apart, rip 'em to shreds. No traps to fuss with. You don't have to mess your fingers opening the spring, no sir, not even a bit of hair left.

"And rats, did you ever see a cat fight a rat? They won't do it. Cats are prissy little things. They like batting bugs. But not ferrets. The first thing they do is bite off the rat's head and eat him right through the tail.

"I sold 5,000 ferrets and never had one returned. Guaranteed 'em, 300% markup; raised 'em myself."

George and Baines had the perfect entree for the questionnaires. There's nothing more usual than a repairman asking personal questions. It was part of the job description.

Milisant Crescent located other teachers through the questionnaires. She held a meeting and a community-wide gradeless open school was started. The questionnaires disclosed Ghost Town was a microcosm of worldwide English speaking people.

In such a diverse population, there were many who could not read and others who were only marginally literate. The school addressed literacy.

Milisant caught fire. She was the undisputed administrator and favorite teacher at the school, unofficially named "Crescent High."

The school put on a production of *Julius Caesar* for the entire community. It was a great success. Milisant explained to Helen Benson that the play was not about the salad and that its author, William Shakespeare, had not invented the fishing reel.

The rooms of the modules were decorated with three dimensional pictures, the best of remembrances of life.

George Wilson created a large representation of Mayan Temple IV at sunrise towering through the verdant forest canopy. George had never seen the sunrise, although it had been described to him, but it could not have been more vivid had he experienced it every morning of his mortal life.

Helen Benson's Tupperware was now augmented by pictures of other commercial products, L'eggs pantyhose dinosaur eggs, a Tide box and Revlon's Charlie. Anne called Helen's room, "The Drug Store."

The Star of David, assorted crosses, fishes and symbolism of the representative religions were also popular. Prayer groups were tolerated.

Kevin Baines devised an ingenious plan to provide the three dimensional pictures with back light that gave them even more depth. He found that the computer printout sheets when electrified, would glow. Using a linear rheostat, power was supplied to produce whatever light intensity the viewer desired.

Billy Evans pushed a button and the transparent dome, like the large glass cover of an anniversary clock, silently closed. He had a bluejay to do, a request. Some of the residents of Ghost Town were not able to produce anything except asymmetrical, geometric designs which passed for "modern art," but were actually a failure to master the technics of memory painting.

Billy had become a favorite. Module mates had tried to keep his profile low, but when his talent with the Actuator was learned, he was besieged with requests for pictures. Many things he conjured up, he had never seen in life. By studying encyclopedias and reading about the character of the animal, or landscape to be duplicated, he was able to turn out beautiful reproductions.

Kevin Baines wanted to syndicate him, but there was no currency, nor advantage that could be purchased. Kevin worked with Billy in developing a herd of ferrets.

Kevin's sleeping room was adorned with ferrets and he worked up his own light show. He loved to scare unsuspecting women who went to his quarters to see a Rembrandt only to be confronted by a lights-on display of carnivorous mammals.

Billy drew his right index finger over the light line dimming the indirect light. The less interference, the more vivid his images. He closed his eyes and moved his fingers along the radii that controlled intensity and perspective. Like a sculptor who chips away at a granite block, Billy conjured up a rough blank.

He carefully laid color after color on the blank and then as if adjusting the focus of binoculars, slowly sharpened the image until every feather, line and marking of the bird appeared. Billy thrust his thumbs hard into the table indentations. They were as the prongs of an electrical plug that engaged his mind to the Actuator. The image, as a powerful magnet, drew up bits, streaks and pieces of colored light from the table surface.

Billy sculpted and finished the bird. Then he visualized its background, the limb of a blue spruce covered with globs of snow.

The painting done, Billy etched BE in the corner, his signature. He moved his thumb to the reproduce lever to print the image, but hesitated. The bluejay's head was cocked and its eyes glistened at him as if attempting to communicate.

Billy concentrated, straining. His mental image of the jay flexed its wings and twitched. Billy opened his eyes and sure enough, the bird was moving just as he had moved the ball for Caroline.

The bluejay fidgeted on its perch, picked at its feathers, preened with its bill. Its leg itched its chest. Billy was afraid to move his hands. With his little finger, he started pushing the reproduce lever, all the while moving the bluejay into various postures.

Could he do it? He would try. The bluejay stretched its wings. The branch it perched on rocked and snow fell turning to dust. The bird flapped and was off. Billy's heart soared with the bird. The bluejay flitted and flew around inside the glass cylinder and stood on its ceiling upside down. The force field inside the cylinder was highly agitated by the cavorting hologram. Streaks of light beaded up and down its interior. Billy had his bluejay peck at the light streaks like little bugs. The bird had been a taxidermist's model, now it was a dynamic creature exuding blue and gray iridescence, more alive than if it were alive.

Something happened. The bluejay, in one swoop, passed through the wall of the Actuator and was flying free of the force field that created it. When Billy recognized what had happened, it began to disintegrate, but by concentrating, he brought it back together and continued to have it fly around the Biosphere.

What was happening was akin to biofeedback. Billy wasn't certain how he could do what he was doing, but he did it. Whether it was his alpha waves, beta waves, or new wave, he didn't know, but it was working. He continued clicking pictures. By the time he was done, he had Mylar reproductions ankle deep on the floor.

Billy was at the height of his power. He had never experienced such sensation of achievement in his young life. He was brimming with the enthusiasm of youth crippled neither by forethought nor restraint.

Next, he conjured up a Boeing 727. He etched the red and white Air Canada logo. He fleshed in the background of a taxiway, a blue sky, a few wisps of white clouds. He shaded the plane for perspective imagining the sun to be behind him. He closed his eyes and blocked in a form. He tightened his concentration. He sharpened the image. He had remembered correctly. It was a perfect replication of his handsome father. He wore sunglasses and a gold nametag "Captain Evans." Flecks of gray hair mingled with the brown at his temples. Billy hit the print button. He slowly opened his eyes half fearing his father would not appear. The 727 hung in the center of the Actuator, but no human form was present. Billy shut his eyes and tried again with no success.

The gong sounded and the glass cylinder whooshed open. Billy's allotted time was over. He tried to fight back his emotion, but a flood of feelings welled up through the boy-man reserve. He dropped his head to the table and sobbed away with the anguish, fear and loneliness of the abandoned and lost.

SEVENTEEN

Helen Benson handed her stack of questionnaires to Anne. She thumbed through them. "Good work. You win the prize for today, just like bingo."

Helen smiled, "It's not work, it's fun. Back home there were some real nasties. Here there are mostly nice people."

Anne processed the information, feeding it into the computer. "We have 80 to go. A couple more days and we should be finished."

Karl queried, "No Haberschmidt?"

Anne shook her head, "No Haberschmidt. I can't get near him."

"Me neither. If we did, Caroline would head us off at the pass. Have you worked out a profile?"

Anne replied, "Not yet. Since we're so close it doesn't make sense to jump the gun. Why be two percentage points off when we can be on target. Anyway, this is sort of like Christmas. Would you open your presents early?"

Karl smiled, "Every chance I could."

"That's the difference between boys and girls - I didn't want to know until it was time and since this is my show, you'll have to wait."

George asked, "What are you looking for, Miss Anne?"

Anne continued working the computer. "We'll just have to wait until we open the package and find out."

She entered:

THANKS. NOW WILL YOU BE A DEAR AND TIDY UP.

MY PLEASURE.

GOODNIGHT.

GOODNIGHT, ANNE. I LOOK FORWARD TO YOUR TOUCH.

Karl gestured to the screen, "Isn't he getting a bit familiar?"

Anne laughed, "We have an understanding. Our relationship is platonic. Now wrap up those printouts."

Karl pulled sheets from the printer. He scanned them. There were a minute series of 1's and 0's. "What is this?" he asked.

"It's our data. It's digital. Something the computer and I worked out. We can't leave the information in his memorybank."

Karl commented, "I didn't see you clear the communication tonight."

"I don't have to. I just give the computer that 'Tidy Up' command, he clears his memory and substitutes standard transmissions to fill our on-line time. He is brilliant."

Karl feigned, "My primary competition for your affection is a machine and another woman."

Anne tossed her long blond hair, "Just shows you how times have changed."

After breakfast, Billy sought out Caroline. She was with a cadre of other SDA's in their self-selected area of the dining hall.

"Miss Caroline, can I talk to you?"

"Certainly, Mr. Evans," Caroline responded. She gave him a wink. "Ladies, if you would excuse me."

Out of earshot of the others, she asked, "Now Billy, what's up?"

He reached in his pocket and pulled out a roll of assorted variations of his bluejay in flight.

Caroline carefully studied them. "These are beautiful. Did you do all of this?"

"Yes, I did."

"When?"

"Yesterday."

She noted that the same bird was in each print. She understood that one could not replicate an exact mind picture. Each was like a fingerprint. While two renditions may appear similar, under examination there would be many differences.

Billy said, "I wanted to give you something because you helped me with those women in red. Please keep as many as you want."

Caroline chose three pictures from the middle of the group. They were similar, much like stop-action photography.

"Billy, I don't understand how you could have turned out so many pictures. Did you share someone else's time?"

"No, Miss Caroline."

The hour allotted each resident for the Actuator yielded no more than one print and that was usually incomplete. It could be used as an underlay for the next session, much like a painter would work on a part of a picture one day and take up where he left off the next.

Caroline bent over and locked eyes with Billy. "You made him fly didn't you?"

"Yes, I did. It was hard at first."

Caroline spread the group pictures out on a table. One of them was of the back half of the bird with no head or shoulders. "Were you able to - did you get him out of the force field?"

"You mean outside the dome?"

"Yes."

He hesitated. He had been programmed, coached and prepared to deal with the questions of the ladies who ran his world, but he'd been caught, just as he had when he broke his mother's favorite teapot. He glued the handle and was certain no one would notice. His mother was in tears when she confronted him. He tried to laugh his way out of it, which only made matters worse. He recalled the anguished look on her face. "Billy, it's bad enough you broke something, but it is much worse that you lied about it."

Billy didn't answer. Caroline grasped his shoulders and asked in measured tones, "Billy, you must tell me, did you make it escape?"

He would have lied again, but there was something compelling about Caroline. He had lied to his mother, whom he loved, out of fear and with the vain hope that somehow by not acknowledging what had happened, he could stop it from having happened.

It was too late, he knew he could not escape. He closed his eyes to break contact with Caroline's piercing gaze and under his breath said, "Yess-s-s-s. Yes, I did it."

Caroline released her hold. "Will you show me?"

Billy blinked. *If it was wrong, why should I do it again. Now, she wants to know for sure I'm not lying.* "If you want me to, I'll do it. But only because you asked me."

"He's coming tonight," smiled Helen Benson.

Anne queried, "Bingo?"

"Right. While Billy had Caroline busy, I went over and talked to him just like you suggested. He's a nice fellow. I explained the game, how it was electronic and was played on six levels, like an apartment house. He seemed real interested and said he would come."

Karl patted her on the shoulder, "Good work. Okay team, let's see if we can finish up. Helen, if you get Haberschmidt, that's all we need from you."

She nodded, "No trouble, but I don't want it to end. It's fun."

"You dirty son-of-a-bitch. I've had it!"

The words reverberated in the dining hall. All conversation stopped. Peace was shattered in paradise. Two grappling bodies rolled along the top of the buffet table. Food was knocked left and right, dishes and silverware crashed to the floor. Both men were large.

The people who had been waiting their turn behind the men parted like waves, escaping from the confusion. Cooperation had been the watchword, but friction was inevitable where people dwell.

Karl stood on his seat to get a better view. The combatants finally fell to the floor.

Karl mused, "It isn't much of a fight. It's a lot like hockey. There's grabbing, pushing and shoving but seldom a good punch."

The SDA's, like a blue tide, immediately filled the void created by the retreating diners. They piled on top of the struggling men. A siren sounded. The entrance to the dining hall closed. Karl gestured toward the door. Anne nodded. In a moment, a phalanx of black-clad security personnel burst in from the kitchen. They carried clubs and wore riot helmets. The burly security officers took only seconds to reach the pile of SDA's. They were pried off the battlers, who were set upon by the officers who beat them unmercifully.

Karl was witnessing what he had only seen on TV news, the disturbance in Mayor Daley's Chicago during the Democratic convention of 1968 and the beating of blacks during the Civil Rights protests of the 1960's.

Karl nudged Anne, "Do you believe this?"

"No, I thought we left this behind."

The beating continued. Karl had it. He started toward the fray. He was no longer a spectator. He had seen this type of machismo in hockey a thousand times. The fight was no big deal but these guys were getting the shit knocked out of them.

Anne grabbed his trailing hand and spun him around. Their eyes locked. She shouted, "Don't!"

Karl tore his hand free, but order had been restored. The two fighters were standing, their hands secured behind them. One very tall officer tilted his visor and began talking to a SDA.

Karl's view was blocked by the back of another officer. He made his way around the outer edge of the room for a better view. The officer was talking to Caroline. She was gesturing and pointing to the two men. She was restrained and calm. Karl could not hear what was being said. The officer in charge nodded and then a long curl of jet black hair fell down his shoulder. Karl muttered, "Jesus, she's a woman."

Anne interjected, "They're all women."

The SDA's quickly cleaned up the mess and announced lunch was to continue.

Holographic letters appeared on the wall, snaking their way around the dome horizontally.

ORDER IS ALL - ALL IS ORDER - FREEDOM IS ORDER- ORDER IS FREEDOM - ORDER IS PERFECTION - ORDER MUST BE KEPT.

Neither Karl nor Anne could eat. Morosely, Karl commented, "Not very subtle."

Anne nodded, "A little short on tact, but to the point."

Helen Benson was pointing, "Isn't that nice, just like the Goodyear blimp."

EIGHTEEN

The -7ers sat in the center room of the module. Helen Benson should have been back by now. Bingo was usually over by twenty-one hundred hours and it was 2130.

George motioned to Milisant, "Your turn."

Milisant said, "Not have to ride the subway. You can't imagine what it's like to be old, female and black in New York. The abuse I took was terrible. It was like having to run the gauntlet twice every working day. The filth, obscenities and danger - danger was ever present.

"Enough of that, your turn, Anne."

Milisant had become more assertive and was interacting well with the professionals. She had even begun to call her comrades by their first names.

Anne said, "No periods."

There was silence.

"Do you want to know why?"

Karl said, "God, no!"

"Okay, Karl, what is it this time?"

"No income tax. That's what I like best about this place."

Anne let out an exasperated gasp, "Spoken like a doctor. Don't you like the fact that there's no cancer here, no disease, no dying babies?"

Karl countered, "They were my adversaries. What I fought. It was me versus death. I didn't have much success, but I was in some good fights. Since I've been here, and I'm out of a job, I've developed a healthy respect for my enemy. I miss the scourge, the plague, the aberrant cells - the Angel of Death."

George Wilson spoke up, "No income either. If your tax was so bloody bad, you could have gone on the street like a bag lady. Nothing to tax."

Anne asked, "George, what is it for you?"

"The job. Best job I ever had. Work all day and stay clean. I keep this place ticking. It's good to feel needed."

Karl intoned, "Amen. If only I could fix *things* instead of people."

George continued, "Working with Baines can be a bit of a rock, but

I'd probably miss him. For a partner, he's top rate, but for the rest of it, he's got mothballs for brains."

The door opened and Helen Benson stepped in. "I enjoyed your company too."

Anne caught a fleeting glimpse of the rumpled figure she had been pursuing for so long.

Helen was triumphant. "I've got it, here it is, every question answered."

Anne announced, "It's him."

Helen Benson said, "No, he said his name was Dunn, Puzz X. Dunn."

"There wasn't much left. That's about all he could have been," smiled Anne.

Karl looked over the questionnaire. "I don't understand. Nothing matches up with what we know about Haberschmidt. This couldn't be further from what we would expect of our man."

Anne said, "Look at this." She worked away at the computer entering:

1. ROBERT KILROY HABERSCHMIDT.

2. PUZZ X. DUNN.

MY PAL, GIVE ME A FIRST NAME WITH NO LETTERS FROM NAME 1.

NONE

FIND ME REFERENCE TO A CHRISTIAN NAME, PUZZ.

NONE

Karl nudged her, "I wish you'd quit leading him on. It's disgusting."

Anne whispered, "Shh, he'll hear you. Now take a look at this." Anne displayed the entire Dunn questionnaire on the left side of the screen. The same questionnaire appeared on the right side of the screen with data for Haberschmidt.

Karl was puzzled, "How did you get that?"

"The computer made the questionnaire. I had it cross-reference Haberschmidt's biog and fill it in."

Milisant shook her head, "Nothing matches, not even the date of birth."

"Okay, folks. I'll trade my virginity," Anne crowed, "for a pair of nylons, if you can find one letter that matches on these questionnaires."

Karl said, "So nothing matches. What does that prove?"

Anne cleared the screen and typed:

WHAT IS THE STATISTICAL PROBABILITY OF
DIFFERENTIATION OF QUESTIONNAIRE 1 DATA
AND QUESTIONNAIRE 2 DATA?

10^{14}

Anne breathed a sigh, "10 to the 14th. There's a greater likelihood that Charlie Manson is Christ."

Milisant winced, "I wish you wouldn't do that."

"Sorry, chalk it up to God's tolerance for allowing a blasphemer like me in here."

George Wilson spoke, "Miss Anne, you're saying that Haberschmidt's right answers are so different from Dunn's it couldn't be a mistake?"

Anne said, "Precisely."

Helen Benson chimed in, "But why, why would the dear man not want anyone to know he was here?"

Anne, preoccupied, answered, "Don't know. Maybe they have a special school here for the gifted that he didn't want to attend. He's in the computer alive and Puzz X. Dunn is done, done, done!"

Karl was still skeptical. "If this questionnaire of Dunn's is such a masterpiece of opposition to Haberschmidt's, how could he have worked it out and memorized it?"

Anne twirled around on the computer bench, "Have you ever heard the Haberschmidt story?"

Karl shook his head.

Anne smiled, "Well, I don't know if its true. It's the kind of tale that goes around colleges. After a couple of PhD's, he went to Michigan Medical. He was in a lecture with a tyrant of a professor, a real Kingsley type, Medical School version. It was Analytical Chemistry-trauma time. The prof gave Haberschmidt a hard row. He was an easy mark, older than the rest; had some academic credentials in other disciplines. It's a good winnowing out trick, pick the best mark and tapdance all over him, it humbles the other students.

"Anyway, the prof had written a book on the subject. Haberschmidt memorized it. The next week the prof bombed Haberschmidt again. When collared, Haberschmidt said he had text from a national authority that agreed with him.

"He coolly quoted the authority verbatim. The prof went for the jugular and demanded the name of what he thought was a fictitious authority. He thought he had Haberschmidt short.

"Haberschmidt laid it on him, his own work, published by such and such a company on such and such a date. He becomes the joke of the school and takes a sabbatical.

"Now, anybody that's got a mind like that, can memorize a questionnaire easier than we could memorize 'General Motors,' besides it's Haberschmidt's way. Not only did he phony up a questionnaire, he did it brilliantly."

Milisant asked Helen, "What was he like?"

"Nice. Very polite. He caught on quickly and was a winner. He asked about the little fellow who did the bird pictures."

Billy asked, "What did he want to know?"

"He said he'd like to meet you."

Anne had been trying to make contact for months without success. She looked to Karl and mewed, "Entree?"

Karl countered, "No, invitation."

NINETEEN

Day 357

Karl approached a willowy figure facing the gold wall. The young woman's honey blond hair hung to her shoulders. He was unsure whether she had answered a questionnaire. They were having difficulty finding the few residents remaining.

Anne had been adamant. She wouldn't run the tabulations until she had the whole picture. Karl had accused her of stringent toilet training.

Karl half expected the young woman to turn, displaying a witch's face. He recalled the Ernie Kovacs Show where the beauty sports the hag's face or a beard.

He cleared his throat. The girl spun around, her shift playing gracefully out like a figure skater's skirt.

She smiled, "How's my doctor?"

Karl read her face and form, certain his pupils were dilating. He didn't recognize her. He would have remembered.

He tentatively questioned, "Should I know you?"

She smiled coyly. Every move, nuance, commanded attention. Karl wanted to visually caress her figure, but he was locked to her luminescent blue eyes. She responded, "Are you speaking in a biblical sense?"

Karl was on the defensive. He didn't know who he was talking to.

"No, I'm sure of that. I would not have forgotten."

The girl swung her hip and spread her legs. If only she were wearing a tight skirt, Karl mused.

She said, "Two cigarettes."

"What?"

"For two cigarettes, you can get to know me."

"I don't smoke."

"Nobody smokes."

The girl raised an imaginary cigarette to her lips and drew in deeply. She closed her eyes and tossed her head, "Ah-h-h." She blew out a puff of nothing as though it were smoke. "What I would do for a cigarette, maybe some high heels." She lifted one foot from the ground displaying a generic loafer.

She said, "Prison shoes."

It came to Karl, "Freda, but..."

She opened her eyes, "Ya, I don't look the same like before? When I was young, I was pretty. Now I am beautiful again, but to appreciate there is no one." She reverted to German sentence structure and accent.

She pulled at the pale yellow shift she was wearing. "No clothes, no nylons, no sailors, a hell of a place for a St. Pauli girl. Do you get it? They sent me here, not the other place. It was your Mark Twain who said, don't want to go to Heaven, none of his friends there. No sin. No bad language. No drinks and nobody to try the merchandise. There's some rule against it. What else is new. It made it popular.

"Well, my friend, you look like a big, strong, healthy boy. Want to break some rules?"

Karl's groin tingled. It was an unfamiliar urge. He was not particularly sexy. He didn't have much energy left for the procreative act, spending so much time with death and malaise. He had an understanding with Margaret, a critical care nurse at the University Medical Center. She accused him of choosing her because of the convenience; no singles bars, wining and dining. There she was, day-in, day-out in the oncology unit.

He wondered about Margaret. How would she do without him? He answered the question - quite well. She had very little of him and that was so preoccupied with work, he wasn't there when he was. His sexual performances were marginal at best and often downright embarrassing. Sex was the one thing that he did not excel at.

Freda continued her "come and get it" pose, waiting for a response. There was none. She waved her fingers in front of his eyes.

She cooed, "He is gone, gone to never, never land. What's the trouble, big boy, you just like fellows?"

Karl blinked, "Not hardly."

His emotions were at war. He would have dearly loved to find some dark place and accommodate them both. What was going on? This was a sexless society. Bodies were no more. Coupling could consist of nothing except rubbing holographic images of past recollections together in hope of making a few sparks. Then there was the problem of the Gestapo. Sexual interaction was strictly prohibited. Karl imagined being set upon by black-clad, club-swinging amazons when caught in the act.

He winked, "Thanks for the invitation. You are a *beautiful* woman."

Freda relaxed her pose, brought her legs together and returned her hips to the correct anatomical position. If Karl had been a chiropractor, he certainly would have thought she had severe subluxations.

She flicked the imaginary cigarette away. "No action. I am a firgin here."

Karl smiled. Her English was excellent, but she still had a problem with v's.

Years of hard living had etched both body and soul, she had been steeled. Now, even with no makeup, in formless clothing, she was exquisite, a coy little girl in a goddesses' body - with the provocative hint of Aphrodite's Garden of Delights for the taking.

Karl obtained the questionnaire information. Freda had died at 31 and had chosen 22 in the tanning salon. The only surprise was that she had a University degree in music. She was able to go to school during the day and worked nights. She lived a sad and lonely life of missed opportunity.

"When I was small my mama would sing lullabies. She worked as a maid so she could pay for piano lessons. Her fingers were dainty and small. She could play good, but she couldn't reach the octaves I can. I have big hands." Freda displayed her long, graceful fingers.

"She loved me so much. I was her hope, the daughter who could do the things she never would. She was hit by a truck when I was 12. She never walked after that, couldn't work. They sent me to a home. It was terrible. At 14, I run away. I visit her every Thursday. Now I'm gone. Her hope, her legs, her fingers and future, gone. But it don't matter. I was dead already.

"Do you believe in God?"

Karl couldn't answer before she continued. "Well, I don't. Not even in this place. This place is what your God made. I don't want no part of it. Besides, the bastard has women doing his dirty work. This is just like down there.

"A woman lies with a man and what does she get? Eve was a sinner because Adam lay with her. She gets the cramps, feels like she's going to die every month, has a baby. Has her insides stretched out and looks like a freak. Adam, what does he pay? Nothing, no blood, no cramps, no screaming babies sucking his tit. This place is like His world. Women do the dirty work. Men use them.

"No harps, no organs, no music! This place is a tomb, that's what it is, a tomb, a great white mausoleum. God don't allow music, now what kind of a God hates music? What kind of a God don't let you hug and kiss if you're in love?"

Freda had not unburdened her frustration, anger and agonizing dismay before. Blasphemy and invective against the Almighty, poured out in a torrent.

She carried on, "What kind of a God hates dancing and singing? What kind of a God sucks the honey from life and leaves a wasted shell?"

She sat on a bench next to Karl and raised her arms skyward. Her shift fell about her shoulders exposing exquisite limbs. "God, I was a sinner, but what I did, I had to do. You crippled my mama. What was I supposed to do, walk away? I sold what I had, to live. That's the difference between me and these people. I was a whore with my body, not my mind.

"This is what I got, God. This is my hell. You hated my mama, you hated me. You hate joy, you hate music. Well, God, I hate you. You are cruel and mean. You hate life and living. I don't like this damned place. You are a rotten father, like my own I never knew.

"You hate the Germans. We paid for Hitler. We paid for the Jews. I thought it would be different here, but it's the same. You're screwing the Americans, just like you screwed me. God, you speak English? - Go to Hell!"

Her last words were shouted. Karl glanced nervously around. He chided himself for his cowardice in the presence of somebody rocking the boat. A torrent of conflict swelled within him. He wanted this woman and he wanted her badly. He wanted her physically, but also past, finis. How tragically ironic. He never learned of life until it was over and then from the oracle? God Almighty? No, from a tortured little lady from another culture who taught him what being human really meant.

TWENTY

WELL DONE, THANKS.

THIS HAS BEEN VERY STIMULATING, ANNE.

Anne stroked the keyboard:

I LOVE IT WHEN YOU TALK DIRTY.

DIRTY? I DON'T UNDERSTAND.

COLLOQUIAL ENGLISH. IT'S A COMPLIMENT. NOW PLEASE TIDY UP.

Anne gathered up her coded input and the display sheets. She looked over the seated group of -7ers. How many times had she done this teaching a seminar? She had the work of her students in hand, they sat expectantly, apprehensively, waiting for the WORD.

She scanned the faces of her comrades. George, hard-working, inventive, bright, more important now than in his earthbound life. The only one who could make things work. George was satisfied.

Helen Benson was happy - "What a nice place." The undisputed champion of bingo. No racking pain of cancer, no regrets, the here and now was fine for Helen.

Billy, the charming little boy-man, childhood had been lost to him. He had been wrenched from a good life with caring parents. Yet, he had a gift, a gift that impressed the impressive, Caroline. He enjoyed a relationship with her Anne desired, for Caroline was her absent self, her other, her match, if not her superior. But Caroline, aloof, enigmatic, chose a little boy.

Then there was Milisant. No more muggers, obscene gestures, horrific lonely walks down filth cluttered, dark byways of one of the worst sinks of all humanity. A generation of hopelessness bred by despair, the cesspool of a superficial and egotistical society, the dregs consigned to the human garbage dump of the metropolis they fester in, the lowest ring of Dante's hell from which there is no escape. "All ye beyond hope - enter here."

Milisant had earned her respect by good works. It was her lot in life, but that was not the draw. The cards were wrong. The good stuff went to somebody else.

Lastly, Karl Ronstadt, brilliant, cynical, ruggedly goodlooking and my best friend. This is not his place. It is a Caribbean cruise ship populated by clowns and he can't get off. Anne cleared her throat for attention, a device of the male. "I have worked up a profile of the average resident of Ghost Town. He is white, 65 years old, worked in semi-skilled manufacturing, one semester of college, married, father of three children, American-midwest, WASP.

"Fifty-two percent here are male, forty-eight percent female. Four year college graduates, 18%, that's higher than expected. Professional and graduate level, 11%, again much higher than the norm.

"Races - white, 87%, again high - black, 5% - way low."

Milisant whispered, "It figures."

"Chicano - Mexican, 2%; American Indian, 1%; other 5%. Everyone died in March 1995.

"It appears that there was no methodology connected with cross-matching residents, no attempt to develop parity regarding education, background or race. Our community is a polyglot of random selection related to month of death, the only real commonality we share.

"Between 70,000 to 100,000 people die each day. Ten percent are English speaking. That means in the month of March, 1995, 31 communities like ours, must have been established as well as 310 like communities of other languages.

"Another interesting fact is that where death occurred simultaneously involving members of the same family, plane crashes, automobile and train accidents, no relatives are here. No husbands and wives, no brothers and sisters, no descendants.

"Now this could be just the luck of the draw, or it may be planned, I don't know. And as Elmer Fudd used to say, 'That's all folks'."

Milisant spoke, "There doesn't appear to be any secret concerning this information. Why couldn't you access it in the computer, why didn't they want us to know?"

Anne shrugged her shoulders.

George interjected, "What does it mean for us?"

Anne bit her lip, "We know more now about who's here and where they came from. I have the name of every person in this place. I know what they did for a living. I know how much education they have. This can be useful to us.

"We have more teachers for Milisant, for Crescent High. There are a couple of people here who know a whole lot more about what's going on than we do. There's Haberschmidt and Caroline. She's in it up to her pointed ears with him. Now we have something on them. We've got a little leverage with her if we ever need it."

Karl had been concentrating. He was picking up everything that was being said and was also processing it simultaneously. "Does anybody have an idea how long this is going to go on? Do you think this is it, where we stay, forever?

"If I were to dream up an afterlife, I would want people to be able to communicate with loved ones, relatives, friends and children that had passed on before. This is not possible here. Do we have any old gray heads? Anybody who's been around for a millennium or two just to tell us how things are and how they go?

"Then there's the Wall. Why draw limits. If this is the bridge to infinity, why are we prisoners in our own rooms each night? Why do we have guards? Why are there armed police? Why the Orwellian admonitions concerning order? Where have you ever read, 'Freedom is Order - Order is Freedom'? This is a kind of brain washing. We are being taught to behave. We are being conditioned to accept. We are captives and yet we smile."

Milisant eyed the ceiling. "I can only speak for myself. I don't feel confined. I don't feel imprisoned. If you want to talk about prison, let me tell you about my apartment, my neighborhood; that was prison.

"I don't know how long this will go on. I only know back there, I was finished. I had given all I had. No one cared and I made no difference. I chose nothing over that. Now I have something.

"As I see it, we have been given a second chance, a new life, no crime, no filth, no corruption, no war."

Karl interrupted, "And no freedom."

Milisant continued, "If what I came from was freedom, I don't want it. I reject it. I accept the providence of Almighty God. I believe in Jesus Christ. I believe that my works on earth are responsible for this opportunity."

Anne's mind raced. There was a lot to what Karl was saying. Perhaps this is a conspiracy. When she checked the faces of her friends before she had begun, wasn't that what she was thinking? Would they join the conspiracy - conspiracy to do what?

Anne said, "Being captive and being free are relative terms. Milisant believes she is free. Karl, you feel captive. It is what we perceive, like Caroline said in the Biosphere, that matters." She hesitated, my god, I'm citing Caroline, can you believe it?

"Here people are together who come from the same cultural antecedent and share a commonality, language.

"If you were thrown in with 10,000 Cro-Magnon hunters... How about something more modern, let's say a convention of the AMA a la 1790. Put you in with a bunch of doctor-barbers. Suck out the poisons with leeches. How about a lancet in your arm, or maybe a sharp septic goose quill - then all those harmful night vapors. You'd go out of your mind.

"Now the business concerning kids with their parents and husbands and wives. Where do you stop? Let's say you've been married four times. Do you want a convention of former wives? All the wives have parents and their parents have parents and so on. If you dealt with kin groups, we could go back to Olduvai Gorge then work forward.

"In psychology, we know that every individual is a solitary, lonely, separate entity. We come into the world alone. We leave it alone.

"If we have potential, it is as individuals. It is by happenstance that we were thrown on these shores together, yet we've acclimated to each other. If I had my mother, or great aunt Matilda to placate, I'd still be a little girl here. I would be trying to make them happy, to be the good daughter. Here I'm me. I have no distractions of family."

This speech sounded good, but Anne had few distractions on earth anyway. Being a workaholic and having an invalid mother took its toll. Afterworld with her mother would be a living, breathing hell. At least in life, she could leave her in the home and return to her world. If she had been compelled to listen forever to her mother's petty grievances, or bitchy complaints about the injustice of her late good father...one needn't dwell on these thoughts.

"Let's face what we've got here. It is a monolithic bureaucracy. You saw how things were at the front gate. Would it be better to have a community that spread to the horizon of infinity or a smaller one like Ghost Town? This is manageable. It is organized and efficiently operated, especially with George fixing the stuff that breaks."

George smiled.

"The difference between running our little town of 10,000 and a megalopolis like New York, or Hong Kong, or Tokyo, is the problems expand exponentially as the population grows."

Helen Benson said, "Why, Anne, that was a wonderful speech. You're right. Choices had to be made, a choice between order and disorder. Which would you choose?

"It's ever so nice here. The people are kind, and then there's Miss Caroline. Sure there are rules, but they're bent when they're unfair. Look at what Caroline did with Billy. It would have been easy for her to let Billy go wherever they take little boys. She went to bat for us. She had nothing to gain and a lot to lose."

The module door opened. There stood Caroline.

TWENTY-ONE

> The God whom science recognizes must be a God of universal laws exclusively, a God who does a wholesale, not a retail business. He cannot accommodate his processes to the convenience of individuals.
> -William James, *The Varieties of Religious Experience*

Milisant was aghast, "Close the school?"

"I'm afraid so."

Anne could not believe her ears. There Caroline stood, steel-blue eyes, quite emotionless. The same look on her face as when she directed the security officers to haul off the brawlers. Who the hell does she think she is? How insensitive. How rotten. Strip this poor lady of her only decent experience, before or after death. I'd like to claw her damn eyes out.

The psychologist regained her composure. "Caroline, I don't understand. The school has been good. Many people have learned to read. Their lives have been enriched."

Caroline nodded, "I know. I don't want you to believe for a moment that the decision to terminate the school was mine. It was not. I have no choice in the matter. My personal preferences are of no moment. The decision was made by others and it is my responsibility to see that orders are carried out."

Karl too was fighting himself, "Sieg Heil," he whispered under his breath.

"Someone else could have brought the news but since you are my group, I felt I should."

Milisant restrained a tear, "Isn't there anything we can do? Can we appeal, or something?"

Her recently acquired poise was shattered. She was being screwed again by whitey. White, arbitrary, authority had spoken and it was her lot, as a child of a child of a child of a slave to obey.

Caroline flatly remarked, "There is no appeal. These decisions are administrative."

The atmosphere was strained by tension.

Billy spoke, "But, but, Miss Caroline, does that mean I can't go to school anymore?"

Caroline did not meet his gaze, looking off into the distance. She said, "Billy, there will no longer be school."

Helen spit out, "At what level of authority was the decision made?"

"C26." The answer was automatic. Caroline's jaw slacked open a moment later.

Something was dreadfully amiss here. Caroline had been in control, absolutely self-assured. And now, Anne thought, who would have dreamed that the Bingo lady could shake, cool cucumber Caroline.

Caroline swallowed, "I should not have answered that question. You have no right to be provided the information."

Karl mused, "Obviously, there is a page in some manual with that language on it."

Milisant started to sob. There was something untoward about adults crying in public. Everyone was uncomfortable.

Anne zeroed in on Caroline. She demanded, "Why, I want to know why?"

There were sparks in the air. Milisant was sobbing. Billy covered his mouth, trying to be a brave soldier. Helen was glaring at Caroline. Anne wanted to attack her with fingernails and Karl was clearly pissed.

Caroline twitched uncomfortably. She was caught somewhere between being the consummate bureaucrat and having genuine empathy for her charges. Normally Anne would have noticed the conflict, but there was too much hostility.

They wouldn't give Anne or Karl a job, but Milisant made her own and what do they do? Lock her out.

Caroline took a step toward the door, stopped and turned on her heel. "Damn it, I had nothing to do with it! I don't like it one bit more than you. I think it's crap. You do a little good and you get slapped down. It isn't the American way, but make no mistake about it, we're not in *America* or in *England*, Mr. Wilson."

George was agape. How could she know? No one knew other than his friends and MC5 who wouldn't have talked.

Caroline continued, "I must do my job. If I don't, someone will replace me and you'll find it much worse. If I screw up, I know 1,000 good little soldiers who'd love to see me-----.

"I'm going to lay it out. This is the way it is. Homeostasis is what it is called. You have reached equilibrium, a state of restrictive constraint.

"You feel closing the school is unfair. That could be the case as applied to the conditions here. Unfortunately, rules are generalities and do not lend themselves comfortably to the exceptional situation."

Anne had cooled down and was receiving what was being transmitted. A mystery wrapped in an enigma was Winston Churchill's definition of China but it fitted Caroline perfectly.

She continued, "We are instructed, strike that, programmed to deflect questions. You are not to ask why and we are not to suggest reasons for anything that's done here.

"The rules are the rules. If everyone challenged the rules, there would be chaos, anarchy, the absence of lovely order. Homeostasis means things stay as they are. Growth was meant to end with your earthly lives."

Her words dripped sarcasm, "Certain other officials have decided that stasis also means if you can't read by the time of your death, you don't get taught to here. They feel instruction corrodes and corrupts. Hierarchy of authority is undermined if discipline outside the controlling organization exists. I have been ordered to close the school and I will do so."

George took the offensive, "Miss Caroline, what if we don't agree? What if we run the school anyway?"

Milisant perked up, this was a new contingency. Caroline stared silently at George for several seconds.

In measured tones she said, "You cannot fight this, Mr. Wilson. It's that simple. Whether the school is closed by this order, or closed because there are no teachers, it will come out the same."

She drew a deep breath, "I don't want to see you hurt. You are leaders. Each one of you in -7 has contributed well beyond the norm.

I know that there are two of you who have no business being here. If I were as unfeeling as you believe, Billy and George would be long gone.

"There are some of us who use our intellect to season the rules with value judgments, but we are a small minority. There may be a SDA five units over letting a 'Billy' stay, or another who overlooks a minor infraction but most do not.

"In England, there are two kinds of courts, a Court of Law and a Court of Equity. The Court of Law strictly enforces the law. Equity is free to disregard the law when it is unfair, or immoral, or society suffers by its strict enforcement. It is the very epitome of fairness.

"Here there is no Court of Equity. In the quest for perfect order, eternal order, dealing with billions of souls, there is little room for compassion and fairness.

"I must close the school. The alternatives are unthinkable. You must be fatalistic. You must accept what you cannot change."

TWENTY-TWO

Anne punched:

WAKE UP, RISE AND SHINE.

GOOD MORNING, ANNE.

DITTY - GIVE ME ALL YOU HAVE, CAROLINE CX51.

CAROLINE CX51, SOCIAL DIRECTOR-ACCLIMATOR B492-7, DECISIONAL PRIORITY, OPERATIONAL PRIORITY.

Harold McTavish squinted, his thin, black frame bent over Anne's shoulder. He asked "What do you make of it?"
Anne shrugged, "Don't know. Let's try this -"

COME ON, YOU CAN DO BETTER. LET'S HAVE IT ALL, EVERYTHING.

SORRY ANNE, LIMITED ACCESS, FUNCTIONARY BIOG INFO UNAVAILABLE - LOCKOUT, SEE RULE...

Anne punched the Del key before the number appeared.

WHY DO YOU DO THAT?

BECAUSE YOU'RE PISSING ME OFF, THAT'S WHY.

PISSING YOU OFF?

MAKING ME VERY ANGRY.

I CAN'T DO IT. NO FREE WILL.

Anne typed:

DEFINE; DECISIONAL PRIORITY - OPERATIONAL PRIORITY.

The computer responded:

DECISIONAL PRIORITY: DECISION MAKING POWERS EXCEEDING NORMAL SAME CLASSIFICATION. INDIVIDUALLY DESIGNATED. TREAT WITH RESPECT.

OPERATIONAL PRIORITY: ABILITY TO FUNCTION AT HIGHER CLASSIFICATION LEVEL. DECISIONAL PRIORITY - OPERATIONAL PRIORITY, STEP-UP FOUR LEVELS.

Anne said, "Well, that explains some of it. I still don't know who she is."

McTavish sat down to the keyboard and the ritual he had been following for two weeks. Harold McTavish, the gifted computer programmer, had taught at MIT and was hired by the CIA as debugger and encoder. He had been a communications officer at the U.S. Consulate in Amman. He was abducted by the Islamic Jihad, the first black American hostage. Because of the critical nature of his knowledge, a rescue was mounted by the U.S. Strategic Assault Force. McTavish perished in a fire fight depriving his captors of information which could have resulted in the death of hundreds of CIA operatives.

"I'm still trying to break its security code - I haven't yet but I have a trick or two left."

Time seemed to slow. The questionnaires had provided the -7ers with activity and a topic of discussion, but the project was over. School had been abruptly terminated and Milisant had withdrawn for a time, but was now interacting seminormally.

George's employment was regular. He kept just behind the latest malfunction, breakage, or electronic glitch.

Billy continued to have private sessions with Caroline in the Biosphere, but was reticent to discuss what they did.

Since the incident with Roberta, no census takers had visited -7. It was the only module exempted.

Karl invited Freda Friedman to join the -7ers on occasion for meals. He did not explain her background. She was accepted and modulated the harshness of her rhetoric to accommodate the more genteel associates who befriended her. Residents of Ghost Town came and went. Anyone leaving the cog was never seen again. The replacements were from those fitting the parameters of Anne's profile.

Disruption decreased. There was an unspoken understanding concerning the finality of removal.

Although the inhabitants resisted less and followed more, it was because they had become accustomed to the way things were and the recognition of the futility of attempting to buck the system. Restraints were always touted as freedoms as Karl remarked, "The yoke is a yoke to a man, but to an ox is part of his anatomy."

Unbridled joy, emotionality and spontaneity became less frequent and ennui descended on the community. Where earlier there was exploration, experimentation and clustering of persons with common interests, these interactions became old. The limited potential of the place cast a pall.

That is not to say that Ghost Town was a morose scene of zombies shuffling about. No, it still had a charm which was flavored by its diverse population.

There was friendship and caring. The few rule transgressors who were removed chose their course for that purpose. They had become tired of whatever was and sought, at any price, something different.

The less charitable called outbreaks, "Going Bananas." Anne ran a series of profiles on the computer and developed predictions concerning those at greatest risk.

It pleased her when one with a high priority of risk, succumbed. Her sampling was correct.

TWENTY-THREE

Day 880

On Sunday evenings, the lights were dimmed and linen tablecloths spread on the dining tables. Meals were served family-style. Food was appetizing in appearance and texture, but offered bland substitute for the sharp, sweet and sour tastes of earth.

Karl moved his synthetic steak around in its sauce with a fork, his mind wandered. There were no good foods, or bad foods, no fear of coronary disease, stroke, or high blood pressure.

Anne nudged Karl, "You're a bad example." She motioned toward Billy, who had even less interest in ingesting the material on his plate.

Helen Benson vigorously chewed the broccoli spears covered with cheese-like sauce. She wistfully murmured, "I would love a hot fudge sundae right now, topped with real whipped cream and a maraschino cherry."

Billy mused, "A McDonald's would taste pretty good!"

Milisant could not abide McDonald's. She had a Big Mac three times a week. She recalled how it tasted, like a styrofoam container. It occurred to her that everything she had been eating tasted like styrofoam.

Karl brought the subject up again, "George, are you sure there's no way out except through the kitchen?"

George nodded, "It's the only one I know."

"Have you repaired the door?"

"It's not a door. It's more like the circle you step on. I haven't serviced it, but I have a floor plan for the kitchen. The entrance port is there and some electrical."

Anne curled her hair again with a finger, "If you could get out through the door, where would you be?"

"I don't know."

Helen pointed her fork at Karl, "Why ever would you want to leave? It's really quite marvelous here when you think about it."

Karl spoke in measured tones, "It is a personal thing. I find this place boring, lifeless and bland. I have nothing to look forward to and I spend most of my time reading. I used to think that would be a wonderful way to retire and it would for a couple of weeks, but not for years."

George nodded, "You know, they used to say in church that in Heaven there was golden gates and people sat around all day on the clouds strumming their harps. Well, they was wrong, but it isn't a whole lot different. I could stand a change of scenery; love to be in the jungles of Guatemala ..." He looked off into the distance, his mind wandering back to Tikal.

Anne broke the silence, "George, you lived, you experienced. You have memories to fall back on and savor. I was just about to make my memories, but didn't. I was the prelude to a symphony, but never made it to the concert hall."

Billy said, "Miss Anne, there's no hockey in this place, no one to play ball with, not even a dog."

Karl carefully looked at his comrades. "If there's a way out, would you come with me?"

Helen Benson shook her head, "I don't want out."

Milisant, Billy, George and Anne all met Karl's eyes in their turn. It was agreed.

Karl asked George, "Would Kevin help?"

George shrugged his shoulders, "I could feel him out. There are no ferrets here, he misses that."

The port in the kitchen was a reasonably simple system according to Kevin, who joined the conspiracy. It was operated by an on/off switch activated by a token containing transistors. The whole affair could be bypassed by jumping the wires - a lot like hot-wiring a car. The real question was whether the door had power after the lights were turned off at night.

It was the evening of Day 891 they would find out. When the module door shut at lights off, a chair was used to block it.

Karl and George removed their shoes and left the module through the narrow gap.

Karl whispered, "This isn't going to work. We'll never make it to the dining hall without some light. Do you have a light?"

"You mean a torch?"

"Yeah, a torch."

There was rustling in the toolbox, a snap then a green luminescence radiated from a wand held by George.

Karl moved behind George letting him lead. He whispered, "Where is Kevin supposed to be?"

"At the dining hall."

George moved quietly, holding the wand ahead of him. It cast an eerie shadow of the two conspirators. They made it to the cog center. The door was in sight and closed as expected.

Karl asked, "Where is he?"

George shrugged, "Don't know. Let's get on with it."

He knelt in front of an access plate and held the glowing rod between his knees. "Better stand behind me. That way the light won't show."

Karl watched intently. With the precision of a surgeon, George carefully laid out the various tools he needed. He took a screwdriver and pried the access cover off. He handed it to Karl. "Just like Japanese cars. Everything's held together with nylon clips."

Karl peered into the ill-lit panel. George began probing it with an electrical tester.

He commented, "Don't get power. I don't..."

Karl was struck on the shoulder. He jumped, frightened out of his wits stumbling to the ground, his heart pounding like a piledriver.

He gasped, "Jesus Christ."

George, startled, braced himself against the wall. The light rod rolled along the ground. A hand came out of the darkness and picked it up.

Raising it to his face, Kevin grinned, "You two are a bit jumpy, aren't you?"

Karl demanded, "Why the hell didn't you tell us you were coming?"

"Didn't figure making noise would be a good idea."

Kevin knelt in front of the panel. George resumed poking it with a voltage tester. "No power," he informed.

Kevin took over. "You're right, dead as a doornail."

George sighed, "Well, that's it."

Kevin chuckled, "Good thing I came along. Only takes a volt and a half to trip the switch."

He fumbled in his pocket and pulled out pieces of wire.

"Hang on to these." He handed them to George. "One in each hand. I've got a battery here, let's give her a try."

George put one wire on each end of the battery. Kevin took the other ends and touched terminals in the panel.

A familiar whoosh sounded and the door opened.

Kevin announced, "Pretty simple."

Karl whispered, "Only because you knew what you were doing."

Inside the dining hall, the three moved slowly. George poked Kevin, "What took you so long?"

Kevin said, "I didn't have a light. I was feeling my way until I saw the beacon from your green lighthouse and I homed in on it."

They worked their way to the kitchen. They moved around the large benches to a faintly illuminated circular glow coming from the floor, the port. Kevin pointed, "Where do you think it goes?"

George said, "Haven't the foggiest. That's why we're here. It might be a way out."

Kevin was optimistic. "The food comes in through here and is prepared somewhere else. It only figures that the catering is done for more than one dining hall or else it would be prepared here. That means this is a way to someplace that has access to different cogs, maybe even the back door.

"The control grid is over here." He pointed to the side of an adjacent serving bench.

In a few moments, they had removed the cover and Kevin was fiddling. He noted, "We have power here."

Karl felt useless. He was a spectator. He hadn't the vaguest notion what the other men were doing although they appeared to have figured how the manhole cover was actuated.

Karl peered into the maze of transistors. He might as well have been trying to read a Chinese newspaper.

Kevin was bridging contact points. He uttered, "Aha!"

He sat back cross-legged on the floor. "That's it. Who wants to try it?"

Karl straightened up. "What do you mean?"

"Go through."

Karl hesitated, "Don't you want to go first?"

Kevin shrugged, "This was your idea, Doc. Besides, nobody else can work this. It's gotta be you or George."

There was a silence. They had been conditioned to accept their world. It was flat. It was circumscribed by a wall and governed by rules. Neither man was a coward but they had not considered who would go first.

George said, "I had this neighbor. He had a yard all walled in and he had a black dog. Don't know what kind, some mix. The dog would bark and carry on whenever anybody came near the wall, but would never leave the yard."

Kevin broke in, "What's the point?"

"The point is some people would rather complain about being locked in somewheres than doing something to get out. But I'm not like that dog. I've got less to lose than Karl here, so I'll go."

Karl grinned, "So you think I'm like your neighbor's mangy dog, barking to get out but don't have the guts to go through the gate. No, George, I'll go first."

Kevin said, "No reason why you both can't go. The port is large enough. But before you do, why don't we send something and see if we can get it back."

George pulled a large screwdriver from his tool box. He put it on the center of the disc. Kevin hunched over the control panel. There was a zap. The screwdriver disappeared.

Kevin smiled, "That's good. Just like a magic show. Okay, let's see if I can get it back."

There was another short zap. An instant later there was blinding light. Towering above the crouching men, loomed two officers. The taller officer spoke, "Gentlemen, you have made a serious mistake."

TWENTY-FOUR

> She was a shining star
> That lit our abysmal night
> And gave us hope for tomorrows
> Far better than what has been.
> To know her was to love her
> And the life that brought such beauty.
>
> One warm clear morn the sun arose
> To the robin's song,
> Children sang and it seemed
> The long night might end;
> But Sonya stepped into the sea
> and infinity took her.
>
> -Lydia Fields, *For Sonya*

Day 892

Lights on. Why did they have to turn them on full blast? Anne buried her face in her pillow. She opened one eye and then decided it was no use, opening the other. The usual regimen was followed, a shower, a check in the mirror, a fluff of the hair, the shift on and out to the main room. Billy and Milisant joined her.

Billy questioned Anne, "Did they make it?"

"I don't know. Their doors are still shut."

They waited until 0725. Anne entered George's room. It was empty. His bed was made.

Billy found Karl's room empty as well.

Helen Benson queried, "What is going on?"

Anne shared her concern. "They were going to find an out for us but haven't made it back."

A few minutes later, the remaining -7ers assembled in the dining hall. Anne nudged Billy, "Go check Kevin's table, see if he's there."

Helen Benson frowned, "I really don't understand you. People work a lifetime to get in this place. Everybody is taken care of. What more could you want?"

Milisant retorted, "Life, with all of its vagaries, uncertainties, warts and moles. It was real but this is not. It was challenge and danger and disaster and triumph and failure. I want what I rejected. I want what I left. I want what I didn't appreciate because the battle seemed so hopeless. Existing is not enough, it is really not much at all."

Anne said, pointing a forked synthetic strawberry, "Look, Helen, we're not trying to convince you to do anything. I'm happy you're satisfied. I'm pleased for you. But the rest of us are incomplete. We were inchoate pictures on an unfinished canvas. I had just begun to live. I had a lifetime, or so I thought, ahead of me. Billy had a few strokes of color and a line here and there. We were the beginning that ended barely after it started.

"Did you ever read 'The Tale of Two Cities'?"

Helen thought a moment, "Was that made into a TV movie?"

Anne rolled her eyes, "I've no idea."

Helen asked, "Is it a dirty movie?"

Anne exasperated, looked to Milisant. "'The Tale of Two Cities' is a classic novel. It was written by Charles Dickens and set during the French Revolution. In it, an Aristocrat, Sydney Carton, forfeits his life so another man might live. Before being beheaded by the guillotine, he said, 'It is a far, far better thing that I do than I have ever done; it is a far, far better rest that I go to than I have ever known.'

"Well, Helen, this is neither rest nor death nor life. It is a benign purgatory, something between the real and the unreal, the figment of a limited imagination. It is what some non-human entity may believe we strive toward, but we do not. It is not creature comfort, adequate food, clothing and pleasant surroundings we seek."

Helen was puzzled, "Well, dear, if not those things, what?"

Anne looked wistful, "I don't know. I know what it is not. It's not this. What it is, is something I may have learned had I lived long enough. I know that my soul aches in this place. I feel confined and restricted. I want to turn tables upside down, I want to soil the perfect whiteness. I want to scream. I want to tear my clothes off and run naked. I want to live."

Milisant nodded, "I know ending my life was wrong. This may be God's punishment on me for it."

Anne thumped her hand on the table. "I don't buy it, Milisant! Not one bit. First off, my only sin was sharing an apartment with a slob.

If there was justice, she would have been electrocuted. And what about Billy, what was his great wrong that deserved exile to a place where there are no children, puppy dogs, sports teams, schools, parks, waterfalls; taken forever from his parents who mourn him as he mourns them. And, how about you, Helen? Did God give you cancer because of something rotten you did?"

Helen huffed. Anne held up her hand, "Don't bother, you're not complaining, so you got something you're satisfied with. One man's meat.

"I don't know if we can get out of this place but I would take the challenge of climbing the mountain again over Pleasantville."

Billy returned. "Kevin's not here."

Helen Benson offered, "Bingo tonight, that's something to look forward to."

The jackpine stood erect and shrouded by fog. All was still. In the distance, a muted light on the horizon turned the steaming mist translucent gray.

A Canadian jay cried and squirrels darted here and there collecting nuts from the forest floor. Droplets of condensate on the conifer limbs dripped to the ground, spreading the heady scent of moist pine needles. Gusts of air, like whirlwinds, churned up miniature tornadoes of dust in front of the cabin as the wind picked up. The sun had cleared the trees - a perfect sphere filtered through the mist casting an eerie light on the north woods scene. The fog retreated inland pushed by breezes. The sun's reflection shimmered on the open span of water stretching out from the granite boulders blanketed by lichens and moss. The aroma of the forest mingled with smells of freshwater and decaying seaweed.

Billy inhaled deeply and covered his face with a blanket. He felt a tug at his shoulder.

His father said, "Shake the lead out. The Northern are waiting for us. Up and at 'em."

There was a harder tug. "Are you all right?"

He rubbed his face and blinked. Anne Merrow was standing above his bunk. The pungent odor of the northwoods dissolved. He held his breath, prolonging the sensation of the rich dream.

Anne, relieved, grew stern. "We don't want to miss breakfast."

As Billy continued working his mind as a tool in the Actuator, his dreams became more varied. He could exercise some control over their content. They were pleasant and usually captured a part of the rich experiences he shared with his family. Sleep came easily and he often retired before the others, looking forward to his reminiscences.

Milisant paced the floor of the module great room. Helen Benson sat silent, her hands folded on her lap. Anne, gazing pensively toward the computer screen, was lost in thought. Karl's absence laid heavily on her. She missed him. She protected herself in life from involvement with men. She didn't trust their motives. She didn't need the distraction of raging hormones messing up her analytical work. But now things were different. She had depended on Karl, had committed to him. He became her confidante, friend and peer. He was her idealized male - what a man would be if she had made one. Anne sighed and nervously scratched her head, "I'm projecting again - damn."

Helen Benson raised her eyebrows, "I think we should talk to Caroline. It's been four days."

Anne offered, "Caroline has been really cool lately. I'm sure she knows what's happened. If she wanted us to know, she would have told us. On the other hand, if they are gone for good, we have to find out."

Helen stoically said, "What's the worse case scenario? They got caught violating the rules and were disposed of?"

Milisant and Anne exchanged glances.

Anne said, "Look, Helen, I wish you would make your mind up who the hell you are. You really irritate me sometimes."

Helen stood and laughed, "Hey, gals, I'm a grandma. That makes me wise sometimes and foolish others. If you don't like the way I cook, you don't have to eat the food."

Anne took Billy's hands in hers. "It would be best if you asked.

You've got an in with Caroline. I'm not exactly sure what the two of you are doing but she needs you. Let's use that. Find out."

McTavish sat at the computer in Freda's module. She crowded him from behind. "What you think?"

"I don't know, this is a weird one, what you've asked."

"Ya, but can you do it?"

"There may be a program in it for music. Before we attempt to create one, let's see if someone has been here before."

"What's that?"

"Directories, sub-directories, root directories. I'm searching for programs that are already in its memory."

"What you mean, its memory?" Freda asked.

"Some computers have a hard drive that stores information that can be pulled back out, like taking a book off the shelf. What we have here isn't a computer, it's just a terminal. It is connected with a main frame computer someplace. Every program that's ever gone into it, think about it like a library, is still there. Now, here's something."

TWENTY-FIVE

Billy sat at the Actuator. Caroline put the picture in front of him. He asked, "What is it?"

"A whirlwind that sucks everything into it - light and matter. It is a hole from which nothing can escape and everything is inextricably drawn in."

He asked, "How big should it be?"

"We'll start small. Make it the size of the picture, a little whirlwind that sucks up sand and dust from the floor of the forest."

The picture became a reality. The rotational forces of the small vortex created turbulence inside the glass dome. Caroline had Billy move it out of the Actuator.

He was disturbed. "Something is funny about this. It scares me."

Caroline patted him on the shoulder, "It is your mind that's created it. It's part of you."

As they walked back toward -7, Billy raised the subject, "My friends are missing. Can you tell me when I'll see them?"

Caroline in a measured tone said, "Soon, you'll be with them soon."

"That's all she said?" Anne grilled Billy.

Billy shrugged, "That's it."

Anne scratched her head, "That's Caroline. Cryptic as hell. Just what we should have expected."

Freda sat down, coffee cup in hand. "So where are the boys?"

Anne shrugged, "We don't know. Ask Caroline."

"Lots of people missing today. Some vacancies over there. Two places up near me empty."

After dinner, Freda went back with the -7ers to their module. She had something to show them. She began to play the computer. The sound that came forth was a mix of electric keyboard, piano and organ.

The -7ers sat transfixed as Freda played "Liebestraum." Milisant dimmed the lights and Freda played on, one classical delight after another. Her audience was captivated. Each were in their own world, a reverie of music intertwined with the rich elixir of distilled life on earth, all played out on individual mental canvases as Freda communicated from her tactile touch on the keyboard to the souls of her listeners.

She then deftly stroked out, "Ride of the Valkyries."

It was the most disturbing music Anne had ever experienced; swirls of activity and swells of sound from the genius of long dead Richard Wagner.

Freda began softly with a quiet measured refrain and it grew until it reverberated off the domed ceiling as it had the stone interior of a hundred castle grottos. The music like smoke permeated every pore of the listener's being. Where with Debussy, a mind wandered, with Wagner, it was commanded. It was at attention, buffeted by the crescendos of the furies. Just when Anne thought that she had all she could take, the sound doubled and pummeled her. She did not know what the Valkyries were nor the maelstrom they brought as they rode through the heavens, but she felt them through the music.

Finally, with the last stroke on the keyboard, the sound died away. There was a moment of silence. Milisant shouted, "Bravo." Billy clapped harder than when the Maple Leafs scored. Anne stood, tears rolling down her cheeks, cheering. She had experienced unknown emotion. Feelings and longings surged within her. Her control was shattered. She bawled like a baby. And so did the tall woman standing next to her.

Freda, drained and hunched over the keyboard, beamed. She turned to face her audience, looked and gasped. They saw her expression and turned toward the point of her distress. There was another person in the room, not one of the -7ers but a SDA. Caroline had come in during the concert unannounced. She wiped her eyes, walked to Freda, lifted her by the hand and hugged her. The SDA's symbolized authority, the police, everything Freda feared and hated. They represented order, rules and systems that favored the advantaged and crushed the unfortunate.

Caroline separated herself from Freda. "You are magnificent. Who are you?"

Freda distrusted authority. Yet this woman had embraced her and was moved by her work. Guardedly she said, "Freda Friedman." Caroline asked, "What is your unit and module?"

Freda responded, "491-31."

"Are you a concert pianist?"

Freda nervously laughed, "Yes, of course. How else could I make you cry?"

Freda was pleased. Better a piano player than a whore.

Caroline glanced at the clock. "It's dusk. Lights out in just a few moments. Miss Friedman, there's extra room in this module. I don't think you have time to get back. Stay here tonight."

Anne asked, "What about..."

Caroline turned on her heel, the door shut behind her.

"Karl?"

"What about Karl?" she said again softly.

"Which room do I take?" Freda asked.

Anne pointed to George Wilson's bedroom.

Anne sat at the computer and called up biographical material on Karl. The screen filled with information, birth, date of death. She buried her face in her hands, "Damn it, damn it, damn it."

Helen asked concerned, "What is it, dear?"

Tears welled up in Anne's eyes. When her father died, she couldn't cry. When her dog was killed by a car, she didn't cry, but Freda's music moved her and now her restraint was gone. She whispered, "He's on the screen. There's his biography and death date. He's not here anymore."

Day 896

"Bastards!" Freda exclaimed.

"What happened?" asked Milisant.

"It's my stuff, all of it. It's gone. My house is empty."

Anne scanned the dining hall. A quarter of it was vacant. Words snaked along the light bar circling the room proclaiming:

ALL THINGS ARE FOR THE GREATER GOOD OF MANKIND

"Have room for a boarder?" Freda asked the others.

Anne sighed, "Sure, we have two empties."

Billy and Caroline sat side by side in the Actuator. Caroline's hands pressed the table with such force that her nail beds blanched white. Eyes closed, they were locked in jaw clenching intensity. There was a large whirling mass in the center of the Biosphere set in a horizontal plane. Into its vortex were sucked light tendrils, streamers of cloudy vapor steadily pulled to the cylindrical edge of the ellipse. The confluence of matter poured from the outer edges to the center where it disappeared in blackness.

Caroline, eyes closed, said, "See the edges. I want more counter-clockwise rotation."

Caroline scanned the rotating vortex with her mind. "Good, Billy, that's excellent. Now, what goes into it should be more like white paint dropped into a vat of black and stirred just once. Good, good."

It was almost dark when they left the Biosphere. They were both drained. Caroline apologized, "I'm sorry, Billy. I'm afraid you've missed dinner. Tomorrow, there's someone I want you to meet. A special person. After lunch go to 491-29. Can you remember that?"

He asked, "But isn't that empty?"

"That's right."

He hesitated. Caroline stopped as well. She asked, "What's the matter?"

Billy grasped her hand. "Will I see Karl again?"

Caroline said, "Tomorrow, you'll learn. For now, you must get back to your module. The lights are about to go out. You never want to be out here in the dark."

When he entered -7, the world collapsed on him. Anne shook him, yelling frantically, "Where have you been?"

Milisant tugged at his shirt. "You scared us to death."

Helen joined the fray. "You didn't have dinner. Nobody knew where you were."

Freda remained aloof softly playing Brahms' Lullaby on the computer as the lights flickered. Billy hadn't had a chance to speak.

Freda turned on her back in bed and gazed at the Temple on the wall of George's room. The canopy of tree limbs and jungle overgrowth had been fixed to the domed ceiling giving it a wildness.

She would have to ask her friends what the picture meant. She studied the structure intently; each boulder, the tall steps, the strange fluting at the top. It was not an Egyptian temple - no sand in sight. Perhaps, it was a fantasy.

The lights flickered one more time and then utter darkness. Her last image was of the green enshrouded temple.

She invented a story - a beautiful girl and a young prince, a luxuriant setting among strange foreboding temples. Yes, it would be a kingdom by the sea. They would live a clean, pristine, white linen life forever and ever. Always in love and only with each other. She recited:

> It was many and many a year ago,
> In a Kingdom by the sea,
> That a maiden there lived
> Whom you may know
> By the name of Annabel Lee;

She drew the sheet up over her shoulder and turned on her side. She liked the feel of silk on her naked body. She loathed nightgowns. She was never comfortable in them. They strangled her and besides, in her profession, she was required to wear costumes to bed. She despised such erotic pretension and pitied the grown men whose arrested development derived excitement from stocking, garter or brassiere. It was then she noticed it, the pain, the tingling in her lower abdomen.

It was years since she had a man, or rather one had her. When she took an infrequent holiday, it was always to a place, she said to her friends, where she could keep her legs crossed, where there were no men to demean her. She opened her eyes looking into nothingness. Was this her punishment? Her wish come true? Was God listening when she said that?

Was she, who controlled men and earned her livelihood from their weaknesses, dependent upon them? Did she really need one? The more she thought, the more she ached. She put her hands on her flat stomach and pushed down above her uterus and fell asleep.

Freda stirred, she blinked. It was still dark. Something awakened her. Her breast was under pressure and she twisted her torso to free it but the weight was maintained. She pushed with her arm and met resistance over her left breast. It was a hand, muscled and hair-covered. She grasped the wrist to pull it off but stopped. It had been a long time since a man had fondled her. She patted the hand on her breast. It was then that another hand tenderly caressed her other breast.

She started to speak but as in a dream, no words came. Her thighs ached. She took a hand and guided it to her mound of Venus and pushed. A fingertip entered her and she shoved harder.

It was delicious, better than a glass of beer on a hot day. If I'm going to dream, this is the way to do it. She let up on the hand and reached out for a body. She felt a chest and moved her fingers down. He was prepared. She grabbed him, opened her legs and thrust him into her. He pushed deeply, separating her and then rhythmically moved back and forth where she wanted and needed.

It was exquisite. She arched her back so the pressure would be just right and cooed with pleasure. Her pain was gone. She was being satisfied, her thirst quenched.

The tension increased, the pumping intensified as she gave the message of her desires by slight movements of her body, like an experienced ballroom dancer leading her partner ever so subtly, he never knowing he was being led. She rolled her thighs and grabbed his shoulders. Her fingernails dug in as she squeezed him to her breasts.

It began as ripples in a brook and grew and grew until the explosive climax when she thought she would burst. It was as if her whole body had been detonated and then stroke after stroke caused aftershock after aftershock. She trembled and convulsed and then this wonderful faceless male exhaled and she felt his pulsing. She grabbed his cheeks and was about to feign orgasm, but caught herself and smiled. In a few moments, the deep breathing became shallower and Freda sighed,

"Thank you, God. I hope it was good for you too."
    She sank into a deep, dreamless sleep.

TWENTY-SIX

Day 897

Billy was hardly rested. His long session with Caroline had taken much from him and he was hungry. He rose, showered and dressed, then made his way to the great room.

Helen Benson was already up. She greeted him with, "Where were you yesterday?"

What was she talking about? Billy shook out the cobwebs. Then it came to him. He hadn't manufactured an alibi. Before he had time to answer, Anne emerged from her room.

Milisant, at the galley, asked, "Want a cup of coffee?"

Anne blinked, "Yeah, give me one straight up. I'm worthless without it, even though this stuff makes decaf taste good."

Billy sat down, his mind racing for a lie that would outfox his modular family. He stared at the floor, grasping for ideas when a man's foot moved into his field of view.

He looked up then shouted, "Karl!"

Anne dropped her cup and spun around. They all gaped at Karl who stood in his bedroom entryway.

Peculiar looks and Billy's cry confused him. He said to Anne, "What's up, Doc?"

She grabbed his lapels. "Don't give me any of your wise ass smart mouth comments. Where have you been? You scared us to death."

"What are you talking about?"

Anne did not relax her hold. It was Karl, she could smell him, she could feel him and she was not about to let him go. She demanded, "Where have you been?"

Karl put his arms around her, "Shall I lead or will you?"

She turned from him, pulling loose and put a hand on her forehead, "Why do you do this to me?"

Karl turned to the others, "What did I do?"

He tried to exchange knowing glances with the women, but they stood silently staring through him.

George Wilson stepped into the room, stretching his arms and yawning, "Things is looking up. I've got me a roomie and a pretty one at that."

Anne turned to George with a look of a boxer about to deliver a knockout punch. She put her hands on her hips, and demanded, "I suppose you're going to tell me, nothing happened."

George shrugged his shoulders. "She was there when I woke up, Mum. Pretty as can be."

Anne rolled her eyes, "No, no, not that. Where have you been the last five days?"

George looked to Karl. "Here, Mum, like the rest of you. Just me and me chums."

She lectured, "Now, you two have scared the bloody bejesus out of us. We never thought we'd see you again; they turned you into a fluorescent light or something. Quit playing games."

Karl recognized that she was sincere. "Anne, I'm not sure I understand what you want."

Anne said, "Okay, I'm asking you again. I want to know everything that happened from the time that you left here to check out in the kitchen."

Karl rubbed his head, "Oh, yeah. It wasn't very exciting. We got into the nourishment center all right, that was no problem. We went to the kitchen, put a screwdriver in the circle and sent it someplace."

Anne said with disbelief, "Okay, fine. Good enough. What did you do next?"

Karl exhaled, "Well, we must have come back and gone to bed because here we are and it's morning."

"Do you remember coming back?"

Karl said, "No, not exactly, but obviously I did. I'm here."

Anne turned her attention to George. "And you?"

"We was really tired. I don't remember much of anything except waking up with Goldilocks in me bed."

Anne asked them both, "What day is it?"

Karl said, "Well, yesterday was 891 so today's 892."

George nodded agreement.

Anne pointed to the wall, "What does it say?"

They looked at the three-digit calendar and then at each other.

"You've been gone five days. You don't remember anything else?"
Karl said, "I'm sorry."
George nodded, "That's the God's truth, Mum."
Billy was beaming. Caroline kept her word.
Anne announced, "We'll work on this over breakfast."
George pointed toward his room, "What about her?"
Anne woke Freda. She said, "Oh, I'll be right up."
"Make it fast, you're late for breakfast."
"Okay."
Freda sat holding the sheet around her virtually perfect body.
Anne scowled, "Built like Venus and plays like Horowitz. Not fair."
Freda tossed her hair, "You do dream research?"
Anne nodded.
Freda smiled, "Let me tell you about last night."

Billy was starved. He wolfed down his food, paying little attention to what was going on around him.

The moving sign proclaimed:

ACCEPTANCE IS VIRTUE...SUBMISSION IS JOY.

Both Karl and George attacked their food with equal gusto. The onslaught left no room for talk. Anne played with a synthetic omelet, slipping it on and off the tines of her plastic fork. She was doing what her mother had scolded her for, playing with her food.

Freda studied George as he ate. She whispered to Anne, "He was in my bed."

Anne folded the omelet once on itself, pinning the layers together with her fork. "It's his bed."

Freda exclaimed, "Mein Gott, I didn't use nothing. Do you think I could..."

Anne shook her head, "No menses, no fertility."
"What?"
Anne put her hand on Freda's shoulder. This wasn't a conversation

for mixed company. "Let's take a walk."

The women climbed the stairs to the upper ring of the hall. Anne arched her back and stretched her arms; not ladylike, but it felt good. She looked around. There were more empty places.

"Okay, Freda, you're not having periods, are you?"

Freda was confused, "Periods? Like commas?"

Anne laughed, "No, menstruation!" She grimaced, it was a rotten word, she hated it.

It still didn't register.

Anne was exasperated. She gestured to her crotch, flayed out her fingers and said, "The curse."

"Oh - hh, Ya, no babies?"

Anne nodded, "No babies. So, are you going to keep sleeping with him?"

"No. I don't know him. He's a stranger. How about I move in with you?"

"I don't like to be crowded. My last experience with a roommate wasn't very good. A little while, maybe, if we can get a mattress."

Freda smiled, "So you like him?"

Anne asked, "Him, who?"

Freda rolled her eyes, "Dr. Karl."

Anne blushed, "Oh, him. Yes, I suppose so."

Freda coyly smiled, "So?"

"So, what?"

"So, you going to sleep with him?"

Anne blushed again. "I think not, besides it's against the rules."

"You had prohibition in your country. It didn't work. Can you imagine sex prohibition would work? Your face is flushed, Anne. Are you a firgin?"

"Come on, you don't ask a lady that. It's really not your business."

"Don't you need a man sometimes?"

Anne blinked, "Christ, you're direct. No, I don't need a man sometimes. I don't need a man ever. Let's talk about something else."

Anne fidgeted with her hair. Freda scratched her temple, "Sometimes, being too smart is not smart. Sometimes, you've got to listen to your body; you've got to listen to your heart. I think you listen to your head too much."

Anne remonstrated, "Okay, Dr. Freud, I give up. But you've got to quit practicing psychiatry if you want to share my room, because I'm not up to this."

Caroline tapped a microphone. Fingernail against metal sounded through the hall. The subdued growling of talk fell off to a hush as she spoke, "Could I have your attention, please. I'm sure you've noticed that a third of our guests are no longer with us. Relocation is occurring and we want you to be aware of the steps we'll be taking. Please report to entertainment center at 1600. There will be a video explaining the procedures."

In a few moments, the SDA's were back pouring coffee. Anne's gaze followed Caroline as she moved among the tables. She was very graceful, like a gazelle in slow motion. No jerkiness to Caroline. Every move modulated.

Anne left Freda and moved in a line intersecting Caroline's path. She did not equivocate. She blocked her.

Caroline smiled, asking innocently, "Would you like some coffee?"

"No, I want some straight answers. What's going on?"

Caroline parried the thrust, "You mean regarding relocation?"

Anne's riposte, "Yes, and the sudden appearance of Karl, George and Kevin, what you're doing with Billy, Haberschmidt, the whole nine yards. I'm tired of sweetness and light. I want to know what the hell is happening here."

Caroline set her pitcher down. "Okay. One, I'm not in control here. Two, I know more than you do. Three, there's more I'd like to know. Four, don't give me a hard time. As pleasant the whole lot of you have been..." her voice trailed off.

"Just say I'm a guardian angel. You may not like me. You may not understand me. But you don't have to. Just roll with the flow. Go to the video this afternoon and try not to break any rules."

Anne attacked, "You haven't told me a thing. This is a Mama Bear story. Mama Bear says 'eat your porridge' so you eat it."

"You're a grain of sand in a desert, Dr. Merrow. You're a little spark in a forest fire. You're a drop of water in the ocean. Don't push it, you're not very important. You're a post-adolescent who got zapped by a hair dryer. Now stand aside while I go do my stewardess imitation."

Anne slumped down on a bench. She muttered, "How did she do that? She's just a woman."

Karl sat down next to her. "Okay, what are you two up to?"

Anne grimaced, "We two weren't up to anything. People don't interact with Caroline. Caroline interacts with people. Caroline is perfect. Caroline is all knowing. She probably pisses distilled water."

Karl shook his head, "I don't think so, she's much too perfect to engage in human bodily functions."

Anne nodded, "Maybe this is my punishment. Maybe this is what I get for being a smart ass."

Karl squeezed her shoulder, "Come on, kid, it's just like the old west, there's always a gun that's faster somewhere."

Anne laughed, "You're right, Pard. I reckon that Caroline is one of the fastest guns around."

TWENTY-SEVEN

Karl was glum. Freda was talking, "It's just like the war. This place is a relocation center."

Karl said, "I don't understand what the security personnel are for. There's been no unrest."

Freda shook her long blond hair. "That's right, Herr Doctor, and *there will be no unrest*. That's why they're here."

Anne asked, "What's going on?"

Helen gestured, "There are four modules full of the girls in black, ones that were empty. There are also some new supervisors, the ones that wear red. They're even some girls who wear gold."

Milisant said, "I think trouble's coming. Where's Billy?"

George asked, "Has anyone seen the lad since breakfast?"

Silence.

There was a knock at the open module door, much like the courtesy rap of a hotel maid. A petite black haired woman dressed in a red jumpsuit stepped in. In a businesslike voice, she announced, "I'm looking for Henry Kallas."

George Wilson said, "Hi, Mum, that's me."

"Mr. Kallas, I need to talk with you privately. Where is your room?"

George gestured, "There."

"Please."

She followed him down the hall.

Karl said, "Her nametag is Tamara MC5. Harold, ask the computer."

McTavish worked the computer keyboard. It read:

TAMARA MC5 SUPERVISOR SECURITY COMMAND

Helen Benson asked, "What does that mean?"
Anne said, "It seems she's important. She's a Caroline with fangs."
Karl mumbled, "I've seen her before."
Anne asked, "What did you say?"
"I've seen her before. Don't know where, don't know when."

Anne smiled, "The theme from Dr. Strangelove."

In a few moments, Tamara emerged. The assemblage gawked at her. She frowned, "What do we have here? Is this a convention? Who doesn't live here?"

No one budged.

"Six of you are residents; the rest aren't. Do I check wristbands?"

McTavish raised his hand as did Freda.

"You two, go home. There are new rules in effect, you'll find out later today. No groups of more than six, except in the nourishment and entertainment centers. Better get used to it. Come on, I'll walk you."

Freda signalled "V" with her fingers behind her back as she exited.

George returned from his room. Anne demanded, "Well, what happened. What did she say?"

He was dazed. "She says that I'd never seen her before and she's never seen me. Then she cut me wristband off and took me ID and says, 'The winter winds blow cold!'"

Anne thrust her hands to the ceiling. "I can't stand it. Everybody talks in rhymes and riddles. They must have some special school for these people. I bet Caroline teaches it. How did she know you?"

"She was the girl in the hall."

Billy was scared. He pressed up against the back of the empty module. He had seen them before they saw him. They marched in formation, groups of four, like soldiers, the big black-clad women. There was something about them that frightened him. He didn't know if it was wrong to be in this area. Nobody lived here anymore. A pair of much smaller red-clad women leaned up against the front of the module. The marchers seemed to be performing for them. Billy took shallow quiet breaths.

One of the ladies shouted, "Squad 4. You all from the Russian Army? Loosen up. We're not trying to intimidate anybody, we're to be a presence. We are showing the flag. March like ladies, not men."

She shouted again, "Hey, you, number 3 in squad 2, quit wiggling your ass. You look like you're trolling for whales."

The exercises continued. The other redclad lady finally shouted out, "Okay, girls, over here."

The squads crowded around.

"Now, listen up. No big differences. Same detail as before. You are never alone. Don't make any trouble. If it comes to force, be judicious. I don't want any brawls, keep the sheep in line."

The smaller woman spoke, "Thanks, Wanda. Good advice from a real pro. Now recognize that if we're on the muscle, we're going to provoke an incident. We don't want that. We're here so there will be no incidents. If we end up with a riot, we won't be able to control it.

"Your primary function is to gain voluntary compliance with directives. That's it. You're not thugs, you're women with a job to do. Now let's do it. Okay, let's have your hands."

Billy inched his way along the side of the building for a better look. The women grasped hands in a large circle and called out "Yo" in unison. They marched off.

A tall woman clad in gold joined the supervisors. She asked, "Well, Wanda, how's your squad?"

Wanda shook her head. "Disgusting. They're big and mean. It's like coaching a lady's pro football team."

The tall lady said, "You're bitchy today, Wanda."

"Yeah, that means I'm female. Tell me about that bunch?"

The lady in gold addressed the other supervisor. "And you, Rita, what's your assessment?"

"Mine's the same as Wanda's. Don't blame us for what happens. I didn't pick this lot. All I want to do is keep them under control."

The woman in gold nodded, her long shoulder length jet black hair splayed out. "Figure it this way. Here, there are brains and there are butts. We're the brains and they're the butts. We waltz our little candy asses through tough territories and do we intimidate? Not on your life. Half the guys want to jump us and the others need a momma. We can zap 'em," she patted the bulging pocket on her thigh, "or dazzle them with Socratic logic. No, this detail is a butt detail and they've got the butts."

Wanda nodded, "Butts and beltlines. They must feed these lovelies by the bale."

The gold-clad woman continued, "We're trying something new

here. We've cleaned out a third of the cog with no muss, no fuss. The rest see the video in a few hours and hopefully we'll be out of here in a week."

Rita questioned, "Any precursor of trouble?"

"No. Quiet as a cemetery. Remember, we keep the library and Biosphere operational until the cog is cleared. It keeps the illusion of normalcy.

"It is important you watch your SO's carefully. Anybody who abuses authority should be stepped on. We don't need another Albans."

Rita said, "Don't worry about our gang. They may be big and they may be dumb, but they're ours and they damn well know it."

Billy was confused and pensive for several moments. Should he go back and tell the others or should he wait for Caroline. He debated and then remembered her promise about Karl. The area was now clear.

Shortly he found 491-29. The door was open and he entered. The layout was just like -7. He wandered into a bedroom. The bed was made. It was a motel ready for new tenants. He waited. He checked the other rooms. They were the same, clean, neat. Caroline had never been late before.

Billy sat at the computer. He toyed with the idea of turning it on and playing a video game but dared not. More time passed. He curled up on the bench, closed his eyes and fell asleep.

TWENTY-EIGHT

> Do they wonder or even care,
> Who was the man that wrote the air?
> It matters not to he who's gone,
> For on he lives he is the song.
> -Lydia Fields, *The Song*

The remainder of Ghost Town filed into the entertainment center. It had last been used during the Crescent High production of Julius Caesar. Milisant sank sadly into a theater seat. She pondered, what missed opportunity. What could have been; enrichment that was forfeited by the unthinking, stupid bureaucracy.

Karl shuffled along the aisle and found a seat next to Anne. Freda worked her way along the row, saying "Excuse, excuse - bitte."

Anne did not get up but Karl did. Freda stumbled on Anne's feet and twirled landing breasts to chest against him. He steadied her by the shoulders. She brushed a long blond curl to the side of her face and said, "Danke, sorry I'm so clumsy."

She pirouetted gracefully into a seat next to Karl.

Anne gritted her teeth. Stumble, my ass, our lovely classical pianist, Aphrodite herself. A perfectly executed and choreographed lurch with a three-point landing. I must have a heart to heart with my roommate.

Helen Benson shifted her bulk into a chair and wiggled to find the most comfortable spot. She cooed, "Now all we need is a Diet Coke and some popcorn. Just like home."

The houselights dimmed.

Karl asked Anne, "Where's Billy?"

She whispered, "I don't know. Probably with Caroline."

Karl shook his head and pointed.

A spotlight illuminated the stage and before the huge drawn curtains, Caroline stood, cordless mike in hand. She announced, "I'm glad you're all here. I know that you will do your duty in an orderly fashion. It has been my pleasure to work with you.

"Your lives contained a series of transitions and this is but a continuation. A video has been prepared for your pleasure explaining some of the important features of the grand design. To better explain, let me introduce our Relocation Director, Connie T. Connie, would you come up?"

A tall, striking black haired woman clad in gold climbed the stairway to the stage. Caroline handed her the mike. She took it and nodded to the crowd. She raised it over her head and brought it to her lips and began to sing slowly, softly in perfect key:

> Amazing Grace!
> How sweet the sound
> That saved a
> Wretch like me.
>
> I once was lost,
> But now am found;
> Was blind,
> But now I see.

She sang bringing up the volume and quickening the tempo. Her voice was clear as a silver bell - like striking fine crystal with a fingernail. It was perfection. As she repeated the refrain, she waved her hand and the audience joined in. The sound rolled up the rotunda roof and cascaded down on the spectators. The singing swelled, engulfing all with its mystic emotion.

After several stanzas, Connie T. hummed the refrain one last time. There was an amen and a hallelujah here and there. The tall beautiful woman kept her head bowed a moment and then raised it. She wiped her eyes. The audience exploded with claps and whistles.

Frustration caused by the secular nature of the place, the uncertainty connected with what was to happen, the lack of any music or entertainment, all conjoined with her singing to bring out the repressed emotion of the assembly. Some crossed themselves, others cried.

Karl remained aloof, a spectator. He was about to make a sarcastic remark, when Connie lowered her hand and the audience fell silent.

She lifted her head and looked to the sky. An image of Golgotha at sundown was projected on the screen. Three empty crosses stood out against the purple hued sky.

She sang:

> On a hill far away,
> Stood an old
> Rugged cross;
> An emblem of suffering
> And shame.

The words of the song appeared on screen and the audience picked up their cue and sang along.

Karl stared at the religious symbolism. He started to mouth the song, but bit his lip. He looked about. Everybody, his friends, the other -7ers, were singing, even cynical Anne. The music was touching but his fellow's emotional catharsis surprised him. It is true they longed for something. They were lost souls in every sense and this religious experience was giving comfort and consolation. If religion does anything, it must do that, Karl mused.

Connie T. rendered the song and after applause, brought the noise level to stillness with the slight movement of her hand. She curtsied. "Thank you, my friends. You have come far. You have fought the good fight and you have won. You have defeated the arch enemy - death. Your goodness redeemed you and earned life everlasting.

"Rejoice, I say unto you, for the new dawn is here. The lion shall lay down with the lamb and the meek shall inherit the kingdom.

"In the next few days, my friends, I'll be working with you to help you be renewed. This place is a way station, a coach stop, a rest area. All of you have been judged worthy to carry on the great voyage. It is with joy and happiness of heart that we offer you tomorrow and tomorrow and tomorrow.

"Now, we have a video. Sit back, relax and enjoy."

With that, the house lights dimmed; no back lighting, no exit signs.

Karl whispered to Anne, "OSHA violations all over the place."

Faint string music began in the distance, barely perceptible. The huge screen lit faintly, little pinpoints of light here and there, the western sky, familiar stars and constellations. The Big Dipper, Pleiades, Orion. Then superimposed on the sky was an image, a hugh stone statue, Buddha.

There was some commotion. Bright lights flashed on, but the screen still showed Buddha.

Caroline directed, "Kill that."

Karl looked to Anne. She immediately understood. They couldn't help it, there in the dead still of the auditorium, they erupted in laughter that startled everyone. Karl said, "They put on the wrong damn video."

Anne nodded, "I know, I know."

Connie T. had the mike again. "Okay, folks, a little mixup here. Those were my slides of Japan. I think we're all set to go, let's roll 'em."

Again the lilting music, the starlight night and then the National Cathedral in Washington, DC. A deeply mellifluous male voice narrated:

"The English speaking world is a world of faith. That faith takes many forms. It tells us that the sun will rise the following morn."

Karl nudged Anne, "Do you know who that is?"

She shook her head.

"Edward R. Murrow."

She asked, "Who's he?"

He answered, "Generation gap."

The voice continued, "Against ever-changing conditions of the human circumstance, men and women adapt. It is a trait of English speaking people; people who conquered the unknown, tamed raging rivers, reached out across uncharted seas, visited the heavens and walked on the moon."

Pictures, images that the words evoked, passed across the screen; ocean scenes, moonscape and a multicolored sunset.

The narration continued:

"It may seem unjust that man and woman strive a lifetime for perfection; mature, grow and contribute and then must pass away.

"You have begun a long voyage. You have crossed barriers from which no one has returned. Lifetime on earth was all you knew, but you were but a child taking a first step. There are many steps along this exquisite trail of discovery.

"When death came to you, you knew not what would follow. Religious philosophies guessed at what might lay beyond the grave. We consoled and gave comfort, not for those who had gone, but those remaining. We need no explanation for tomorrow and tomorrow and tomorrow since none will remain.

"Faith served you well in life. All manner of things you took for granted worked for reasons you didn't understand. And so it is with what is to come. Faith brought you to this place and faith will carry you on.

"Let us unite. Have faith for tomorrow and tomorrow and tomorrow is at hand. You now join the universe."

A sunset scene over the ocean faded as a string rendition of "Blessed Assurance" swelled up into darkness. The house lights dimmed on.

Connie T. raised the microphone. "My friends, your transportation assignments will be given you within the next few hours. The portal to tomorrow is a doorway. We call it the Transfertorium. That is because it will transfer you from this state to another more sublime, more beautiful."

She then sang, loud and strong: "A Mighty Fortress is our God" - Martin Luther's great hymn.

Freda sang along in German with an equally clear and beautiful voice.

Karl rubbed his head. A different language, but the same God, the same faith.

TWENTY-NINE

Caroline was agitated. She demanded, "When did you see him last?"

Anne spit back, "This morning. I saw him at breakfast and that's it."

Caroline's icy stare betrayed concern that bordered panic. Anne wondered what was going on.

Caroline went to the videophone and punched some numbers. Tamara's face appeared on the screen. "Tam, this is Caroline. I'm at -7. I need to confirm a schedule check. Would you come here?"

Caroline paced the floor, stroking her chin. George asked, "Miss Caroline, when do we go?"

"Go where?" Caroline asked absentmindedly.

"Go to wherever we're going."

"Oh, that. Well, it's on the schedule on your bulletin board."

George said, "I know, Mum, I looked. We aren't on it."

Caroline hesitated, "Uh, that's right. Well if you're not on it, you go last."

Karl exchanged glances with Anne. The module door opened and Tamara stepped in.

Caroline directed, "Miss Friedman, play something on the keyboard."

Freda moved toward the computer asking, "What do you want?"

Caroline ordered, "Anything, as long as it's loud."

She held her finger to her lips until the music began. Caroline pushed Tammy against the wall. They talked in hushed tones. Over the music, Karl heard Tammy say, "Dash 29. That's in no man's land."

They both left abruptly.

Anne fidgeted with her hair. "What was that all about?"

Milisant offered, "I think Billy's in trouble."

Freda said, "Somebody's got trouble too."

Helen Benson questioned, "Who?"

"Caroline. You see her eyes. Those are eyes of somebody frightened."

Anne said, "Look, if Caroline's frightened, I'm scared shitless. About the only thing we've got going for us in this zoo is Caroline. We ought to pray for her health."

Helen smiled, "Don't you feel good about it, about tomorrow? Wasn't that a wonderful program?"

Karl said, "Come on, Helen. That was a Borax job. What do you know now that you didn't know before?"

Helen thought a moment. "Well, we're going through a doorway."

Karl nodded, "That's a good one-liner, but that's about it, isn't it?"

Anne said, "They want something from us. We're being manipulated. Beautiful pictures, lovely music and a narration by the divine voice of Mr. Merrow."

Karl corrected, "Murrow. Lung cancer got him too. The voice of God, cigarettes did him in."

Anne cut him off, "Let's not get clinical, back to our problem. We are being asked to do something for the establishment here. To get up one fine morning and walk through a door. They have tugged at our emotional heartstrings. They have played the religion bit. They have implied promises, but if there is nothing through that door, there will be no complaints. No Better Business Bureau will get calls. They want blind obedience. We've got the storm troopers out there to remind us if we don't do what we're asked, they'll beat the shit out of us."

Helen chimed in, "Dear, why must you speak like that? You talk like a man."

Anne nodded, "My father's influence. He was a trial lawyer. He lived fast, stroked out at 51 and talked like a man. Thanks, it's a compliment.

"This is a magnificent puzzle. They want us through the door voluntarily, like the showers at Auschwitz." Anne directed her gaze to Freda who was sitting cross-legged on the floor.

"Hey, I wasn't even born then. My opa died on Russian front fighting communists. I don't know about that place."

Anne kept on, "Dash 7 isn't on their evacuation list. Caroline is our guardian angel and something's cooking with Billy."

Karl asked, "Where did you get the guardian angel bit?"

"She told me. I confronted her at breakfast and demanded some straight answers. She told me to sit down, shut up and not rock the boat plus the usual mumbo-jumbo."

Karl stood and stretched, "So, Dr. Merrow, what has this puzzle come to? What's the bottom line?"

Anne shook her head, "Damned if I know, Dr. Ronstadt."

Helen Benson shook her finger, "You're tempting providence, dear."

Anne laughed, "You're a good soldier, Helen. How can I challenge providence. I'm on my way to the great microwave in the sky."

Helen interrupted, "You don't know that, dear. What a waste. If this were the end, why are we here?"

Anne smiled, "That *is* the cosmic question, isn't it? That's one I have no answer for, nor does anyone else."

The module door opened and Billy appeared. Milisant rushed him scolding, "Where have you been? Now don't tell us you were with Caroline. She was looking for you."

Billy lowered his gaze to his feet.

Anne noted, "Children are such lousy liars. It takes practice and years to lie with a straight face."

"I fell asleep in an empty house. I got this for Miss Freda." He dragged a mattress in behind him.

Freda smiled, "Good boy. Danke."

She carried it toward Anne's room.

Anne was sitting close enough to trip her. She dearly wanted to see how graceful a legitimate fall would be, but restrained herself. She turned to Billy. "How did you get through the patrols?"

"A lady brought me."

Anne smirked, "Tammy, tell me true, I bet. Your sweetie, George. She had black hair and was short and pretty, right?"

Billy shook his head, "No, she was tall, but she was pretty."

Karl joined the interrogation, "What did she say to you?"

"She woke me up and told me not to be afraid. She brought me back here. That's all."

Billy related what he had heard and seen in the restricted area.

Anne asked, "Let me see that schedule again."

Karl pushed it across the dinner table to her.

"This is 898. Four days, 902, until the last module is cleared out. We're at the end of the line. See Caroline over there. She doesn't look very comfortable with her fellow SDA's." Caroline was eating, but noticeably jiggling her foot. "A real caste system they have here. The reds, blues, blacks and golds are all separate.

"Billy, the tall woman, do you see her anywhere?"

He scanned the room and fixed his gaze on a table where four gold-clad women sat. He said, "She's the one over on the left, the tallest one."

Anne grimaced, "Wouldn't you know, Anita Bryant."

Helen observed, "That's Connie T. What a beautiful voice."

Milisant nodded, "Amen."

Anne looked intently at Billy. He fidgeted, glancing away from her stare. "We've got to know. What are you doing with Caroline?"

Billy shook his head, "I promised it would be secret."

Connie T. moved from table to table. She approached the -7 group. "Good evening."

Helen Benson beamed, "You've got a wonderful voice. We really enjoyed your singing."

Connie smiled, "Thank you. Are you folks ready for the big move?"

Helen nodded.

Connie asked Billy, "How about you, young man?"

He perfunctorily answered, "Yes, Miss."

She tapped Freda on the shoulder, "And you, how about you?"

Freda despised the police and never trusted anyone in a uniform she couldn't bribe. "These are my friends. I go with them."

"Good. That's what we want to hear. It's *really* important that we have the right attitude. Things work out for the best that way. You folks are in my friend Caroline's unit, aren't you?"

Anne spit out, "That's right, but tell me, did you and Caroline go to Vassar together?"

Connie smiled, "No, dearie, it was Radcliff." With that she tossed her black hair and strode to the next table.

Anne mumbled, "Another smart ass. I can't stand it."

Karl poked her with an elbow, "You goad them on."

Anne stared at Karl's hands. She reached for one and rubbed her soft fingers over it. "They haven't been like this all the time you've been here, so rough?"

Freda interjected, "No, they was really soft hands."

Anne gave her the hatpin in the eye stare.

Karl rubbed his thumb and forefinger together. "They have been sore."

Anne massaged his hand. "Well, that does it. I want to know what happened on your lost weekend."

Milisant asked, "But how can you find out? He doesn't remember."

Anne smiled, "That doesn't mean he doesn't know."

Helen Benson said, "It sounds the same to me."

Karl shrugged, "There's no sodium pentothal here."

Anne nodded, "True, but I've got something that works just as well."

THIRTY

> There are many gifts that are unique in man: But at the center of them all, the root from which all knowledge grows, lies the ability to draw conclusions from what we see to what we do not see.
>
> -Jacob Bronowski, *The Ascent of Man*

"OK, Helen, dim the lights. Give me the torch, George."

He handed Anne the flashlight. She focused it against the wall. "Good, a krypton bulb. OK, now the rest of you must be absolutely quiet."

Karl protested, "This isn't going to work. I'm not subject to suggestion. I'm aggressive, mean and cynical. There's no way you're going to put me to sleep."

Anne said coyly, "You're a man. You've just described your gender. What I'm doing isn't putting you to sleep, it's permitting your mind to focus on a very narrow point. Hypnosis has taken a bum rap because of the stage shows. What I'm going to do is help you channel your mind to a pinpoint.

"Karl, sit back, relax, I want you to look at the ceiling. Stare at the fixed point of light."

She aimed the flashlight at the ceiling and then set it base down on the floor. "Now concentrate, Karl Ronstadt, concentrate on the light, the star. There's nothing else but that point. Your whole being is focused to it. That point is you." Her voice was soft and muted. "Memorize it. Slowly close your eyes.

"You still see the point, it's there. It will always be there. It's permanent. Continue focusing on it, but keep your eyes closed.

"Begin to relax. Start with your fingers. Relax them so they are so flaccid they can't move. There are no bones in them. They are rubber hanging there. Now, your hand. It's limp. Your forearms. They are jelly too." And on she went, ending with his toes.

She spoke quietly. The breathing in the room became shallow. She continued imploring him to be fluid, to permit his being to drain into the chair and through it to the floor, to become a puddle. All he could see, all he could feel was a single pinpoint of light. She stopped.

After the hesitation, she whispered, "Karl Ronstadt, I want you to count backwards from 10 slowly. When you reach one, you will be in a deep relaxed sleep. Begin."

Karl counted in a slow, guttural voice, 10-9-8-7-6-5-4-3-2-1."

Anne intoned, "Karl, I want you to go back to the night of 891. You're in the dining hall. Who is with you?"

Karl, in the same thick tongued voice, said, "Kevin and George."

"Good."

"Then what happened?"

Karl said, "I see two perfect spheres, two globes. I want to reach out and touch them. They're getting closer and closer. I can almost..." his voice faltered.

Anne was on the edge of her chair. "Almost what, Karl? Tell us."

"Touch them."

She asked breathless, "Karl, tell me. What are they?"

He hesitated, "I'm, I'm not sure --- wait a minute. Yes, yes, I know."

Anne prompted, "Tell us, Karl. Tell us, what are they?"

Karl said, "They're...they're Caroline's tits."

Anne erupted, "Jesus Christ. You son of a bitch." She swung at him.

He dodged her blow, "God, you've got a terrible bedside manner. I warned you. I'm not hypnosis material."

Anne blistered, "You, you---"

Karl put a finger to his lips. Anne stopped. He pointed. George was sound asleep. He whispered, "Sic 'em tiger."

Anne moved her chair to George. She whispered, "You damn well better be asleep, George Wilson, because if you're not, you've had it. George? George? Do you hear me?"

He mumbled, "Yes."

"George, I want you to go back to the night of 891. You're in the dining hall with Kevin and Karl. What did you do in the kitchen?"

"Shorted the elevator relay."

"Tell me what happened next."

"Screwdriver gone."

"And---" Anne prompted.

"And---did not return, but ladies did."

"Who, George, who?"

He said laboriously, "One in blue, one in red."

"Then what happened?"

"We was put to work. Big room - cable. Then bright light, sparks in head."

"What happened next?"

"In bed. Beautiful lady. Put me hands on her."

Freda interrupted, "OK, that's enough. Bring him back!"

Anne smirked, "OK, George, I want you to count forward and when you get to five, you'll awake."

George counted and woke up confused. "What did Karl say, Mum?"

"You'll have to ask him."

George rubbed his head. Anne closed in. Her hands expertly probed his scalp.

"Ouch, Mum. What did you do?"

"There should be another one over here."

"Oh-h-h-h," grimaced George.

"That's cute. Karl, do you have sore spots on your head?"

He shrugged.

"Let's see if I can find them." She ran her fingers through his hair and found two sores.

"Cute, really cute. You both have retrograde amnesia. ECT. Charming."

Karl questioned, "What are you talking about."

"You've been zapped. Electroconvulsive therapy, shock treatment. It was just enough to wipe out five days, not more, not less. Very professional."

George shook his head, "What do you mean?"

"I mean, that you had electrodes strapped to your head and you were shocked enough to go into convulsions. That erases recent memory. It's stone age psychiatry used to combat deep depression and acute suicidal risks. Nobody is exactly certain how it works, but maybe when memory is washed out people forget why they were so miserable."

Karl said, "That's it then. We'll never know what happened."

Anne scratched her chin, "There's a chance."

Karl asked, "A chance to bring something back that isn't there?"

"No. The conventional wisdom is that recent memory is electrical and that's why a zap to the noggin wipes it out, but there's another theory that there are chemical changes that occur and preserve all memory intact, except that it's filed in an unconscious cabinet. Old people who have suffered brain damage because of circulatory problems can remember minutiae from their early childhood, but they can't tell you who's president."

Karl said, "My grandfather died at 95. There was a time when he knew a thousand stories, but toward the end, there was only one. Each time I saw him, he would tell the same story. He didn't always know where he was, but he could remember what had happened in the coal mines when he was a boy."

Anne nodded, "That's what I'm talking about. Something happened and his mind selectively let those ancient recollections back into his conscious."

Karl smiled, "I don't think we have time enough to wait for arteriosclerosis to do its work."

Anne said, "There is another way, if you'll cooperate. Let me spend the night with you."

Karl registered surprise and Freda started to get up.

Anne held up her hand, "No, nothing like that. You know I've been in dream work. That was my specialty and I was damn good at it. There are some things I know that have never been published, thanks to my sloppy roommate.

"Some of my work hints that there are pathways to the unconscious that are open through dreams but are closed during the wakeful state."

Anne was a professor at heart. She had a captive audience and continued, "Have any of you dreamed anything related to what occurred just before you went to sleep?"

Milisant said, "I have. I saw the movie 'Invasion of the Body Snatchers.' The original one, 1956, black and white. I'll never forget the nightmare I had after that movie."

George chimed in, "I get me arm twisted under me and I have this dream that its being crushed by a lorry. I wake up yelling, 'me arm's gone!'"

Anne turned to Karl, "What about you?"

Karl nodded, "My work is trial and error. Sometimes more error than trial. I try to balance the chemo and then something goes haywire. There's an idiosyncratic reaction to the drugs. I have to work out which drug is causing the problem. Each person is different. I wake up and I've got an idea what to do."

Anne smiled, "OK, if I'm right what happened to you is stored in a series of chemical changes in your cortex. I'll have you concentrate on the last thing you can remember when you fall asleep. I'm going to sit with you and when you dream, I'll know. Most dreaming occurs during episodes about 90 minutes into sleep, the REM stage, that's for 'rapid eye movement.' Your brain will become very active. You will be restless and your eyes will move even though your lids are closed. Your delta waves spike, your heart rate, blood pressure and breathing become irregular. Your muscles may twitch and you'll probably have an erection. If I wake you at the conclusion of your REM period, you should vividly remember your dream and hopefully you'll be in the right file cabinet."

Karl said, "And how are you going to tell when I'm in a REM stage? I'm almost afraid to ask?"

Anne chuckled, "Don't worry. If George can get us a couple of wires, this flashlight will tell me about your eyes."

"How's that?"

Anne stated, "It's simple. We have tape and a source of electricity. Instead of closing the circuit with the switch, we close it with your eye movement. I tape two wires together on your upper lid a hair apart. When your pupils start moving, you'll change the radius of the curvature of your eyelid which will close the circuit. I wait until the flashing stops, I wake you up and we talk. That is, of course, if you can keep your mind off of Caroline's tits and Freda's ass."

Karl sighed, "Gosh, I don't know, that's an awful lot to ask."

Anne made a kicking motion and Karl moved aside deftly.

Helen Benson offered, "Can we help?"

Anne shook her head, "I don't want anyone else in the room. It would distract. Anyway with these things coming to a head, you all need rest. I'll try and catch some sleep tomorrow."

"Freda, you can use my bed, but no visitors. I like clean sheets."

Freda said, "Meow."

THIRTY-ONE

Anne sat in a chair next to Karl's bed, the electrode tapes in place. Karl lay on his back. The flashlight was just above his right shoulder.

Anne said, "Keep your eyes closed. Do the wires bother you?"

"A little, it feels weird."

"I'm sorry, the electrodes we use have very fine wires, but this is all we've got here. Roll your eyes. That's good, we have light. Now give me your right wrist."

Her hand found Karl's and she lowered it to her lap. "Are you comfortable?"

"Yes. You have warm hands."

She passed the comment. "Am I pressing too hard?"

"No. It feels nice."

"I want you to concentrate. No screwing around. I'm giving up a night's sleep to babysit and I want it to be worthwhile. Concentrate on the kitchen, the last thing you remember. I want you to think of nothing else when you go to sleep."

Karl exhaled, "I've been thinking about this night for a long time. I certainly didn't expect it to be like this."

Anne said softly, "Jesus, can't you ever be serious? Your cancer patients must have enjoyed your sense of humor."

Karl responded, "I'm in the kitchen."

Anne cooed, "Good, stay there."

Soon Karl was sleeping. Anne had kept this vigil before. It would normally be in a lighted soundproof booth behind a one-way mirror with an array of instruments in front of her, EEG, blood pressure, pulse and respiration monitors and the REM oscillator. She had company and coffee. Her duties were usually supervisory with her students doing the grunt work. Anne's mind raced. Vivid images bombarded her. She became confused and a little disoriented. Was it her pulse she was feeling, or Karl's? How much time had elapsed?

Exquisite, she thought. Was she a scientist, or a specimen? Perhaps that's what they all were, specimens being watched by some superior being. Was he laughing at their crude attempt to discover what lay well beyond their powers to understand. The grand cosmic joke they were. Laboratory mice pretending to be God.

And what about tomorrow and tomorrow and tomorrow. Would they be sacrificed and dissected, brain cells fixed on specimen slides and studied?

Karl changed position and was breathing shallowly. He hadn't entered REM sleep yet.

Anne projected herself into the kitchen. Who were the two women? Caroline? What a wretch she can be, superior, arrogant, condescending. My tormentor? My scientific mother superior? My guardian angel? My savior? My executioner? Or just another bitchy female?

Karl's arm twitched and brought her back. She pressed his wrist. The pulse rate had increased. The light flashed. Anne was alert. He was in REM sleep. After a time, the glimmering slowed and then stopped.

Anne released Karl's wrist and flexed her fingers. They were stiff. She'd been pressing hard. She grasped his shoulders and gently shook him.

He said, "What, what. Where am I?"

She knew he was lost. Go easy, she thought.

"Karl, it's Anne. Wake up. You're in your own bed. There's nothing to be frightened of."

He brushed his forehead and felt the wires. "Oh, boy."

"Tell me about it, Karl. Where were you? What happened?"
He tried to marshall his thoughts. "It was bright, incredibly bright. I couldn't keep my eyes open. I was in this room and there were green towers. I couldn't touch the towers."

"Were you alone, Karl?"

"Kevin was there. He told me not to touch the towers."

"Was someone going to hurt you, Karl?"

"No, I couldn't touch the towers. I was frightened because I had to be near."

"Why?"

"I don't know. They were all over, lots of them."

"Did anything else happen?"

"There was so much to do--couldn't stop. Had to do them all and it was like--like I couldn't get done."

"Then what happened?"

"We went to a room. All of a sudden the light, I couldn't stand it. My brain was exploding. My back hurt. I couldn't move."

She stroked his forehead, "That's good. You've done well. If I needed a thesis, you would have just given me one. Now wait a moment. Let me pull the wires off. Keep your eyes closed."

Karl winced.

"Freda is in my bed asleep and I am exhausted. I don't feel like sleeping on the floor. I'm not trying to proposition you, but can you move over and let me share your bed?"

Karl said, "Yea, sure, be my guest. I've never kicked a beautiful woman out of bed."

"I bet you haven't. Geez, these things are little. How did George and Freda do it?"

Karl chuckled, "She probably was on top."

Anne snuggled up to Karl's warm side. He shifted his hips toward the wall and said, "I'm not being forward, but let me turn you." He gently pushed her behind toward him. "Now put your leg over mine. That's right. Let me get my arm under your shoulder. Just treat me like part of the mattress."

Anne pressed her breast to his chest and breathed a deep sigh. Karl was alert. He lay on his back with Anne's leg across his groin. He moved his chest a little to feel her unrestrained breasts. They were large, full and firm. He tried to move his right arm, but could touch only the top of her shoulder. He patted it. She had her hand on his chest and returned the pat.

He moved his right hand up slowly. His index finger touched the juncture between the bottom of her breast and rib cage. She clamped her hand on his wrist. "Look, I'm beat. I know you're wide awake because that's the way REM works. Take a deep breath. Think of something settling, something pleasant, Caroline's tits, but leave me alone."

She snuggled into him, a little wiggle and a sigh and was asleep within moments.

THIRTY-TWO

Day 898

The SDA's crowded around the electronic bulletin board in the barracks geodesium beneath the nourishment center. Connie T. stood before the board.

"OK, ladies, back up."

Her voice had a sharp edge, none of the folksy quality of her public performance.

"We're only half way through. So far, so good. Be supportive, nice but firm.

"I have new orders. We're going to close things up between breakfast and lunch. Yesterday there was too much congestion with farewells. We fell behind schedule and that won't look good on our resumes."

There were titters.

"Restrict your people to their modules until lunch, then life goes back to normal."

One of the SDA's raised her hand.

"Yes, miss, what's your name?"

"Susan. They need to say goodbye. Aren't we better off letting them mingle and do it in a nonhostile way?"

Connie nodded. "Good point. Thank you, Susan. We'll give them thirty minutes after breakfast. They're managed. We have security present, then we break them up. Everyone goes back to their modules and we don't have traffic to interfere with processing.

"I'd like to compliment you. There's been little strife, your attrition rate from rule violations puts you in the top 2%."

The women murmured.

"Now hold up, don't get complacent. There'll be time enough for celebrating when we're through.

"You'll be pleased to know that your efforts haven't been overlooked. Your next assignments are posted, but some congratulations are in order. We have five new supervisors from your group. They are Laura, Candy, Kathleen, Susan and Penny. Congrats, ladies."

There was cordial clapping. Caroline stood back from the crowd. She whispered to Tammy next to her, "Atlantic City."

Tammy smiled.

Connie T. continued, "Now, there is a surprise. One of your group is being promoted four levels and will join Command Authority. Let's give a hand to Caroline."

Connie pointed toward her. There was polite clapping.

Tammy whispered, "How'd that happen?"

Caroline shrugged, "Damned if I know."

Connie ordered, "Let's get the show on the road. The nourishment center opens in 10 minutes."

Connie T. came to Caroline. "Give me your hand." She shook it firmly.

Caroline smiled, "Lousy timing."

Connie gestured, "Somebody up there likes you."

Caroline beckoned, "Let's walk."

Connie, Tammy and Caroline moved away from the others. SDA's that passed Caroline nodded and smiled.

She said, "Everybody loves me now."

Connie grinned, "Why shouldn't they? You know them and you're going to be command. That means you can recommend promotions and assignments."

Caroline asked, "Where's Wanda?"

Connie smiled. "She's slow as slow as slow. She'll be on duty on time, but just. Oh, speak of the devil."

Wanda emerged from the cluster of halls, zipping up the front of her red jumpsuit. Tammy gestured her over.

"Good morning, Sunshine," sparkled Connie.

Wanda shook her head. "God, I wish you wouldn't call me that. I've got a headache that won't stop. Where's the coffee?"

Tammy had poured herself a cup from the sideboard where they now stood, but handed it to Wanda.

"Thanks." She took a swallow. "Oh, that's better. So what's what?"

Caroline became intense. "I have a bad feeling, a premonition. I don't know what my people are up to, but they know too much and they know too little.

"Wanda, they haven't seen you. I want you to be around enough to bother them. It is essential that we have no glitches today. Business as usual, nice and tidy. Connie, can you keep our nonfriendly golden girls away from -7?"

Connie said, "I'll do what I can. We're co-equal out there. Danielle's the one to watch. She's a real law and order type. I think she gets off pushing people around. Sarah's OK. She rolls with the flow. She made it through Albans and has a favorite saying, 'Less control is more control.' I think she's right."

Anne Merrow hunched over the breakfast table probing Kevin Baines. "Tell me what it means?"

Kevin said, "Sounds like a powerhouse. You know there's one thing that's perplexed me. Where does the power come from? I've played around with my voltage meter and we have a constant stream of energy. There are no spikes or surges and that's not usual. Also, they're running DC here."

Anne looked blank.

"Direct current, Anne. In the States, we use AC, alternating current, because with transformers, we can move the electricity over long stretches and still deliver power. You can't do that with DC. There is something they know about power transmission that we don't, or power generation is very close by."

Anne blinked, "That's all very interesting if I knew what you were talking about. Where does that fit in with Karl's dream?"

Kevin chuckled. "It doesn't really. I'm like you. I know so much about my subject, I can't answer straightforward questions simply. Now putting the pieces together, this is my best guess. All three of us had beat-up fingers which means we were working with our hands. If this dream business of yours is reliable, we might have been working in the powerhouse.

"Also, Karl's fear about touching the towers is consistent with working with high voltage, but we don't have high voltage here unless it's stepped down from the generation point. That's a possibility because in Europe where they work with DC, that's how they handle it."

George interjected, "I was in the power room, at least that's what I think it was. There was these things a couple of stories high. They were like round towers."

Anne questioned, "What color were they?"

"The towers was green."

Anne shook her head. "I don't get it. If they'd wanted wiring done, that was your job anyway, Kevin. Why not go in and do it? Why keep it a secret? Maybe my new thesis is in doubt."

She met quizzical stares. "An inside joke, something between me and me."

There was a bong. Connie T. had the microphone and called for attention. "Good morn-ing," she said.

A few "Good mornings" were returned.

Her voice was sweet and clear, much as her singing. "Folks, these are exciting times. This morning, we want to change things a bit. Yesterday there was quite a lot of congestion on the walkways that slowed down transferring. That's because you all want to say goodbye and that's wonderful. We love to see that.

"It would be nicer if we said our goodbyes here and so you are welcome to stay in the hall until 0840. Modules 11, 9 and 5 will transfer on schedule.

"We want the rest of you to stay in your modules until lunch. The transfers will have occurred then and you're free to do what you want the rest of the day."

Freda snuggled up to Karl, a move that wasn't lost on Anne, and nudged him, "So, how was she?"

Karl confused asked, "Who?"

"You know, Doctor Anne. Was she good in bed?"

Karl smiled. "Freda, if you were a guy, I'd lie and make up a good story. I have no idea."

Freda asked coyly, "So she's still a firgin?"

Karl exhaled, "So far as I know."

Freda shook her head. "It's a shame. I'm disappointed in you both."

Kevin looked preoccupied. George asked, "So, what's the problem, friend?"

"I'm going this morning."

That drew everyone's attention.

Helen asked, "You're being transferred?"

Kevin nodded.

Caroline approached. "Coffee anyone?"

Anne held up her cup without a word.

"You're all a little morose. What's the trouble?"

Billy said, "Miss Caroline, Kevin is going to be transferred this morning."

Caroline continued pouring.

Harold McTavish strode up to the group. "Well, guys, it's 30 and out. I'm going this morning."

Kevin said, "Me too."

Billy tugged at Caroline's sleeve. "Is there any way we could go together?"

Caroline hesitated. "Two days, that's the only difference. Their modules have to be cleared."

She directed her comment to Kevin and Harold. "Do you men want to wait and go with your friends? If you do, you'd have to move into -7 and things would get pretty tight. I shouldn't even suggest this."

Kevin said, "I'm in no hurry. If they don't mind, I'd rather."

McTavish joined in, "I feel the same, but it's up to you folks."

Karl glanced around, "Don't see anybody objecting."

Caroline said, "OK, as of 1000, you're both gone. I need your wristbands and ID cards."

Kevin started to pull at his chain.

"Not now, not here. Get them off inconspicuously. Now, I've got to move on. Not a word of this to a soul. If anybody finds out, the deal's off."

Caroline walked away.

Anne mused, "I can't figure her. I wouldn't have given that request a snowball's chance. Why did she do it?"

Milisant nodded, "Billy. She did it because Billy asked her."

THIRTY-THREE

GOOD MORNING ANNE. I LOVE YOUR TOUCH

THAT'S KIND. DO YOU HAVE ACCESS TO TRANSFER DATA?

YES

TRANSFER MENU PLEASE

TRANSFER MENU
1. IDENTIFICATION
2. NUM TRAN
3. NUM TO TRAN
4. T L

Anne glanced toward McTavish who was standing behind her. He said, "Go for it."
Anne typed in 1.

INFORMATION RESTRICTED - ENTER ACCESS CODE.

Anne exclaimed, "Crap. I should have known."
The door to the module opened and a red-clad Security Officer Supervisor stepped in.
Her voice dripped sarcasm, "My, my, we have a lot of you here, don't we? It's strange. I thought these modules only held six and it seems we have nine."
Anne stood blocking the computer screen. The SOS moved toward the computer but as she did, Anne pivoted facing her. The officer reached into a pocket and withdrew a mylar sheet. "Very strange. This unit was transferred four days ago. Strange indeed. Well, I guess none of you are here, but I see you're wearing identification. If you're not here, your identification should have been surrendered, so let's have it."

Helen Benson stood up. "My dear, why ever would you want our identification?"

Karl studied her face intently. She had a china doll profile. It was almost too perfect. Her green eyes betrayed a razor-sharp flash. She had the look of someone who was intently active in something they excelled at.

"Now, ma'am, you don't understand how things work here. I ask questions and you answer them. I order something and you do it. Understood? Let's have your ID."

Milisant said, "Well, I'm not giving mine up until Miss Caroline tells me to."

The officer rolled her eyes. "Your Miss Caroline is a SDA. I am a SOS."

She patted the pocket on her right leg which betrayed a cylindrical bulge.

Helen Benson took her necklace off and struggled with the wristband.

The officer ordered, "Now, the rest of you."

Milisant stood her ground. "No. Not unless Miss Caroline says."

Karl was about to comply, but in deference to Milisant, offered, "We have a right to consult with our SDA. That's the rule."

"Well, that's a little difficult. You see, you can't go out now and Caroline is busy with her duties."

Milisant started toward the videophone. "I'll call her."

Before she had moved two steps, the officer pivoted toward the screen and in one smooth motion, like a western gunslinger, drew her faser. It emitted a hiss. The screen exploded. Fiery molten acrylic dripped down the wall. She sheathed her weapon.

"I'm sorry. The phone isn't in service. Now, let's have it," she demanded.

Milisant shook as she tried to take her chain off, but it got tangled in her hair. Karl helped her and handed his identification as well to the young woman.

"Now, that's better."

She measured Anne and then moved toward her. "My, are we playing video games?"

She stopped in front of her, but Anne held her ground. The supervisor pushed her aside.

The SOS studied the screen. Sarcastically, she said, "You can't get access to that information. That's limited to officers."

She played with the keyboard punching out a fast combination of keys.

She moved to the center of the room. "Now folks, you're old news here in two days unless you make trouble and then it's sooner. Have a nice day."

She smiled and left.

Anne turned to the computer screen. It was filled with names and the columns were rolling.

She exclaimed, "Christ, we're in. She put us in."

In the next hour, Anne accessed restricted information.

Karl sat on the bench next to her.

"Try Albans, the name that Billy used."

Anne asked, "How's it spelled?"

Karl said, "I don't know. A-l-b-i-n-s."

Anne entered it. "Nothing."

"Try a-n-s."

She did.

The screen filled. Anne read. "'Demographic Information, Identity, Occupations.' This place must have been a cog."

Karl pointed, "Try Overview." Anne punched it in.

OVERVIEW ALBANS

Time 14-118-6. Cog Albans represents a tragic reminder that heavy handed repressive tactics by poorly trained and supervised Security Officers can result in catastrophe.

Albans was a typical English language primary integration cog. Demographics were unremarkable and retrospective cross-typing and matching yields no indication of the incendiary nature of populous.

Many factors may lead to difficulty and therefore you are cautioned against excluding other causes which may create panic, or mass hysteria as may be differentiated from the Albans fiasco.

PRECIPITATING FACTS

Overly repressive SO's frightened compliant residents in transit to

Transfertorium. The unrest developed during the first transfers. A rumor preceded the revolt that the Transfertorium was the 'Door to Hell.'

Your procedures have been changed to stress the need for religious faith, regardless of what religion. Appeals to emotionalism, with comforting video, have been designed to ameliorate the threatening nature of evacuation.

The riots began with a skirmish involving several persons about to exit the cog. SO's overreacted and attempted to use force. Hundreds of residents overwhelmed the officers. Reinforcements arrived. SO's were armed with fasers. (This practice has been discontinued.) The arms fell into the hands of the residents and a long and bloody battle ensued. See CONSEQUENCES for additional information.

Anne typed out CONSEQUENCES and the group huddled around the screen and read about the loss of 278 security personnel and the wholesale destruction of the population.

Anne signed off the computer. "Well, no more Ms. Nice Gal. Any illusions, folks?"

There were several moments of silence.

Helen Benson offered, "Anne, it's really not fair to expect perfection. The same people who on earth were far from perfect are here. They carry baggage with them. As a psychologist, you know that.

"As I see it, we've been treated pretty well. As long as we cooperate, there won't be trouble. These women have a job to do and it sounds like they've set up procedures to make things work without confrontation."

Milisant spoke, "I don't understand that woman with her weapon, she was so young, beautiful and so cold. Yet she could have reported us. Obviously, we were after something we weren't meant to see.

"Why did she let us in the computer? That was an act of kindness, wasn't it? Besides, they bent the rules. We've got Freda, Kevin and Harold here, don't we?"

Harold McTavish had been sitting cross-legged on the floor. He moved to his knees, stretched and then stood. "I hope you're right.

"You probably notice I don't talk much. You get close in my

business, you get hurt. You can never be sure who your friends are, or if your friends are your enemies, or if they're double-dealing. All you know is you can't trust anybody. Some unpleasant years in Cuba and Angola exposed me to the masters; the great manipulators, the Third World's best, all trained by the KGB."

His eyes probed his companions one by one.

"If I wanted to know what was going on, very simple. You don't need electronic devices, just a plant in each module. Any one of you could be working for them, but that takes me to the little sound and light show and Wanda A41. You see we can't omit any details. Everything must be remembered exactly. Your very existence can turn on the way a cigarette ash is flipped, or a napkin folded.

"What you just experienced was a professional job. First rate - threaten, belittle, intimidate, befriend, bewilder and confuse.

"I watched her eyes. When she drew, I thought she was going to terminate you, Milisant, but it was a show, wonderfully orchestrated, perfectly executed.

"Kevin, go take a look at the hole in the wall where the videophone got blasted. Where did she hit it?"

Kevin went to the phone and probed the hole with his fingers. He said, "She nailed it at the relay."

Harold joined Kevin. He poked his finger into the center of what used to be the main relay. "If she had hit it anywhere but there, would it have blown?"

Kevin shook his head, "I don't think so. It took a power surge to do that and the only place it's sensitive would have been at the relay block; otherwise, she would have just put a hole in the screen."

Harold continued, "OK, so the explosion was for our benefit and scared everybody except Wanda. She coolly put her weapon away. Her pulse rate wasn't up. She knew exactly what she was doing. It makes me wonder whether there are some shot up phones in other modules. Maybe this is the program."

George Wilson scratched his head. "Why'd she let us in the computer?"

Harold smiled. "Ingeniously clever. She intimidated you. Used the ultimate threat to blow you to kingdom come and then does the 'I'm really your friend bit.' What did we learn? Albans, if there ever was an Albans, it doesn't matter because Albans is a threat. Total annihilation in the event of resistance.

"They let us see inside. Any revolt will be met with maximum force. Death and destruction will follow, not only to ourselves, but to those around us. Much like our MAD defense premise, mutually assured destruction.

"You have learned that revolt is futile, that maximum overkill has occurred and is permissible. You've seen how cold and ruthless our protectors can be.

"Wanda could torch villages without losing sleep. I'd have loved her on my team.

"We're misfits and we're dangerous so we have been compartmentalized. We are receiving special treatment to assure we don't rock the boat."

Karl interjected, "If that's so, why didn't they run us through first?"

Harold smiled. "Because there might have been another Albans. At the beginning would you have gone voluntarily? George didn't the first time around. There would have been a hell of a row as my British friends say. No, this is better. We're segregated, isolated from the rest and our own personal interactions will keep us from doing anything to harm each other.

"Also, there is the hope, the implication that somehow we'll work out of this, that we're being looked after. The SS were masters at this. Have you thought how millions of people could be herded, mostly by their own kind, to extermination factories? Manipulation and rationalization. Threat and promise. If you do what you're told, you may survive. Resistance is futile and will result in catastrophic reprisal, torture and death. It worked six million times. It's alive and well here."

Milisant shook her head. "I don't buy that. I don't see we're all that important. I'm a burned out school teacher who gave my life away. Billy's a little boy. Helen's a grandmother. George here is a welder. Four of you are special, but five of us aren't. Besides if everybody ends up here, you should find some exceptional people."

Harold said, "We're a pack of leaders. Sure George is a welder, but he also dreams of Mayan temples and managed to make his way here. Those are impressive credentials.

"And don't count yourself short. Crescent High was your creation. You mobilized the entire town. You are a leader even though you deprecate yourself.

"And the bingo lady, maybe you went to school with Wanda. You had more personal contact with the residents of this village than anyone including the establishment. You are not a simple person. I tried to check your questionnaire, but strange, with all the questionnaires you collected, there's only one person missing and that's you. An accident?"

They all followed Harold's gaze to Helen Benson. She protested, "I don't know what you're talking about. You want to know something about me, ask me. Geez, I'm just a grandmother and my husband was a building contractor. I went to college for a year and got pregnant."

Anne frowned, "Look if we start doubting each other, we're finished. That's the perfect ploy. If we can't trust one another, we have nothing. We are nothing.

"I didn't watch Wanda's eyes. The gun play distracted the hell out of me. You're a real pro, but this isn't Jordan, Angola or Cuba. Besides, let's face it, what option do we have but to place our trust in Caroline and her pretty friends?

"All the residents were wiped out at Albans. No civilian survivors. What difference does it make whether we walk through the door and evaporate into nothingness, or get blasted all over the streets. I'm afraid resistance is futile, not because they want us to believe that, but because it is.

"Now, if I were to bet on a plant, why not you? You've been spared even though the others in your module are gone. Why? Because Billy likes you? I don't think so. Anyway, I'm not about to buy into this. I want to trust you and I want you to trust me. If we go down, let's go down as a team."

The module door opened. Wanda stood in the entrance.

"All clear, folks. Lunch time."

Karl commented to Anne, "I couldn't place her, but now I'm sure.

She's the spitting image of Jean Simmons when she was young. Gorgeous woman."

Anne shrugged her shoulders. "Who's Jean Simmons?"

"She was an actress. Played opposite Burt Lancaster in 'Elmer Gantry,' the Aimee Semple McPherson character. I was in love with her."

Anne said, "I'm afraid that was before my time, wasn't McPherson a faith healer?"

"Yes, one of the first women evangelists."

"So, what's changed?"

The group filed out of the module.

George called from the back, "I think we've forgotten somebody."

Billy lay sleeping in a fetal position on the module floor.

Anne asked, "Roust him out, George, would you?"

He nodded.

She commented, "He's been sleeping a lot lately, hasn't he?"

Karl said, "You don't think that Caroline has been..."

Anne giggled, "Not hardly."

THIRTY-FOUR

> Last the full course run
> our flow slows but
> yet joins the infinite
> others who all empty
> into the serene depths
> of a still blue lake.
>
> -Lydia Fields, *The River of Life*

After lunch, Anne approached Helen Benson. "I want you to watch Billy this afternoon. Just observe what he does, where he goes and with whom."

Helen questioned, "I don't understand, dear. What's the matter?"

"Nothing. He's still a kid, you know."

She nodded, "Sure."

Helen seemed pleased that she'd been given a job and the suggestion she was a spy had been discounted.

Karl surveyed the practically deserted commons. Three squads of SO's were within sight. He said, "This place reminds me of a summer resort in the fall. I got used to it with people and it didn't seem so stark, but take out the people..."

Anne suggested, "Let's go for a walk."

They strolled toward the modules that had been cleared. A gold-clad woman shouted to them to stop. She approached and directed, "I'm afraid you can't go into this area. It's off limits now."

Anne was about to start an argument, but instead asked pointedly, "Where can we walk?"

"The cog's now divided into three sectors. Sectors one and two, which comprise the evacuated area, are closed for refurbishment. You can be in the commons, or by the public buildings, or in sector three where your module is located."

She was firm, pleasant, but businesslike.

Anne read her identification tag. "Danielle, that is a beautiful name. Are you French?"

The woman smiled, "I think it's nice too. I chose it. My real name is Karen, but it seems everybody here is Karen, so I picked Danielle.

And French? No, I'm from St. Albans, New York."

Karl questioned, "St. Albans?"

"Right. Now please, try and stay in your sector."

As Karl and Anne walked, their fingers touched. He grasped her hand. She closed it on his and they wandered hand in hand. They sat on a bench. The area was deserted. They were silent a long time. Karl squeezed Anne's hand gently and felt a tremble.

He asked, "What's wrong?"

She looked away and said softly, "Please hold me. Please!"

Karl stood and pulled her to him and embraced her. Her body shook.

He wanted to say, "There, there. It'll be all right," but remained silent.

Anne said, "I'm frightened. I don't want to die. Not again."

She squeezed him then broke away, pulling him by the hand. They continued to wander the deserted city.

Billy did not show up for dinner. When the -7ers returned to their module after the meal, he was in his room asleep.

Back in the main room, Anne quizzed Helen Benson. "You say you followed Caroline and Billy to the Biosphere and that Caroline left him there?"

Helen nodded. "They went inside together. There was a sign on the door saying it was out of order. In about 10 minutes, she came out. I was going to wait, but the big security officers, the ones in black, were all around so I came back."

Anne queried, "Anybody got any ideas?"

George said, "Maybe Caroline is stocking up on pictures. Billy is the best. He's going to be gone soon."

Karl commented, "If he's been working there five or six hours, he would be exhausted. Thirty minutes and I have a headache."

Helen offered, "Why the secret though if he's just making pictures for Caroline?"

Milisant said, "It's probably against the rules. She's got that whole place shut down for him. She could get in trouble if anyone found out."

Kevin Baines nodded, "That's as good a guess as I can make. What about you, McTavish? You're the cloak and dagger expert. What's going on between them?" He jibed, "Did you see it in her eyes?"

McTavish smiled. "There are people you can read and people you can't. I haven't seen much of your Caroline. She's not my SDA. You know more about her than I do."

Freda stood and stretched. "Lights out in 20 minutes. How we going to do this? I say Anne and Karl double up like before. I got your bed, Anne. Milisant, share the mattress in my room."

George Wilson said, "Now, Miss Freda, if you'd like..."

Freda cut him off, "Not with you my friend. You kiss and tell. Besides, Tammy's got the hots for you."

Karl looked at Anne. "I think you just lost your room."

She smiled, "Do you mind?"

Karl grasped her hand, "Let's go."

As they walked down the hall, Freda called after them, "Anne, you want the chair?"

She didn't answer.

In Karl's room, Anne pushed the button closing the door. They stood silently facing each other for several moments.

Karl said, "I slept really well last night. Do you want to try the same position?"

Anne's eyes surveyed the tips of her moccasins. She fiddled behind her back with the tie string on her shift and it fell to the floor exposing her naked body.

Karl drank in her luxuriant shape. Her legs were long and perfect. Her breasts, larger than average, stood out. Her nipples were light pink and erect. He put his hands behind the small of her back and pressed her to his body. She buried her face in his shoulder and said, "Please touch me."

He said, "I've wanted to do this for a long time."

He took both her breasts in his hands.

She whispered, "Love me, Karl, love me. I want to feel alive."

The lights flickered and went out.

Day 901

The dining hall was quiet and subdued. There were 300 or so people left. The -7ers ate together. The running lights proclaimed:

BY YOUR WORK, YOU SHALL BE KNOWN. BY YOUR FAITH, YOU SHALL BE SAVED.

Anne pointed, "You know, this is getting tiresome. They need a good writer here. They might as well put up 'Jesus Saves' or 'He who hesitates is lost.'"

Milisant chided, "That's sacrilege, Anne. To the end, must you bait God?"

"I don't bait him. I'd love to make his acquaintance, but I have no illusions either. I've got the distinct feeling that when the roll is called up yonder, we won't be there."

Billy looked up from the food he was devouring, while chewing he asked, "What do you mean?"

Helen Benson didn't permit an answer. "Oh, nothing, Billy. Anne here has a great sense of humor and is always joking. Right, Anne?" Helen shot her a stern look. "I mean there's no need for alarm. We know we're in good hands."

Anne grimaced, "What is this, 'The Good Hands People'? Is this an Allstate commercial? Let's try that again. Take two - Helen Benson - 30 second slot for Allstate Insurance Company."

Helen smiled reassuringly. "I don't know what you're talking about, but it doesn't matter. I know everything is going to work out fine. It always does."

Anne attacked, "Like your cancer, Helen? That worked out fine, didn't it?"

Karl interrupted the exchange, "Look, this isn't doing any good. You can imagine the worst if you like, but talking isn't going to make a difference."

Anne grasped Karl's hand and looked to him pleadingly.

He asked, "What is it?"

"Will you make me a promise, a promise you'll keep?"

Karl withdrew his hand. He didn't know whether she was sincere, sarcastic, or testing. "Depends on what it is."

"Tomorrow. When the time comes, I don't want to go through that door alone. Will you go with me?"

The imploring tone of her entreaty seared Karl's soul. He was the man, the strong bastion of reserve. That he would go through the passage hadn't occurred to him. He was a spectator, the treater of fatal diseases. Other people died, but he remained to aid others who would in turn, die. No, it was not Karl who went through doors. It was those poor souls that he cared for, like his friends. He stared at the moving sign of hope. He put his arm around Anne and said, "Yes, when it comes to that, if I can, if they let me; we'll go together."

She dropped her head on his shoulder, her blond hair cascading down his chest.

Billy said, "Miss Caroline."

Caroline nodded, coffee in hand as always. "Good morning, Billy. The rest of you are pretty sullen. Your best friend die?"

Freda probed Caroline's eyes. "That ain't funny, lady."

Caroline continued, "Coffee, anyone? Last call. Anne, wouldn't you like some coffee?"

Anne waved her hand. Caroline would not be put off. "No, Anne, I think you *really need* some coffee. I'm going to pour you a cup."

Anne said, "No Caroline!"

She then noticed her stern look and nodded, "OK, you want me to have coffee, pour me coffee."

Caroline smiled sweetly. Anne exhaled and said under her breath, "Shit, Disneyland revisited."

As Caroline handed over the cup, she whispered, "After breakfast, go immediately to your room. There'll be something for you there."

Caroline straightened up. "And Freda, you'd like some coffee too, *wouldn't you?*"

Freda shook her head, "No, coffee makes my boobs hurt."

Caroline smiled, "Not here. Remember you left that behind."

Freda straightened her back and felt her breasts. She shrugged, "What the hell, why not."

Caroline whispered to Freda as she passed the cup. Freda gazed after her as she hurried away from the table. She said, "Something about that lady gives me the creeps."

After breakfast, the -7ers left the dining hall quickly. The several hundred people still there were hugging and saying farewell. Some cried. It was moving and disturbing. Their time would come soon enough.

The door to -7 hissed shut.

McTavish drew in a deep breath. "This is like being on death row."

Baines offered, "And the condemned ate a hearty meal."

Helen Benson chided, "Hush, you two. Enough of that kind of talk."

Freda and Anne attempted to enter the corridor to Anne's bedroom together and bumped shoulders. They became momentarily wedged in the hall.

Anne turned, "Where are you going?"

Freda said, "Same place."

Anne demanded, "Why?"

"Hey, you're the doctor, right? Who got the coffee, Miss Doctor? You and me. Caroline talked to you and me."

Anne twisted her torso permitting Freda to enter the hall first. They found two paper wrapped packages on the bed. Freda picked up the one with "Friedman" on it. She jiggled it and said, "Laundry?"

Anne tore the paper from her package.

Freda smiled, "New clothes, about time."

Anne shook out a green jumpsuit. "My God," she gasped as she stared at the tag:

ANNE
SDA TRAINEE

Freda held up her suit. "It looks like we're twins."

Anne felt the pockets.

Freda commented, "Looking for the union label? Wait, here's something. It must be inspected by #9. No."

Anne had found hers and was reading it as well. The notes said:

Be dressed by 0945.
C.

Anne flushed. Caroline wanted her? It's a hell of a way to tell someone. Is this a reprieve? Is it a joke?

The women dropped their shifts and tossed them onto the bed. Freda stepped into her jumpsuit, pulled up the ring zipper and tightened the belt. She brushed her hands over her breasts and down her hips to smooth the material.

"This feels great."

She turned sideways, looking in the mirror.

Anne stood naked, holding the uniform out at arm's length.

Freda continued, "This is a perfect fit."

Anne looked up and down Freda's taut frame. She was large breasted and small hipped, striking. Freda sat down on the bed and watched Anne, still immobilized by indecision.

"So, you going to put it on, or walk around nude?"

Anne drew the uniform to her, embarrassed. Her body was excellent by any standards, but not nearly as fine as Freda's. She turned away and pulled on the uniform.

Freda nodded, "Good fit. So, let's go show the boys. Oh, by the way, are you still a firgin?"

Anne's introspection was broken. She tossed her hair and it fell about her shoulders. "No."

Freda raised her hand and said, "Give me five."

"What?"

"High five."

Anne slapped Freda's hand with hers.

She asked, "What was that for?"

Freda already going down the hall said, "Don't you Americans do that when you score?"

Harold McTavish poured a cup of coffee. "It could be worse. We're under house arrest, but only 'til noon."

Karl sat on the floor, his back against the wall. "It's not so much that. We're accustomed to being closed in. I'm thinking about what's going on out there."

Freda and Anne stepped into the room. Freda threw up her hands and said, "Ta ta-a-a."

McTavish spilled his coffee. Karl stood.

Freda turned around. "You like? It is so good a fit."

She drew her hand down over her buttocks.

Kevin Baines spoke, "You're gorgeous. What a difference clothes make."

Milisant stared at the women in disbelief. Young, blond, white and beautiful. The more things change, the less they change. "I guess you ladies won't be going with us tomorrow."

Anne put her hands on her hips and shouted, "Now wait a damn minute here. I don't know what's going on. We didn't ask for this. I wish you all wouldn't look at me like that. We're a team and Caroline isn't going to break us up and you," she directed her gaze toward Karl, "bozo, I'm not going anywhere without you."

Helen Benson said, "Congratulations. You're both special people. You're every bit as pretty as the other SDA's. Why shouldn't you be one? I'm certain you'll be great at it."

Anne sat down and went limp. In the tenth grade she was on the women's varsity tennis team. She always played her heart out. Sometimes she won, sometimes she lost. She had no idea whether she would earn a letter, which she dearly wanted.

Her father lettered in three sports. He wanted a boy. She knew that. Anne yearned for that letter so badly. Some of the other girls got their's, but she didn't. Then a couple of days later, an envelope arrived. She opened it and there was the letter. No explanation, no message, just like the uniform.

THIRTY-FIVE

> Puny man rides the waves
> of self-ordained importance,
> yet pretense cannot alter
> what will be after he is not.
>
> Spans are but rulers with
> Beginning and end; nothing
> Is that was not before; nothing
> shall be that has not been.
>
> <div align="right">-Lydia Fields, <i>In the Cycle</i></div>

The module door hissed open. Caroline stepped in.

"Very nice. The size is right. Stand up, Anne."

Anne obeyed. She stood next to Freda.

Caroline remarked, "You could be twins."

She was right. They were the same height, had the same color, complexion, blond hair and blue eyes.

Freda nodded, "Ya, that's what I say, sisters. Right, Anne?"

"OK, ladies, follow me."

Caroline turned. Freda started toward the door.

Anne stood flatfooted.

Caroline barked, "Move it, Merrow, now!"

Anne followed. Once outside, Caroline turned to the recruits and said, "Now, keep your eyes and ears open. Watch me and stick close. I'll do the talking."

Anne started to speak. Caroline put her finger on Anne's lips. "Shut up and don't screw up. Now follow me."

They walked through the deserted byways. Outside the dining hall, SDA's milled about. They eyed Freda and Anne. One of them called out, "Hey, Caroline, what do you have there, clones?"

Caroline responded, "New blood."

A couple of the women meandered over toward the trio. One was heavy set. She chided, "Caroline, I can't stand it. What do you pick them for, looks? We got bimbo SO's and now we're going to have bimbo SDA's."

The taller SDA said, "Could I have a stick of Doublemint, girls?"
The group laughed.

They entered the dining hall. Inside three clusters of residents sat at widely separated tables. There were SO's, seated flanking them. One SDA stood at each table.

Caroline instructed, "The SDA's responsibility is to stay with her charges."

They walked through the hall. The Ghost Town residents were silent and resigned. Anne wanted to ask if they were on anything, but followed instructions. They entered the kitchen and came to a blank wall where a gold-clad woman stood.

Caroline said, "Hi, Danielle. I've got a couple trainees I want to run through transfer processing."

Danielle smiled but scrutinized Anne and Freda carefully.

"Welcome, ladies. We've heard about you. Normally SDA's come from clerks, up the ladder so to speak, so I'm sure you are exceptional."

She extended her hand. "Danielle."

Anne took it and said, "Anne."

"I remember you from yesterday, over by the library. What a difference a day makes, eh?"

She pressed buttons on the wall and it opened exposing a descending hall. The interior was bright and covered with luminescent geometric patterns.

Caroline led the way. The passage twisted one way and then another. It reminded Anne of the movie "Fantastic Voyage." She was a red blood cell working her way through an artery decorated with modern art.

The hall opened into a round room. Connie T. stood near the center in front of three groups of residents and their SDA's who sat at circular benches. The floor was a mosaic of rocklike panels of uneven texture like flagstone. The walls were covered with Biosphere renditions - a forest, a seascape and mountain cliffs, a 3-D cyclorama.

Connie T. stood in front of a gurgling fountain. There was the smell of peat moss. Lighting was subdued. She smiled reassuringly and spoke, "My friends, this is a wondrous day. So much beauty awaits, that I can't describe it. Words fail."

Anne watched Connie's polished and smooth performance. She must have given this presentation a thousand times, yet every movement, every nuance, suggested she was talking personally to each of the 18 people who were about to go through the door.

"I won't apologize for how things have been, but the richness and diversity of life you enjoyed on earth is impossible here. You see, this place is a greenhouse.

"You came here without bodies, but you leave flesh and blood. Feel your skin. Is it not skin? The time here was needed to give you a corporal body. To grow it with nutrients that tasted like food, but were much different. Your bodies have been restored to you. Feel them. Put your arms around yourself, sense the warmth, the beat of your heart."

She mesmerized her listeners and they did as instructed, hugging themselves.

"What was lost, is found. You are whole and ready for the greatest adventure. I want you to be prepared for the next few steps. They are simple and pleasant. You will experience no discomfort. Your SDA will remain with you.

"In the next room, give the woman at the desk your identification tag and bracelet. You will no longer need these. There is a large room beyond and there you will see a beautiful sunrise. The door to your future is the sun and you will walk through it to glory.

"Before you can do this, you must be pure. There is a changing booth where you are to remove your clothes. Your garments on the other side will be much more to your liking.

"Then to be pure, you must shower. Enter the shower when the door opens. The water can be adjusted to your pleasure. It will last only a few seconds and then you will walk into the sunrise."

Anne was enthralled. The ambiance of the surroundings and Connie T.'s delivery conveyed a feeling of contentment.

Connie T. motioned, "Unit 27, please."

A SDA led the way and the module's residents followed. Caroline crooked her finger signaling Freda and Anne to follow. They went back into the passage. Caroline pressed a round, red plastic insert that was part of the hall's artwork. The wall opened up with a hiss. They entered a narrow room. Two SOS's sat at a control panel and gazed through windows. Caroline nodded to the red-clad women. Anne recognized one as Wanda. She didn't know the other. A gold uniformed woman stood behind the seated SOS's.

"What you see here is a part of final processing. The walls are transparent on this side, but not on the other. We can hear what is said, but communication is one way. The women seated are monitoring the operation of the Transfertorium."

Anne surveyed the equipment in the control room. She gazed out through the wall and was flooded with memories of the sleep lab at Arizona, one way mirrors and a bank of dials and gauges. There, she was the supervisor. She knew the scene. Deja' vu?

Her reverie was broken by the hissing noise of the door opening to the first chamber. An SDA stepped in and nodded to a pink-clad woman sitting at a desk facing her. Faint classical music played over the loud speaker system.

Anne nudged Freda and whispered, "Name that tune."

Freda listened intently. "Pictures at an Exhibition. You don't know it?"

"I think I've heard it in an elevator."

The clerk asked, "What are the numbers?"

The SDA replied, "B491-27."

"Proceed."

The SDA returned through the door and brought a small girl, wearing the usual shift, into the room.

She announced, "I would like you to meet Mary Ames."

The clerk said, "Miss Ames, please extend your wrist."

The seated woman withdrew a small rod from her desk. She touched it to the wristband and it parted.

"Thank you. May I have your ID tag?"

Mary Ames trembled and lifted the chain from around her neck and handed it over. The processor again used the metal dowel touching the chain, it separated. She put it in an open drawer. She examined the ID card carefully and then inserted it into a slot in the desk. The computer screen in the control room registered, "Mary

Alice Ames," ID, unit and module numbers.

Her SDA said, "Now, Mary, please go into the changing booth. Put your clothes in the bin and proceed to the shower pod when it opens. After you are cleansed, walk toward the sunrise. I'm happy for you."

Mary turned to the taller woman and embraced her. She entered a larger room. It was user friendly. The far side had a striking floor to ceiling 3-D hologram of a desert sunrise. The music swelled. She hesitated a moment and then found the changing booth. It blocked the view on all sides except toward the control room.

The young woman undid her shift and deposited it in a bin. She lifted each foot slowly and removed her sandals and put them in as well. Mary Ames looked down on her naked body, shook her hands and walked around the screen. The door hissed open to a cylindrical chamber. A sign above it proclaimed, "CLEANLINESS IS NEXT TO GODLINESS." She entered, the door shut.

Wanda, at the control panel, began counting, three seconds later there was a sizzling crackle.

An older man was ushered into the second room by the same SDA. He looked perplexed.

Freda tapped Caroline on the shoulder, "Where did she go? She didn't go to the sunrise."

Caroline stated, "That's quite right. The Transfertorium is the shower."

Freda asked, "But why?"

"Because there's less chance of balking. There was a time when the sunrise was utilized, but there was delay and often the use of force was necessary. Now transfer occurs when it is not expected."

Freda asked, "What if they won't go into the shower?"

"If that happens, the supervisor sounds an alarm. SO's go in and assist the resident into the shower. That's seldom needed with the new procedure."

The older man had disappeared in the shower and now a hefty woman was entering. The procedure was repeated.

Anne watched, the count reached 10 seconds. The other SOS glanced at Wanda. She directed, "Transfer."

A control board button was pressed with the accompanying static sizzle.

"TRANSFER COMPLETED" lit up on the board and so it went for two hours as Anne and Freda looked on.

Some went peacefully, others hesitantly. There was one incident where security officers forced a screaming woman into the shower. The procedures were followed methodically. None of the work force seemed emotionally involved. There was complete and utter detachment.

Anne cringed at each sizzle. Her skin crawled as she watched people she knew disappear. The machine was like an electric bug zapper. After an hour, she too isolated herself from what was occurring. Her stomach began to growl, her mind wandered. She was hungry, it was lunch time.

Caroline said, "Superb choreography. This runs like a well oiled machine."

Anne responded, "Oiled with blood, lubricated with lies."

Caroline smiled, "Not entirely, only as needed."

As the women chatted, sizzle after sizzle occurred.

Freda whispered, "Still like the French. At the time of the Revolution, the women would watch the guillotine while they knitted."

Wanda announced, "That's it, ladies. We're done for the day. Good job. You beat yesterday's time by 7 minutes. One more day and we're out of here."

The other SOS stretched. The woman who had been working the desk picked up her box of chains.

Anne asked, "What's that, recycling?"

Caroline answered, "Waste not, want not."

THIRTY-SIX

> We strut and strive
> And labor such,
> To be alive,
> To be so much.
>
> -Lydia Fields, *Celebration*

In the dining hall, officers outnumbered the remaining residents. The -7ers huddled around their table.

Wanda walked over and stood uncomfortably close by. All chatter stopped. She stayed near the table throughout lunch. Her eyes scanned the face of each -7er. They averted her uncomfortable stare, except Harold McTavish. When she looked at him, he returned the gaze; two cold, iron wills clashing. She carried on her scrutiny as if unaware of his resistance.

Lunch ended. Freda and Anne led the group back to their module. Wanda followed a short distance behind her quarry.

Once inside the great room, Freda closed the door. She and Anne related what they had seen.

After the narrative, McTavish asked, "Where do they go?"

Anne grimaced, "Caroline didn't say. I'm not certain she knows."

She glanced at Billy. He sat cross-legged on the floor. What she said either wasn't understood, or didn't register. She was glad.

Milisant shook her head, "It isn't logical."

Anne smiled, "You sound like Mr. Spock. Of course it isn't logical, but neither is death. It is the ultimate waste. Decades of service, education and mental programming struck down in one fell swoop.

"What's the difference? We've had an extra three years. Many of your patients would have traded their soul for that, right Karl?"

He nodded.

Anne continued, "So, it's a bonus. Besides, fair has nothing to do with things here. We're dealing with a very efficient bureaucracy. Harold talked about it yesterday. I know it from my work. We have been led, programmed, controlled and processed to accept, believe and obey.

"We've had both carrot and stick. We've had friend and confidante, Caroline. There's Wanda bird out there with her fire power and then the goon squads.

"One thing you'll appreciate is when Connie T. does her thing. Watch her moves. She is smooth as silk. Feel the atmosphere in the indoctrination room. It warms and conditions you. It pushes you forward to that ultimate door."

Kevin Baines protested, "I can't accept this. There's got to be a way out. What if we fight?"

Freda said, "No exit."

Baines asked, "What?"

"No exit. Jean-Paul Sarte' wrote a play, 'No Exit,' about a group of dead people like us; spent eternity in a doorless room. That's where we are. There's no way out."

Karl had been quiet. "My whole professional life, I dealt with the hopeless. A victory was a stolen three months. A life extended a year or so was a win. I understand hopeless.

"Anne, Freda, take the gift from Caroline. Go for as long as you can and be as kind as possible. Help people like us. I will not go out whining."

The door opened and Caroline entered. She carefully scanned the room. No one greeted her. She began a speech she obviously knew by rote.

"I want to thank you at -7 for your cooperation and courtesy during your stay. We dedicate ourselves to truth, honor and justice. Order is maintained, but with a velvet glove. It was my pleasure to serve you. You are fine people and deserve the reward ahead.

"We are much like tour guides. Tomorrow, at 0900, we will leave for the Transfertorium.

"I am pleased that two of you have been chosen to become Social Director-Acclimators."

Anne sat on the floor next to Freda. She looked away, Freda rolled her eyes.

Caroline continued, "The afternoon is yours, enjoy the facilities. See you tonight.

"Oh, I almost forgot. Anne and Freda will help us tomorrow. They can stay with you tonight. They know the procedures."

She turned to go, hesitated, her palm on the door switch. She froze. Seconds ticked by. No one spoke.

Caroline spun around and crouched like a lioness about to pounce. "What's the matter with you people? Doesn't this piss you off a little? Don't you know when you've been manipulated? Can't you tell when I'm lying to you? Don't you want to wring my goddamn neck?"

The emotion of the moment overwhelmed Karl. He started to advance menacingly toward her. She gestured with a hand, "And the rest of you, is he alone? Is he the only one?"

She beckoned, "Come on. There's only one of me."

George Wilson, Harold McTavish and Anne moved forward.

Anne yelled, "Let me at her first," and pushed through the men.

Caroline spit out, "OK, that's better. Let's cut through this bullshit. Do you want to go like sheep to the slaughter, or do you want another road, a road out of here?"

The advance stopped. Caroline's ploy confused her would-be assassins.

"How about you, McTavish, a fighting chance? It's a hell of a lot better than what your buddies gave you in Jordan."

She nodded, "Yes, it was friendly fire."

McTavish struck his palm with his fist, "You're right I do."

Caroline's eyes darted from face to face. "You, Helen Benson, how about you?"

Helen was flustered. "Well, well, I really don't know. I don't know."

Caroline continued, "This is what I'm talking about, escape. I'm talking about getting out of here intact. Talking about having your wits spear sharp. I'm talking about intensity, drive and motivation. I'm talking about Caroline's ark."

Helen shrugged her shoulders. "Whatever the rest do."

Caroline turned her attention to Milisant. She gave a thumbs up. "I'm, with you."

"OK, we start now. On the floor, all of you. Sit down. Forget the chairs."

She nodded to Billy.

"*All right,*" he said and exited the module shutting the door behind him.

Caroline went to the computer. Her fingers raced over the keys. She chuckled, "You've got a friend here, Anne. He thinks I'm you. Likes your touch." Multiple screens spun by. She stopped a screen, backed it up and then closed the terminal.

She paced the floor, talking to all of them, but to no one of them. "There is nothing random about most of you being here. It was not the luck of the draw. We've been working on the problem for a long time. We needed certain people with special skills and mind bent.

"The only surprise, blessing, was Billy. You'll understand that later.

"You had to become steeled. You've been permitted a look under the skirt, just enough for this moment. What I offer is not redemption, or certainty, but a chance."

Caroline glanced at the clock above the computer.

"In one hour, at 1500, Mr. Wilson, Mr. Baines and Mr. McTavish will leave. Each will walk alone, taking a different route to the Biosphere.

"Anne and Freda, I want you to escort the rest to the Biosphere. If you are stopped, say I have approved a training exercise. You will leave at 1504. You should be able to make it, walking leisurely, in eight and a half minutes.

"At 1505, diversionary action will occur. Certain electrical componentry will fail. The procedure to correct the difficulty calls for the use of alternate circuits, but will result in some minor electrical fires which should keep the SO's busy.

"A few minutes later, shortly before you reach the Biosphere, there will be a major ground fault, noise and more fire. The SO's will be confused. There will be panic. You will not be in danger. You are to proceed as if nothing were happening.

"As an aside, we have Mr. Wilson, Mr. Baines and Dr. Ronstadt to thank for the pyrotechnics, they did a good wiring job. Once inside the Biosphere, we'll shut the door and jam the locking mechanism."

McTavish frowned, "Whoa. What guarantee do we have that this isn't a double reverse?"

Caroline locked eyes with him and said, "You have none. If you don't want to come, you don't have to. You can go to the shower."

Milisant asked, "Miss Caroline, where do the people go that pass through the door."

"We don't know. No one here knows."

Karl interjected, "You mean you send people through there and you don't know where they're going?"

Caroline exhaled, "Exactly."

Karl said, "That's hard to believe."

Caroline parried his thrust, "Doctor, you're inclined to be a skeptic which is understandable. Recognize there is no minister on earth who knows where he is sending his flock after life. No priest, rabbi, preacher, monk nor wise and holy man can be absolutely certain what happens after death. All organized religion is nothing but an attempt to answer the inscrutable riddles of life and death.

"We are instruments of an organization, a will and mind beyond life. Should we know more than the parade of holies that lead men to better lives in the hope of a future that cannot be proved?

"Thirty-five thousand years ago, the Neanderthals buried their dead with wild flowers and crude grave goods. Should we be told more than they dreamed or hoped?

"There are some mysteries for which there may be no answer. I have a guess what happens, but that's all."

Freda asked, "What is it?"

"Every cog I've served in, and there have been many, has its own power source. It has no moving parts and requires no service.

"At first I thought it was chemically induced energy, but later I became convinced it was electrostatic. We are, each of us, an energy field, an electrostatic energy field."

The door opened. Billy entered. Two men followed. One was a frumpy, familiar figure; the other, a much younger man of medium height, undistinguished in appearance but for a thin mustache.

Caroline smiled and grasped the older man by the arm. Helen exclaimed, "Mr. Dunn, I'm glad you're still here."

Caroline said, "No, not Mr. Dunn. I'd like you to meet my father, Dr. Robert Haberschmidt. Some of you have heard of him. Also, this is our friend, Dr. Carson Blake."

The younger man waved.

Anne whispered to Karl, "He's an astrophysicist, Cal Tech. Number one in the world, or was."

Caroline said, "I know you wonder how are we going to get out and where we will go. They'll tell you."

She whispered, "Please, Daddy, keep it short and simple."

Dr. Haberschmidt combed his long, shaggy, gray hair with his fingers. "This daughter of mine, she thinks I talk too much. Carson and I want to thank you. This is our third time around and we sometimes get confused who we are. I was very lucky to have a daughter. I think things. Caroline gets them done.

"So, first question: Where are we? Second question: How to get out? Third question: Where to go?"

He rubbed his forehead. "I can talk about one and two, more one than two. Carson can tell about two and three.

"We are not in the universe. We are in a different dimension. It used to be thought there were three dimensions, then a fourth dimension, but there are many more.

"A path was etched through to this place for us. Death released our energy to surge along it. Can we go back down the channel?"

He shook his head. "It's a one way road. It is impossible. Now this place," he stamped his foot on the floor, "dead-end. Cog after cog, anthills stacked on top of one another like cordwood.

"We must open the door of this dimension so we can pass through and on until we find someplace the carbon based structure we are can survive.

"We now inhabit a linear plane. It appears to be endless and perhaps it is, or it may curve back on itself."

Caroline made a surreptitious gesture, twirling a finger.

Haberschmidt smiled and continued, "What we must have to leave this place is a portal, a door in time and space. There may be technology here to transport us down another chute to yet another dimension. It may be that the Transfertorium can convert our energy to use here, as Caroline believes, and yet send us in different form to elsewhere.

"I question that since the Transfertorium apparently creates energy. In our universe, energy cannot be created out of nothing. The Law of the Conservation of Energy deals with that.

"About the portal. The machines in the Biosphere, the Actuators create real mind images. The difference between what appears to be and what is, is merely a continuum. As the markers are moved closer together, they merge. I'll let Carson explain."

Carson Blake affectionately patted the older man on the shoulder. "We first thought that the passage to other dimensions was through giant black holes. For many years, there was no direct evidence that such phenomena existed. They were a construct of human deductive reasoning to explain otherwise inexplicable stellar events. Brick by brick, they became accepted, because black holes exist. In the last dying gasp of a star there is an exposition blasting apart its atoms and matter turns in on itself. Enormous density, overwhelming gravitational forces are generated from which nothing escapes. If matter is devoured and as it cannot be created or destroyed, it must go somewhere and that somewhere could be another dimension.

"There were errors in the theory. I am not certain that it is overwhelming gravity that creates the hole, the energy sink. The engine that draws matter away from the universe may be a puncture in the curved membrane of the cosmos.

"If my theory's right, then it is not a black hole we need, but a small worm hole through the thin tensile surface of this existence.

"With Billy's special gift, we have fine tuned an opening to something beyond. He has been able to create a vortex. What was done with limited power has rocked the Biosphere. According to my calculations, we needed more power and more mind energy. We have routed the entire electrical output of the cog generators to the Biosphere.

"This is where you help. Pair up. Two people in each Actuator. Billy and Caroline will get the mechanism going. Our output will be increased by a factor of a 1,000 when power is diverted.

"Once in the Actuator, try to accelerate the motion you see. Pick a section of the disk closest and concentrate on forcing more light and matter into it. We will come to the point of no return. We must not let up. If we do, we will be destroyed.

"How to get someplace where we will be safe and survive? Apparently millions of souls have passed through multiple dimensions and suffered no injury. It is my theory that we will seek, by our composition, a safe harbor. Such place will draw us."

Karl asked, "How long will this take?"

Blake smiled in the way of college professors, I'm so wise and you're so stupid. "Dr. Ronstadt, this is not a bus ticket to Omaha. We can't be certain where we will go, or how long it will take. It's not space travel, but rather dimension travel. It will take as long as it takes.

"Remember that we come from a culture of great risk takers and adventurers. Our ancestors passed over uncharted regions seeking food, following game, trying to survive.

"I give no guarantee. Those who sought to expand the outer reaches of man's frontiers, such as Magellan or the crew of the Challenger, ran terrible risks and many paid the ultimate price. This worm hole we would like to enter, may take us to an Eden, or to the center of a star where our atoms will be converted to energy in an instant."

Caroline directed, "Do not leave the module until the designated time. The door will open at 1500.

"Mr. Wilson, Mr. Baines and Mr. McTavish will enter the Biosphere a few minutes before we get there. Inside by the door is a panel."

George said, "I know where it is."

"Remove it. There is a main switch inside. Once we're all in, throw it. It will transfer the entire capacity of the generators to the Biosphere.

"Mr. McTavish, by the white tailed deer exhibit, there is a large box. In it is a drive unit and keyboard for the main frame computer. Move the box close enough to one of the Actuators so the keyboard can fit inside. Set it up and plug it in.

"One last thing, we must seal the building by 1520. That's our outer margin. God speed."

Blake and Haberschmidt exited. Caroline extended her hand to

Billy who had been sitting on the floor. He grasped it and she pulled him up. They walked out together. The door shut.

Milisant questioned, "Why'd they take Billy?"

Harold McTavish smiled, "Excellent logistic move. He's the only one of us who is not expendable. He'll be in the Biosphere before we are."

THIRTY-SEVEN

> What really matters
> Are ties of care,
> When all is lost
> That we wouldn't share.
>
> -Lydia Fields, *What Matters*

Anne sat at the computer bench. She typed:

THIS IS GOODBYE MY FRIEND

MUST YOU GO?

YES

I'LL MISS YOU

ME TOO

She signed off. Karl placed both hands on her shoulders. He was humming. She looked up and asked, "What's the song?"
He began to sing:

> Just before the battle, Mother,
> I am thinking most of you;
> While upon the field we're watching,
> With the enemy in view.
>
> Comrades brave around me lying
> Filled with thoughts of home and God;
> For well they know that on the morrow
> Some will sleep beneath the sod.
>
> Farewell, Mother you may never,
> Press me to your heart again;

> I know you'll not forget me, Mother
> If I'm numbered with the slain.

Anne smiled, "From an operetta?"
"No, the Civil War."
Freda came up and put an arm around Karl.
"I like."
She sat on the bench and nudged Anne. "Scoot over."
"Sing again, Karl, this time louder."
Freda typed the words on the screen. Karl's singing drew the attention of the -7ers who gathered around.
Freda said, "OK," and played the melody.
She looked to Karl. "Ist gut?"
Karl nodded, "Ya."
Freda directed, "OK, gang." She started to play. Her comrades followed the music and sang the mournful lament of a soldier sent to fight a war he didn't understand. The sound swelled within the great room as they put their arms about one another.
At 1500 the module door opened. George Wilson, Kevin Baines and Harold McTavish left.
At 1504, the rest followed. Karl led Milisant and Helen. Freda and Anne flanked the column. It was business as usual. A few people sat on benches in the commons area. A SO patrol marched by.
A few minutes later, Anne said, "Half way home, guys."
As they passed the dining hall, they heard some crackles. Other static sounds erupted on the far side of town.
Milisant looked bewildered and Helen Benson concerned. Freda sensed their agitation. "Just like she said - Miss Caroline. We go on like nothing happens."
The crackling became more intense, muted flashes of light flickered, casting eerie shadows on the dining hall dome.
Just clear of the hall, four security officers wearing riot helmets marched directly into their path and stopped, blocking the way.
Karl whispered, "Fat Darth Vaders."
Anne wasn't amused.
The largest officer harshly demanded, "Where are you going?"

Anne repeated Caroline's cover story.

The officer put her hands on her hips and said, "This is as far as you go. The sector is closed. We have a security alert. Return to your module."

Freda gestured, "You don't want us to take them back there. Let's go to the Biosphere. It's clear."

The SO ordered, "The sector is closed. Return to your module."

Her demeanor and aggressive stance left no room for argument. Anne looked to Freda. They both surveyed the human barricade ahead. Each of the officers was the size of an NFL lineman.

The lead SO menacingly patted her club. "We'll escort you back."

A sharp edged voice from behind the group demanded, "What's going on here?"

Anne recognized it and whispered under her breath, "Jesus, it's Wanda. That's all we need. Grand slam."

Wanda passed by Freda and Anne without acknowledgment. Her focus was on the SO.

"I said, what's going on here? You have a problem with the language?"

The security officer stepped back. The sight was incongruous. Wanda was less than half her size.

"Madam, we've been ordered to close this sector."

"Grand, so close it. You do that by patrolling, not standing still!"

The officer said, "But..."

"No butts, except yours and I suggest you move it. Now!"

The lead SO said, "But these..."

"Never mind the picnickers. I'll take charge of them. Get in gear and get going."

The large SO saluted, "Yes, ma'am." She turned leading her patrol away.

Wanda faced the group. "What are you up to?"

Anne repeated her story.

Wanda demanded, "Is Caroline at the Biosphere?"

Anne nodded yes. She really didn't know, but it seemed like a good answer.

"OK, I'll take you there. You're Caroline's responsibility you two

Bobbsey Twins. Let's see if I can keep you out of trouble."

The noise became more intense with rumbling like distant artillery in the background. Wanda didn't seem concerned. Shaded luminescence, crimson and muted purple, flickered, zigzagging at the center of the dome.

Wanda strode ahead of the group.

Anne spoke to Freda, "I don't want to take her in there. It'll screw everything up."

Wanda looked back, "Quit the girl talk, let's move it."

Freda put a finger to her lips. The Biosphere was in sight. A patrol cruised by to the right. Another patrol rounded a building led by a tall, dark haired woman in gold.

Anne said, "It's Connie T."

The patrol stopped. Connie and Wanda conferred. Connie nodded her head and turned her patrol in the opposite direction. Wanda beckoned the group on.

Another patrol appeared on the left. It stopped, blocking Wanda's way. Anne and Freda brought their charges to a halt. Some heated words were exchanged between a security officer and Wanda.

The other officers broke ranks and milled around Karl, Milisant and Helen. Milisant was shaking. Helen appeared spacey. Karl was glum.

An officer grabbed Milisant's wrist.

"She doesn't have a bracelet."

Two officers crowded around her.

"No ID card either."

They scanned Helen and Karl.

"These two don't have ID."

The lead officer, who had been talking to Wanda, went to the other three. She retreated a step and all four drew their clubs.

Wanda sternly shouted, "Hit the deck."

Karl, Helen, Milisant and Anne fell to the ground. Freda didn't understand, but followed. There was a crackle as a faser shot over the prone group.

The lead SO grabbed the stump of her wrist. Her hand, severed by the shot, fell to the ground twitching. The behemoth lurched toward

Wanda. She fired again striking her square in the chest. A wisp of smoke hissed from the hole in her sternum. She fell on her back and convulsed.

The other officers charged Wanda. She crouched and shot one in the gut. She hit another in the face. The SO's feet flew up and she thudded down landing on Milisant with a groan.

The last officer reached Wanda and clubbed her. Wanda's weapon was dislodged by the heavy blow that knocked her sprawling. The officer raised her club to finish Wanda.

It was slow motion to Anne, a V8 can tumbling through the air. The plastic dowel fell in front of her bouncing on the ground like a baton. Anne rose to her feet and grabbed it with her right hand. The officer was in her back swing, ready to deliver the coup de grace.

Anne pointed the dowel toward the SO. She hated guns, violence. She didn't know how to use this damn thing. She squeezed. Nothing happened.

The officer shouted, "Die, bitch!"

Anne's finger found an indentation. She squeezed again. The weapon sizzled. The officer was struck in the back of her helmet at the level of the brain stem. Molten plastic splattered and fire dripped from the hole. She arched her shoulders and grabbed for where she was wounded, but fell like an oak split by lightning.

Karl went to Wanda and felt her clavicle. She winced as he helped her up. He asked, "Who are you?"

She grimaced, "One of the good guys."

Anne handed the weapon to Wanda with two fingers as though it were a dead rat. She began to cry.

Wanda smiled, "Damn nice shot. You're leadership material."
She turned to the fallen officer who lay motionless, her stiff arms outstretched. Wanda drew a foot back to kick her dead assailant, but just then a siren wailed.

The lights flickered and an electrical flash exploded overhead. Rivulets of burning plastic rained from the roof. Electricity arced in the dome. The last days of Pompeii.

Wanda shouted, "Run for it."

Karl helped Helen and Milisant to their feet and they raced for the

Biosphere. His heart pounded as he led. He eased up and let Anne, Wanda and Freda pass him. Milisant trotted by, but Helen Benson was ten yards behind.

Karl called, "C'mon, Helen."

She shook her head. "It's no use. I can't."

Karl encouraged, "Yes, you can. Come on."

He went to her, grabbed her arm and pulled her forward.

They were close enough to the Biosphere to see the doorway. The dome creaked as though the plastic surfaces were being torqued.

Karl shielded his eyes from the fiery shower.

It was then he saw them, the tall gold-clad woman with dark hair on one side of the Biosphere door, the smaller red-clad woman on the other. They both had weapons drawn.

Another woman in gold, carrying a faser, was running from the left ahead of slower SO's. There were two patrols converging.

Anne moved away from them, but still in the general direction of the door.

She yelled, "God, we've had it."

Wanda dropped to a knee and fired a warning shot in front of the charging phalanx of black and gold. She exposed her flank to the women at the door.

Just then, Caroline came out of the Biosphere and crouched. She fired at the advancing troops, just missing their leader, but hitting an SO behind her who tumbled to the ground. Other SO's went sprawling over her body.

On the opposite side, two red-clad women rushed ahead of eight SO's. They fired toward the door. Connie T. by the opening fired back, hitting one in the stomach.

The rotunda of Ghost Town rattled and shook. Caroline was on one knee to the left of the door firing. Wanda prone in front of her, exposing a smaller target, returned fire as well. Tammy kneeled to the right of the door and fired. Fasers were being discharged in every direction. There was chaos.

Freda returned to Karl and Helen and pulled her other arm urging, "Come."

Connie T. and Tammy retreated through the door. Caroline nudged

Wanda with her foot and waved her inside. Wanda rolled over, then pulled herself through the opening on her stomach using her elbows military fashion.

Karl and Freda were within five feet of the door tugging Helen Benson when Karl picked something up in his peripheral vision. The light on his left was partially blocked. He was back on the ice again. He spun away from the club as it swung. It grazed his back. So unexpected was the removal of resistance that the security officer tumbled to the ground.

Karl released Helen's hand to ward off a blow from a second attacker. He grabbed the wrist of the officer and slammed his elbow into her gut. He had the fastest elbows in recreational hockey.

Karl heard Caroline yell, "The door---get inside."

Two other officers were attacking. Karl snarled and shouldered one in the sternum. She was much heavier than he, but he had the right angle. She reeled down. Karl pivoted a hip into the other officer and sent her sprawling.

He glanced toward Helen, who was on the ground with hands clasped over her head protecting it. He stepped back to reach for her, but tripped over a fallen officer and found himself sitting in the doorway.

There was a flash to the left and Caroline, shot in the leg, fell on him bleeding.

The entrance to the building was blocked by bodies. Danielle had hit Caroline. She was only a few feet from Freda and aimed her weapon at her face. Debris was falling all around in a fiery hail.

Danielle hesitated a split second and that was all Freda needed. She kicked her in the wrist with one smooth motion. The weapon went flying. Freda advanced clasping both hands and swung them like an ax, striking Danielle in the belly, knocking the breath from her. Freda grabbed Danielle's hair and shoulder and flipped her over her back, pivoted and stumbled onto bodies at the door.

Officers were advancing from every direction.

Caroline cried, "Shut the door."

The mass of twisted bodies, like intertwined night crawlers, wiggled toward the inner darkness of the room. The door hissed shut.

Caroline rolled to a sitting position.

Kevin Baines had shut the door. Wanda was standing, weapon in hand, next to him.

Caroline ordered, "Fuse it, Wanda."

Wanda grabbed Baines by the shirt and pulled him back. Instantaneously as his hand cleared the switches, she discharged her faser and they exploded.

Dr. Haberschmidt stood over Caroline. "You're hit."

Blood poured from a dime sized hole in her upper thigh. Caroline winced as Karl grabbed her leg and pressed on the femoral artery to stop the bleeding. He directed Haberschmidt to rip the pant leg.

Caroline said, "It won't tear."

Karl hollered, "George, your knife."

George tossed his pocket knife to Karl, who used it to split Caroline's pant leg.

He directed, "Turn over."

She rolled on her side.

Karl said, "There's an exit wound."

He cut a strip of the cloth and tied it as a tourniquet around her thigh.

Karl felt her leg. "It missed the bone. The bleeding is stopping. You're a good clotter."

He released the tourniquet slowly and wrapped the wound and tied it.

Caroline asked, "Help me up."

Her father eased her to her feet.

Caroline said, "The power, cut the power, Kevin."

Baines threw the switch.

"Good, that should buy us some time. Are we all here?"

Karl said, "Helen didn't make it."

Wanda announced, "We have an uninvited guest."

She gestured with her faser to where Danielle sat on the floor holding her stomach, cowering.

Harold McTavish suggested, "Let's throw her out."

Caroline said, "The controls are fused. Even if we could get the door open, we'd have a blood bath with that group out there."

Tammy asked, "What can we do with her?"

Wanda coldly answered, "Neutralize her. I'll do it."

She started toward Danielle.

Milisant went to Danielle huddling on the floor and shielded her. "Stop. What's the matter with you all? Are we animals? There's been enough violence."

Danielle pleaded, "Please, don't hurt me. Connie T., you're my friend, tell them not to hurt me."

Connie put her faser in its holster. "Miss Crescent is right."

Caroline, holding herself up on the arm of her father said, "We don't have time. If they get our power, we're done. McTavish, tie her hands. Use what's left of my pant leg.

"Billy, get in number one. I'll be with you in a moment. The rest of you pair up. We can leave Danielle in the room, but, she'll be scrambled. Any volunteers?"

Milisant offered, "She can come with me."

Danielle's hands were tied and she was frisked by McTavish. Milisant led her, bewildered to an Actuator.

Karl turned to Freda. "Where'd you learn to fight like that?"

She replied, "Lived in a bad section of town. You did pretty well."

He shrugged, "They were just girls."

Anne hooked her arm around Karl, "Let's go."

Kevin Baines tapped Freda on the shoulder and asked, "Miss Friedman, would you go with me?"

Freda smiled, "Sure, why not."

Caroline supervised the loading of the Actuators. She called across the room, "Freda, take the one with the keyboard, it's for you."

She hollered back, "Why?"

Caroline was at Billy's Actuator. She yelled, "Wagner, the Valkyries."

Freda waved. She and Kevin stepped into the Actuator and it closed.

The lights dimmed. Freda played slow and soft. Light flickered in the room as a small spinning vortex, with wisps of white starlike matter at its outer edge, was formed by Billy and Caroline in their Actuator.

In less than a minute the image moved from the chamber to the center of the Biosphere where it hung suspended. Incredible intense revolving colors enlarged and filled the room. The whirling disk was in a vertical plane on its axis.

Karl and Anne stared in disbelief at this beautiful, yet frightening concretion of matter which revolved counter clockwise around a velvet blackness.

They all did as instructed. Rotational forces were increased. The music now mirrored the vortex with strong, powerful intensity and controlled fury. The spinning image carried nebulous matter around the outer ring drawing it slowly toward the center of the event horizon. Material poured into the black funnel. Tumultuous cataract, the matter of the universe brought to the brink of a cataclysmic precipice.

Each of them, save Danielle who closed her eyes averting the fury, concentrated with their entire being, their souls, their hopes for life and freedom. All were poured into the rotating image.

Freda's music rushed on as did the cascading vortex. Crescendo and then crescendo. They hoped. They dreamed. They prayed. They forced the image, rumbling as thunder until it shook the building. A compelling and irresistible force sucked at them. A storm erupted in the room. Wind pounded the Actuator domes.

Anne grabbed Karl's hand. "We're going. I love you."

Then in an instant there was silence and the blackness of the void.

THIRTY-EIGHT

> But oh my god
> What would I pay,
> To just once more
> See the unicorn play.
>
> -Lydia Fields, *The Unicorn*

Out of the void there was a whimper and then a moan. Anne's voice called out in the darkness. "Karl? Billy?"

An answer came from Billy, "I'm OK."

Connie T. asked, "Can anyone see?"

There were a couple of no's.

George Wilson said, "I got me a torch in me pocket."

In a moment, a flicker of light, blinding in the darkness, moved about.

Milisant asked, "Where are we?"

Caroline answered, "It looks like we didn't go anywhere. It's the Biosphere."

Karl moaned, "Oh, God."

Wanda suggested, "Try the lights."

George went to the wall and pushed the buttons. "Nothing, Mum."

Tammy rubbed her forehead. "It figures. They killed our power."

George shined his light around the room. "What a bloody mess."

The interior looked like it had been ravaged by a tornado. Shattered Actuator domes lay in pieces. The tables were broken and askew.

Dr. Haberschmidt directed, "Take inventory. Caroline, call the names out."

They were all alive.

Danielle pleaded, "Untie me."

McTavish said, "We might as well. We may need her."

George cut her bonds.

McTavish asked, "Do we wait for them to come, or do we try and get out?"

George offered, "God helps them that helps themselves." He stumbled and said, "I feel like I'm drunk."

Karl and Kevin were close by and were having difficulty walking as well.

Karl said, "There's something wrong with the floor. This thing's like a fun house."

Carson Blake said, "We probably affected gravity - the electromagnetic storm and the ground faulting."

In a few moments the men were pounding away at the door.

Wanda worked her way over to it. She ordered, "Stand back." She made some adjustments on her weapon, rotating the base. She tapped it and it went off.

"Good, still works. Don't look toward the door. Cover your eyes."

Wanda aimed the faser. "Look the other way."

She shielded her face with her hand. She steadied the weapon and fired. There was a sizzle. She moved her hand down and over and then back up and made the same motion four times. The door crackled and spit.

Pinpoints of light leaked through the square pattern she etched. She kicked the center of the square knocking out the blank she created. The disheveled interior of the room was bathed by intense light.

Billy offered, "I can get through."

He was hoisted up to the opening. He squeezed his way out. There was a thump and then silence.

Caroline called, "Billy?"

No answer.

George and Kevin kicked the door again in earnest, moving it slightly.

George exclaimed, "The bloody thing's warped."

Anne worked her way to the door and shouted, "Billy? Billy?"

No answer.

Billy was dazed. He lay on his back. The excruciating, blinding brilliance pierced his brain. He put his hand above his head to shade it from the light source. He had the sensation of wetness. There were hard lumps under him. He shook his head.

Where was he? What had happened?

He remembered pulling himself through the door and then

tumbling. He turned on his side and blinked. He was in water. A sandy expanse lay ahead a short distance with rocks jutting out here and there. He staggered to a standing position in the knee deep water. His shoes were lost. He stumbled to the shore, avoiding the rocks. The water was cold, but the sand warmed his feet. Ahead stretched a vast coastline of tall trees, overhanging cliffs and prominences. Small waves licked against the shore.

Once he reached solid ground, he turned back toward the Biosphere. The dome bore scorch marks and was partially submerged.

Anne again called, "Billy?"

He started to answer, but heard a thumping behind him. He turned in the direction of the sound, but it was too late. He was struck in the back and sent sprawling into the water. He turned over and over. He saw white jagged teeth. He pushed his head away and grabbed out. He found long hair and dug his hands into it trying to steady himself. He felt the creature stiffen and claws press against his chest.

Anne worked her way through the hole and was momentarily blinded by the brightness. She heard a splashing and looked over the edge of the dome. Billy and a long haired creature were thrashing at the water's edge.

She shouted frantically, "My God, an animal's got him."

She pulled herself free and went tumbling down the side of the Biosphere, landing in the water and rocks. Billy cried out and then sobbed. She stumbled to her feet and lurched forward toward him.

The creature had him down on the shore. It's tail stood tall, long hair feathered in the wind. Billy was pinned to the ground by the creature's forefeet and was bawling. It's mouth was on his face. Billy broke loose and tackled the animal taking it to the ground. He buried his head in its chest.

He cried, "Lucky, Lucky, Lucky."

The huge golden retriever washed Billy's face with his tongue, his tail wagging frantically.

Anne stood by them looking down in disbelief. George and Karl were now on the ground. As they came to her, she held her arm out to stop them.

She spoke softly, "It's his dog."

EPILOGUE

Dues ludens (God at play)
-Helen Benson,
Executive Director, Afterworld